Max's To-Do List

1. Acquire new company and partner.

2. Talk brother into asking partner's daughter to marry him.

3. Host party so said proposal will take place.

4. Speak with butler about guests and refreshments.

5. Become completely distracted from all of the above by butler's niece.

1. Replace usual uniform with sexy black dress.

2. Finish making chocolate desserts.

3. Keep Max's brother from flirting with women other than his intended fiancée.

4. Explain to Max that his butler, my uncle, is sick. Offer self as replacement.

5. Try to run party smoothly while falling hopelessly in love with Max.

Dear Reader,

It's another wonderful month at Harlequin American Romance, the line dedicated to bringing you stories of heart, home and happiness! Just look what we have in store for you....

Author extraordinaire Cathy Gillen Thacker continues her fabulous series THE LOCKHARTS OF TEXAS with *The Bride Said, "Finally!"* Cathy will have more Lockhart books out in February and April 2001, as well as a special McCabe family saga in March 2001.

You've been wanting more books in the TOTS FOR TEXANS series, and author Judy Christenberry has delivered! *The $10,000,000 Texas Wedding* is the not-to-be-missed continuation of these beloved stories set in Cactus, Texas. You just know there's plenty of romance afoot when a bachelor will lose his huge inheritance should he fail to marry the woman he once let get away.

Rounding out the month are two fabulous stories by two authors making their Harlequin American Romance debut. Neesa Hart brings us the humorous *Who Gets To Marry Max?* and Victoria Chancellor will wow you with *The Bachelor Project*.

Wishing you happy reading!

Melissa Jeglinski
Associate Senior Editor

Who Gets To Marry Max?

NEESA HART

HARLEQUIN®

TORONTO • NEW YORK • LONDON
AMSTERDAM • PARIS • SYDNEY • HAMBURG
STOCKHOLM • ATHENS • TOKYO • MILAN • MADRID
PRAGUE • WARSAW • BUDAPEST • AUCKLAND

To Corinne Everett, fellow author and friend, for
indefatigable support and breathing lessons!

ISBN 0-373-16843-8

WHO GETS TO MARRY MAX?

Visit us at www.eHarlequin.com

Printed in U.S.A.

ABOUT THE AUTHOR

Neesa Hart lives in historic Fredericksburg, Virginia.
She publishes contemporary romance under her own
name, and historical romance as Mandalyn Kay. An
avid theater buff and professional production
manager, she travels across the U.S. producing and
stage-managing original dramas. Her favorite to
date? A children's choir Christmas musical featuring
The Pirates of Penzance.

Books by Neesa Hart

HARLEQUIN AMERICAN ROMANCE
843—WHO GETS TO MARRY MAX?

Dear Reader,

I first had the idea for this book when I was six years old. I had thirty-five Barbie dolls and three Kens. The odds weren't so good. Besides, Ken liked to wear clothes that matched Barbie's, and that didn't seem, well, quite as alluring as my brother's G.I. Joes, which had all those neat uniforms.

I made do with Joe while my brother wasn't looking, but wistfully longed for a Barbie doll companion that was up to snuff. The thought reoccurred to me when I went to college—the odds there for me weren't much better than poor Barbie's! This time, there were no G.I. Joes to be had, although there was a Marine Corps base right up the highway.

Still, the thought lingered, and—this truly is the best part of being a writer—eventually I got to see it through to the end. Max is a special guy. He charmed me from the beginning, and had, I thought, just what it took to turn a woman's head even if G.I. Joe was in the room down the hall. Hope you enjoy him as much as I did!

Neesa Hart

Chapter One

She looked good in black.

Sidney studied her reflection. She hadn't thought she'd like it, but now that she wore it, she had to admit she was glad she'd splurged on the outfit. Auspicious occasions, her uncle Philip claimed, demanded auspicious clothing. And being in the Hudson River valley home of Max Loden, financial guru and world's most enigmatic bachelor, she supposed, was just about as auspicious as it got.

The luxurious fabric, which had seemed so incredibly impractical, highlighted the best aspects of her figure with exquisitely tailored perfection while somehow managing to downplay her flaws. It skimmed her hips and fell gracefully to the floor, giving her an air of sophistication she suspected she was going to urgently need. The short jacket, with its structured shoulders and waist-trimming fit, inspired her Miracle Bra to new levels of achievement.

Perhaps, she thought whimsically, she might survive this encounter after all.

"What the hell is going on here?"

Or, maybe not. Sidney took a deep breath before she turned to face him. At the fierce look on his face, she had to stifle a grin. She could easily picture him saying, *fee, fi, fo, fum.* Sidney schooled her countenance into an appropriately solemn expression. "Hello, Mr. Loden."

"Mad Max," as his enemies and even some of his friends

called him, was everything she remembered and more. Elegantly clad in a black tuxedo, he towered over her. His melt-her-kneecaps gaze swept her from head to foot. "Sidney." He sounded simultaneously baffled and annoyed. "Where's Philip?"

She straightened the lapels of her catering jacket to disguise the customary nervousness she felt in the presence of the indomitable Max Loden. It was his eyes, she'd decided years ago. They had a way of dismantling her. "I'm afraid you're stuck with me," she said. "Uncle Philip's not here."

His razor-sharp gaze darted around the spacious kitchen of his Hudson River home—although, Sidney mused as she thought of the sprawling structure, the term was loosely applied. Her staff had seized the kitchen, and were functioning at their usual peak efficiency. Rows of hors d'oeuvre trays lined the stainless steel countertops. Three of her pastry chefs put finishing touches on an assortment of desserts and handmade chocolates. Champagne glasses, freshly polished, stood in neat rows, and her assistant busily rushed about making careful notes of each procedure. Evidently done with his inspection, Max met Sidney's gaze. "What do you mean he's not here?"

"Uncle Philip isn't well."

That turned his generally fierce expression into a full-blown scowl. "Not well? He's ill? What's wrong with him?"

She refused to let the bulletlike pace of the interrogation rattle her. "He has the flu."

"The flu—are you sure?"

"Very. He was extremely upset that he couldn't be here for you this weekend." She clasped her hands behind her back to keep from fidgeting.

"Hell." Max rubbed at the muscles of his neck. The motion, she noted, spread his black jacket open to emphasize a broad chest that had been rumored to make women swoon.

Sidney made a mental note to thank Philip for encouraging her to abandon the jeans and sweatshirts she usually wore when she supervised a party this size. Although she spent her time behind the scenes, and would generally remain invisible to Max's guests, both the cut and the cost of the black jacket and trousers boosted her confidence. "Uncle Philip sends his regrets," she told Max.

"His—" He swore. "Is he going to be all right?"

The question would have surprised many, she knew. Max Loden had something of a reputation. People called him all sorts of names—compassionate was not generally one of them. Had it not been for her uncle's long relationship with him, Sidney, too, might never have seen behind Max's implacable facade to the heart of this amazing, if daunting, man. She tilted her head to one side to study him. "I'm sure he will be."

"Does he need anything? Has he seen a doctor?"

Not for the first time, Sidney decided that every story she'd ever heard about "Mad Max" Loden was completely unfounded. No man could inquire after the health of his butler with that rough and tender voice and be missing his heart, no matter what his critics said. "Yes, he has. And he's quite fine. I stocked his refrigerator and his pantry before I left."

"The flu can be dangerous for a man his age."

Heartless indeed, she mentally scoffed and felt her inner knot of tension begin to unwind. Even Philip's home was another of Max's flagrant generosities. While most butlers lived in their employers' homes at their employers' whims, Max had provided Philip with a personal retreat for his off-duty hours. "Yes, it can. That's why his doctor confined him to bed."

"Is someone with him?"

"A neighbor."

"You're all the family he has."

"Except you," she said quietly.

He stared at her for long, disconcerting seconds, his silver gaze searching her face. Everything else about him was dark. His hair, his expression, his countenance, even his voice. But those eyes were positively brilliant. "Shouldn't *you* be taking care of him?" Max prompted.

"He wanted me to take care of you instead."

Max lifted one eyebrow in an expression she was willing to bet sent his employees scrambling. "That sounds like Philip."

"He knew this weekend's house party was exceptionally important to you. He briefed me that your brother, Greg, is considering an engagement to Lauren Fitzwater. That, with any luck, Greg will finally muster the nerve to ask the young lady to marry him—and that you hope the relationship will further your efforts to merge Loden Enterprises with Edward Fitzwater's electronics company."

Max's eyebrows lifted. "Philip's in top mental form, I see."

Sidney nodded. "He also explained that the younger Mr. Loden probably wouldn't respond favorably to that information, and that you'd prefer discretion from the staff. Without Philip here to command them, he was worried they might not understand the importance of decorum. Since the Fitzwaters and several of your investors will be present this weekend, this particular event could prove both profitable and beneficial to your long-term goals."

"It could," he agreed.

"And, knowing that, Philip was extremely concerned. He knew how much you have riding on this event. He'd already employed my staff to assist your own for the weekend, and, in his absence, he asked me to supervise." She finished the speech and breathed a mental sigh of relief.

Max studied her for long seconds. "Philip told me you're in business for yourself now."

The note of admiration in his voice almost felled her. Not in her wildest imagination had she pictured him admiring her for anything. Not when his first impression of her had been as a miserably unhappy adolescent who'd cowered from him for no apparent reason, and every subsequent impression would have been formed while watching her cater his friends' parties and assist her uncle. Though she'd seen him from a

distance, this was their first substantial conversation in years.
"I am," she said.

"You run a temp agency." He drummed his fingers on the
counter. "Waitstaff and caterers," he clarified, still holding
her captive with his gaze. "As Philip explained it to me, you
started the business after your divorce."

She cringed. Uncle Philip, it seemed, was certainly quite
liberal with the details of her private life. She wasn't prepared
for the idea that Max Loden had an intimate view of her
failures. "That's true."

"And you supply extra personnel for large events and
household needs."

"And parties like this one."

"I see." He continued to stare at her.

"Was there something else you wanted, Mr. Loden?"

"Max." His voice was nearly a whisper. He seemed to be
studying her. Without warning, he grabbed her hand and
tugged her toward a door at one end of the kitchen.

She gave him an anxious glance. "Is something wrong?"

Max looped his fingers under her elbow as he hurried her
toward the pantry. "Maybe."

Sidney decided not to resist. If she did, he'd probably make
a scene. Max loved scenes. It was one of his quirks. "Chip,"
she called out to one of her assistants, "Can you take those
lobster crepes out when the buzzer rings?"

"Sure." He lifted his eyebrows.

Sidney ignored him. Max steered her into the relative quiet
of the pantry. The door swung soundlessly shut behind them.
"Why are you here, Sidney?" His voice had dropped to a
low rumble.

The only light in the cramped space came from the slight
space around the door. With a sharp tug on the string, she
switched on the overhead light. A mistake, that, she mused.
The single light bulb made his expression more fierce. Gathering her calm, she met his gaze. "Uncle Philip—"

Max cut her off with a wave of his hand. "I know. Philip's

sick. He asked you to stand in. You haven't answered my question, though. I want to know why you agreed.''

"I'd do anything for him. He was very worried that he—"

"Couldn't be here." Max moved a step closer. "You told me. But Philip told me that you almost never supervise parties yourself. You leave that to your assistant." His eyebrows drew closer together. "Kelly—" She could almost see the gears turning in his brain.

"Lars," Sidney supplied.

Max's nod was short. "That's right. You run the business and assist your clients with event planning, but she handles the events on site. Isn't that right?"

"Uh—"

He nodded. "It's right. So I want to know why you made an exception in my case."

"Well, I—"

"Why did you decide that this particular event needed your personal touch?"

Gritting her teeth in frustration, she resisted the urge to tell him it was rude to interrupt. "I knew uncle Philip was particularly worried about not being here, and that he'd rest easier if he knew I was."

He frowned. "Is that what he told you?"

"Not in so many words, but he was very agitated about missing this event."

Max watched her through a narrow-lidded gaze. "Is that the only reason?"

She swallowed. "What other reasons would there be?"

He raised one hand to rest it on her shoulder. The slight pressure of his fingers eased her closer to him. "I don't know, Sidney. You tell me."

Her breathing turned shallow. He couldn't possibly know the effect he was having on her—the effect he always had on her. By design, she saw him rarely. Most of what she knew about Max, she knew from her uncle. She stayed out of his way whenever possible simply because he had this ability to melt her bones. "Max, I—"

His fingers tightened. "Damn it," he whispered.

"What's the matter with you?"

"Damn it," he said again.

"Max—?"

His eyes drifted momentarily shut. When they opened again, she saw the resolve in them. "I want you to stay here this weekend."

Sidney blinked. Oh, Lord. Not that. "Excuse me?"

"You heard me. I want you to stay here."

Vintage Max, she mused. No explanations. No common-sense argument. Direct, and straight to the point. What Max wanted, he was used to getting. She'd been afraid of this when she'd spoken to her uncle. Max had a lot riding on this weekend. He'd want to make sure someone was covering for Philip. He couldn't know that three uninterrupted days with him would shrink her into a bowl of nerves. "I don't think—"

"There are twenty bedrooms in this place, not including the guest quarters where Philip usually stays when we're out here. You could have the apartment to yourself."

"Really, I—"

"Your staff is going to stay, aren't they?"

She reached for her patience. "Not all of them. Only the few that I'll need for early morning. You have an ample household staff to cover whatever happens during the night. You won't need any extra help until your guests start moving around tomorrow."

"I want you to stay."

She stifled a groan. "I know you—"

He leaned closer to her and said, with a soft insistence that curled her toes, "I'm serious."

She couldn't decide what he meant by that. "I can see that."

"Philip would stay."

"It's Phillip's job to stay."

"He won't like it if you leave."

She recognized the lightning-fast change in strategy. He

wasn't getting his way by bullying her, so he'd switched to guilt as a maneuvering tactic. "He doesn't like being sick, either, but he is. I had planned to stay with him tonight."

Max eased his hand down her arm to cup her elbow. There was something oddly intimate about the slight heat of his fingers seeping through her jacket. "I appreciate your concern about Philip. I'll send someone over to take care of him."

Sidney felt herself losing ground. "I really feel I should check on him myself."

"He told you to stay here, didn't he?"

The man was too insightful, that was his problem—and he was making it her problem. Philip had argued with her for nearly an hour. Somehow, Max knew it, and didn't hesitate to use the knowledge to his advantage. "I think you can understand why Philip would want—"

"Didn't he?" Max prompted.

She squelched a sigh of irritation. Max knew Philip well. "Yes."

Philip had worked for the Loden family for forty years. Two days after Max's birth, he'd been promoted to senior butler. And he considered the care and tending of Max Loden his life's work. When Sidney had informed him that she planned to leave her assistant in charge overnight, Philip had pushed himself up in his sickbed and given her a sound lecture on the importance of personal service. Sidney had no answer for that. She certainly couldn't explain that she was sure to be wearing her heart on her sleeve by the end of the weekend.

"Then what's the problem?" Max persisted.

Sidney frowned at him. "Uncle Philip doesn't run my life, you know?"

"He runs mine pretty well."

"And he can't right now. He needs someone, and I want to be there for him."

"By driving home at two o'clock in the morning? Do you have any idea what kind of people are on the road at that hour?"

"Overworked caterers who are being harassed by their clients?"

His scowl darkened his features. "Drunks and criminals."

"I'll be careful."

He uttered a mild curse. "It'll be almost four when you get there. You'll get three hours sleep, and then drive back out here tomorrow. That's inefficient and foolish."

Blunt as usual, she thought irritably. "There's more to life than efficiency, you know."

His expression told her he thought that was ludicrous, and barely resisted the urge to tell her so. He shook his head instead. "What are you going to be worth to me tomorrow night, or the night after, if you're exhausted?"

"I assure you, you won't have any complaints."

"I know I won't if you stay here."

"Why are we arguing about this?"

"Because you aren't giving me my way." He reached for the wall phone. "I'm going to send Charlie to your house to pick up your clothes."

Sidney recognized the name of one of Max's chauffeurs. "Max—"

He ignored the warning note in her voice. "Really," he said. "I left Charlie in town with the limo. It's a stretch. I never use the damned thing. Too pretentious, and parking's impossible." He punched a couple of numbers.

"Then why have it?"

He shrugged. "Because I'm supposed to. People expect it."

Sidney abruptly pressed down the receiver button. "Max, stop it. This isn't going to work."

He ignored her. "Of course it will. If you call someone to pack a bag for you, Charlie can swing by your place, get your stuff, then stop at Philip's on the way here to let him know your plans have changed."

"That's not—" She drew a deep breath. "I'm not staying."

"He can be here by midnight if I call him now."

"I hadn't planned to work all weekend." Sidney said.

That stopped him. "You had plans?"

Plans like fighting her way through her accounts, and trying, somehow, to dig her way out of the mess her tax accountant had left her holding. Plans like taking care of her uncle. Still, they were her plans, and while Max might have succeeded in taking over the lives of his family, her life was her own. "Yes. I do."

"Hell. Can you cancel them?"

"Maybe I don't want to. And why is this so important to you, anyway?"

"I just want you here to take care of things, Sidney."

Something about that didn't ring quite true. She frowned at him. "I know you'll miss Philip, but—"

"I'm not trying to be a jerk about this, you know."

"Really?" She raised a knowing eyebrow.

He stared at her. She pictured him rummaging through his mental bag of tricks for a new strategy. "I'll make it worth your while," he said softly. "What am I paying you for this? Four, five thousand for the weekend?"

She gritted her teeth. "There hasn't been time to discuss the terms of the contract. Philip got sick this afternoon."

"Did you already have an event for this weekend?"

"That's not—"

"Did you?"

"Yes."

"Did you have to cancel it?"

"I spread my staff out, and brought on some extra people. We're fine."

His low whistle parted her hair. "I hope you're charging me a premium for this. How much overtime are you shelling out this weekend?"

"Don't worry. I'll make sure the bill hurts when you pay it."

"I doubt it. Look." He covered her hand where she still had her finger on the phone. "Whatever you're planning to bill me, I'll double it if you stay."

"Why?"

He stared at her for several breathless seconds. "Because I've got a lot riding on this weekend and it'll make me feel better if you're here."

"For a man with a renowned sense of business acumen, paying twice my fee for a little personal security seems a little rash."

He shrugged. "Don't let it get out. The stock market might crash."

Not even a hint of humor showed in his expression. Sidney searched his face for some indication, even a flicker of evidence that he wasn't absolutely serious. Finding none, she released a careful breath. "Are you going to let me out of the pantry—or do you plan to hold me hostage in here until I agree?"

"Will it work?"

"I can be kind of stubborn."

"So Philip tells me."

"I really feel like I should check on him tomorrow."

"If I send someone over there tonight to make sure he's okay, can't you go in the morning?"

"I'd have to drive all the way down there and back in time for lunch."

"I'll go with you. I'll drive you." She started to shake her head. His fingers tightened on her hand. "I want to."

The quiet insistence chipped away at her resolve. "You have guests."

"So?"

The question shouldn't have surprised her. Social niceties generally eluded him. "If this weekend is as important as you say, you should be here to entertain them."

"My guests expect to sleep until eleven-thirty, then take advantage of my pool, my tennis courts and my bar. If we leave early, I'll be back for the important stuff. No one will miss me."

There was something profoundly sad in that statement. Max had everything money could buy, and none of the things that mattered. Not for the first time, Sidney wondered how, and why, he'd surrounded himself with such superficial people. When Max entered a room, he immediately took up all the available space. Dynamic and compelling, he left a vacuum in his wake. Anyone who failed to notice was a self-absorbed fool. Deliberately, she dropped her voice to a whisper. "You aren't going to give up, are you?"

"I rarely do."

"So I've heard."

He tilted his head to one side. "Say yes, Sidney."

She hesitated. Why, oh why, did he have this effect on her? What was it the man did that made her want to simply melt into the floor? She'd seen him less than ten times since she'd come to live with her uncle Philip, and every time, he had the same, unnerving effect on her. "Max—"

He held her gaze with intense scrutiny. "Say yes."

It was that boyish charm that did her in. It had never ceased to amaze her that people found Max Loden irascible and ruthless when she found him so irresistible. "Are you sure you can get someone to stay with uncle Philip tonight?"

He squeezed her hand. "Not a problem. I've got a full staff of people in the city who love Philip. In fact, I'll get Gertie to go over there with some chicken soup. Unless I miss my guess, she's got a soft spot for your uncle."

"He likes her, too." Her uncle spoke often and warmly of the older woman who took care of Max's New York penthouse.

"See? Problem solved. Do you want Charlie to pick up your stuff?"

"Yes, no—oh, I don't know. This is too complicated. I can't think this fast. I like to plan things more than five minutes in advance."

"It doesn't have to be complicated. Just let me take care of everything."

Just like he always did, she thought. Max Loden, general manager of the universe, caretaker of the downtrodden. She thought of all the reasons she shouldn't—even prepared a quick list in her mind—but as she prepared to tell him no, he trailed the tip of his index finger along the back of her hand. "Sidney," he said, his voice a rumbling whisper that set off a fluttering of butterflies in her belly. "I thought you were a customer service fanatic."

She was going to lose, she realized. He was going to captivate her, just like he did everyone else. "I am," she blurted, more to herself than to him.

If he sensed her inner turmoil, he ignored it—or rather, capitalized on it. "Then make the customer happy." His thumb found the pulse in her wrist. "Make me happy, Sidney."

She could no more resist that pleading tone in his voice than she could fly to the moon. Waging silent war with the warning bells in her head, she hesitated for long seconds, then nodded. Max's gaze flared with satisfaction as he brushed her hand from the phone and again punched the numbers. With a few efficient words, he set the wheels in motion to take over her life—or her weekend, at least.

When he pressed the receiver into her hand a few seconds later, she couldn't meet his gaze as she explained the change in plans to her uncle. He seemed relieved. She frowned at the sound of his racking cough. "Uncle Philip, are you sure you're going to be all right?"

"Fine, fine," the older man told her. "Gertie's soup can cure anything. How's Max?"

Sidney glanced at him. "Stubborn as ever."

"Good. I told you that you should stay there. Max is going to need you." He coughed again. "You can't imagine how much, Sidney."

That made her smile. "I'll never be able to replace you, you know."

"You'll do fine. Make sure someone pays special attention to Greg Loden."

"I know. Keep him away from the gazebo." According to her uncle, the younger Loden's favorite seduction spot was the picturesque gazebo in the grove of apple trees near the foot of the estate.

"And keep the women away from him."

"Got it. Anything else?"

"Don't let Max turn into a tyrant."

"Too late for that."

His slight laugh warmed her. "And don't worry about me. I'll see you tomorrow."

"All right. We'll be there by nine. Good night, Uncle Philip. Promise you'll call if you need me."

"My word, my dear. Good night."

"Good night." Sydney slowly replaced the receiver. She raised her gaze to Max's. "You win." He still had that probing look that made her feel oddly transparent. She drew a deep breath.

"Good." He pushed open the pantry door. "I guarantee that I'm always in a much better mood when I win. Do you want Charlie to bring you some clothes or not?"

"I guess not. I can make do for tonight." Sydney followed him back into the kitchen. Her assistant, Kelly, could lend her whatever she couldn't scrounge in Philip's apartment.

He jammed his hands into his trouser pockets as he turned to face her once more. "I'm glad we settled that. And I meant what I said, I'll double your fee just for giving in."

His voice was a sultry whisper that reminded her of a hot summer wind: strangely welcome, and more than a little disconcerting, as if a storm was sure to follow in its wake. Worse, he smiled at her. At the sight, her heart skipped a beat. Max Loden's smile, she'd long ago determined, was like a well-preserved piece of art: he displayed it on the rarest occasions and it never failed to impress. "I'll see you later, Sydney."

And then he left.

The room went suddenly still. The vacuum caused by his absence, she mused. Like the aftermath of a hurricane, unnatural silence settled on the bustling kitchen. Sydney turned to find her staff watching her with wary eyes. "What?" she prompted.

Kelly Lars, her assistant and best friend, shot her a grin. "That was him," she said. It wasn't a question.

Sidney nodded. "Yes. That was Mr. Loden."

One of her pastry chefs, a young woman who'd joined Sidney's team several weeks ago, leaned one hip against the counter and exhaled an audible breath. "Wow."

Chip Meyers, who'd worked for Sidney for several years, gave the girl a sympathetic look. "It's not usually like this, Becky. Most of the places we work, we never even see the people we work for. This is a little different because Sidney is friends with the guy."

Kelly laughed. "I'm not sure I'd say *that* exactly."

Sidney shot her a warning glance. "Kel—"

"Well, you're not," Kelly insisted. "You've talked to him—what? A dozen times in twelve years?"

Sidney suppressed an irritated retort. "My uncle is his butler," she explained to her overly curious staff. "Uncle Philip has been with the Loden family for forty years. He's known Mr. Loden all of his life. You're here this weekend because my uncle hired you to augment Mr. Loden's staff. I'm here because uncle Philip couldn't be."

Becky was busily wiping her hands on a dishtowel. "You didn't mention, when you asked me if I wanted this assignment, that we'd be working for a human stick of dynamite."

"You're not." Sidney's voice was sharper than she'd intended. "You're working for me." The dynamite, she silently added, is my problem.

Chip frowned. "You know, Sid, when you told me the guy made his living making toys, this wasn't what I was expecting."

"Toys?" Becky asked.

Sidney exhaled a slow breath. "Max Loden makes his living making money. AppleTree Toys is just a part of the Loden Enterprises empire."

Becky's eyes widened. "AppleTree—oh my God! *Max*

Loden. That Max Loden?'' Her expression changed to awe. ''I can't believe I'm in Max Loden's house. And that he looks like that.''

Kelly laughed. ''What did you expect him to look like?''

''Well, I expected he was like, sixty at least.'' Becky leaned against the counter. ''I had no idea he was such a— well—such a stud. My kid sisters love those dolls.''

Chip laughed. ''So do the rest of the girls in America. That's how we ended up working in digs like this. Who knew a guy could make billions selling dolls.''

Becky warmed to the topic. ''I remember when the Real Men collection came out. I was so jealous of my sisters. When I played with Barbie dolls, all we had were Ken and Alan to date Barbie and all her friends.''

''That was a man's kind of world,'' Chip countered.

Becky glared at him. ''Then along came AppleTree Toys with the Real Men collection. How many are there? Six?''

''Eight,'' Sidney supplied. ''Max got the idea from watching his friend's daughters play with their dolls. There were never enough males to go around.''

Kelly snorted. ''Very insightful.''

Becky nodded. ''Lucratively insightful. I remember reading that. So he conceived this entire line of male dolls. Each one has his own personality. There's a stockbroker, a park ranger, a football player, a doctor—I can't remember the rest. Anyway, the Max doll is the central figure. Supposedly, his staff named the doll after him.''

''They did it without his knowledge,'' Sidney said quietly. ''By the time he found out, the ad slicks had already gone out. At the time, AppleTree toys was operating on a shoe-string, and Max didn't feel like he could justify the expense of pulling the ads.'' She paused. ''He doesn't like it.''

''Yeah, well,'' Becky continued, ''like it or not, the Max doll, and all his friends, are phenomenally popular. My sisters have a zillion of them, and all their accessories.''

Chip raised his eyebrows. ''They have accessories? No guy

I know would be caught dead with anything that could be called an accessory.''

Becky laughed. ''Not even if the accessory is a twin-engine airplane?''

''Well—''

Kelly came to his rescue. ''What she means, Chip, is that the Real Men dolls have an entire line of fashions and play sets that suit their individual personalities. I have it on very good authority that when the Max doll pulls up in his Jag roadster, it sends any self-respecting Barbie doll into a swoon.''

Chip flexed his biceps beneath his white chef's jacket. ''I'll bet he doesn't have Chip the super chef.''

Becky swatted him with the dishtowel. ''Those dolls are so popular, the advertising slogan for the line is Who Gets To Marry Max? When little girls drag their dolls out to play, that's the first question they ask.''

''They're not the only ones,'' Kelly quipped. ''Every society reporter and fortune hunter in the country keeps asking the same question about who'll marry the real Max Loden.''

Chip shook his head. ''So that's how 'Mad Max' made his millions.''

Sidney lost what was left of her indulgence. ''Don't call him that,'' she said firmly.

The three looked at her, wide-eyed. Kelly placed a hand on her arm. ''He didn't mean—''

''I know,'' Sidney assured her, and managed a slight smile at Chip. ''I know you didn't. But I don't want to hear that name again while we're here.'' She paused. ''For that matter, I don't want to hear it after we leave, either. Max Loden inherited his father's company on the verge of bankruptcy. Thanks to the success of the Real Men dolls, he earned enough capital to bail out some of Loden Enterprises' less successful public ventures. He took an ailing company, put his mind and effort behind it, and made it grow. Just because his methods are a little unorthodox, and just because some of his adversaries think he's a little—eccentric—doesn't mean we're going to disrespect him. I trust I've made that clear.''

Chip looked sheepish. ''I'm sorry, Sidney. I didn't know you—''

''It's all right. He's heard the name before, I'm certain. But I don't want him to hear it from us. Mr. Loden is paying every member of this staff extraordinarily well for their service.''

Becky nodded. ''I'm getting twice what I did for the last house party I worked.''

Sidney tugged at the points of her jacket. ''Most of you are. So in addition to your service, he's going to get your respect, too. I'd like you to alert the rest of the staff to that. If I hear anything that even hints at disrespect, I won't hesitate to let someone go.''

Becky and Chip stared at her, astonished. Kelly alone seemed to sense the volatile nature of her mood. ''Chip,'' she said, with the soft authority Sidney had always admired. ''I think now would be a good time for you to find Mr. Loden's chef and decide how the two of you want to divvy up the kitchen responsibilities. Do you have the punch list I gave you?''

He nodded. Kelly waved him away with a sweep of her hand. ''Good. Becky, I'd like you to gather the rest of our staff in about ten minutes so we can brief them.'' She scanned the kitchen, then tucked her clipboard under her arm. ''We've got two hours,'' she continued, ''and I'm going to make sure the guest rooms are up to spec.''

As Kelly picked up a tray of chocolates, Sidney gave the confections a final, assessing glance. The shaped candies were Sidney's personal trademark. Individually made, each candy represented a guest's personal interests. Before a major event, she interviewed her clients to determine how best to serve their guests. The chocolates, which her staff placed on the pillows of the guest room beds or at each place setting for meals, were a special touch her clients usually raved about.

Kelly paused on her way to the door. "Sidney, would you like to instruct the rest of the staff, or shall I?"

Sidney gave her a grateful look. "I'll do it."

"You're sure?"

"I'm sure." At her friend's dubious look, Sidney laughed. "Don't worry, I've delivered my last avenging angel speech for the day."

"All right," Kelly agreed. "I'm going to deliver the chocolates, then." She inspected the tray. "You know, these look really good, Sid," she said. "Even if you did make them at three this morning. No one makes them as well as you do."

Sidney shrugged, unwilling to discuss why she'd been unable to sleep the night before, and had decided to personally make the chocolates—a duty she generally would have delegated. "I enjoy doing it. I hadn't done them in a while, and I wanted to make sure I hadn't lost my touch."

Kelly gave her a shrewd look, but silently hoisted the tray of chocolates to her shoulder. As she strolled past Sidney, she whispered, "Sure you don't want me to put the Cupid on Max's pillow, Sid?"

Sidney frowned at her. "Did you listen to a word I just said?"

"Every one of them. That's why I asked."

"Kel—"

"Okay, okay. He sure is cute, though." She sailed out of the kitchen without a backward glance.

Sidney almost laughed out loud. Max Loden was many things. Daunting. Charming. Elegant. Ruthless. Brilliant. Maybe even handsome. But never, *ever* had anyone described him as cute. Sidney sometimes doubted that Max had even entered the world as a baby. Instead, he seemed to have walked onto the stage of his life full-grown and ready for battle.

When his parents died, leaving a twenty-five-year-old Max full responsibility for his brother, his two sisters and his father's struggling corporation, Max had taken the reins like a man born to lead. He'd made a lot of money, and a lot of enemies along the way. Sidney's uncle, Philip Grant, had seen him through all of it. And while the world found Max's eccentricities, razor-sharp business acumen and incomprehensible ability to take the wildest risk possible and make astounding profits from the venture both infuriating and intimidating, Philip adored him. His adversaries and even his colleagues claimed he had no heart, that he placed profits above people and that he'd step on anyone who got in his way. "Mad Max," they called him. And as far as everyone could tell, he liked it.

But Sidney had never believed it, for reasons she'd told no one—not even Philip. On a cold rainy evening, years ago, not long after she'd come to live with her uncle, Max Loden had given her a gift so generous, so unthinkably extravagant that she'd tucked it close to her heart and used it whenever her confidence had needed it most.

He would never remember the incident, she was sure. She'd been fifteen. He was a college student bound for glory. Everyone agreed it was his destiny. She'd been afraid of him, and hadn't known why. In those days, however, it seemed she had feared everyone. Even then people talked about him. He had what Philip called presence. He always seemed to be involved in terribly important, terribly serious business. While his brother and sisters were enjoying the carefree life afforded them by wealthy parents, Max appeared to know, somehow, that his destiny would be different—that, too soon, he would bear responsibilities far too heavy for most men's shoulders.

Yet on that night, for reasons she might never know, he had stepped off his constantly spinning world to give Sidney's self-esteem a desperately needed transfusion. And, in that instant, she'd mentally cast aside his critics as shallow fools and envious naysayers. And "Mad Max" had become, forever known to her alone, as "Max the Magnificent."

Chapter Two

When Philip Grant recovered from the flu, Max decided two hours later, he would kill him. He stood in his study where he scanned the assembled guests on his terrace. The only light in this third-story room he used as a refuge came from the festive lanterns and mini-lights Sidney's staff had strung through the trees. Dark clouds blotted out the crescent moon.

Which, he thought in a burst of grim humor, seemed wildly appropriate. The clouds of his temper had begun gathering earlier that day. His mood had rapidly progressed from foul to rotten. Greg, who had trouble committing to wearing the same tie all day, was predictably balking at the idea of betrothing himself to Lauren Fitzwater. Never mind that Greg had made certain promises—promises that Lauren had every reason to believe would lead to marriage. Greg was experiencing a very predictable bout of jitters. Max had been prepared for that. Max liked to think he was prepared for just about everything.

He had assured Greg, and meant it, that Lauren was the best thing in his life. Max's desire to see Greg settled went far beyond the simplicity of a multimillion dollar corporate takeover.

Everyone needed stability.

Max should know. He'd spent his whole life without any. Stability, he'd learned, was the remedy for loneliness. So he'd strengthened his brother's resolve, and considered it all part of a day's work.

And while Greg's burst of misgivings had proved mildly irritating, the beginning of his descent into hell hadn't happened until later. His gaze narrowed and found Alice Northrup-Bowles downing a glass of champagne as she flirted with Max's senior vice president. Damn the shrew. Her presence alone was enough to rattle him.

And then there was Sidney Grant. Sidney with her wise, intelligent eyes and that cocky little smile that made him want to kiss it right off her full mouth. What the hell was Philip thinking?

The old man was too shrewd, Max realized, not to know that his employer's interest in his niece ran deeper than common courtesy. While Max had never told Philip the story, the evening years ago when he'd discovered Sidney in his parents' library had left an indelible mark on him. He didn't know why, and had long since given up trying to figure it out. He'd found her holding a dust rag in one hand, weeping over the broken remains of a porcelain figurine. She'd looked so desolate. Something in the bend of her shoulders, her tear-filled eyes, had struck a note in Max that had never stopped ringing.

The encounter hadn't lasted long. Less than five minutes as he recalled, but he'd walked into that room, with no earthly idea why he felt moved to comfort her. And in the end, she'd comforted him. She'd told him how her twice-divorced mother had remarried again, had decided that Sidney's presence in her home would make it too difficult for her new stepchildren to accept her as their mother. Philip asked his younger sister to send Sidney to him. Sidney's mother had needed little prompting. She'd put her fifteen-year-old daughter on a bus the following afternoon.

Max remembered his sense of horror as her story unfolded. Even his parents, who had always remained slightly detached from their children's activities, wouldn't have contemplated anything so unspeakable. Sidney had mopped her eyes as she'd told him the tale, then apologized for burdening him with it. She'd started crying, she'd said, and that was how she'd broken the figurine. She was on her way to find her uncle Philip to report the incident.

Max had shaken his head, handed her his handkerchief, and assured her he'd handle everything. She needn't worry about the broken figure. "I'll take care of it," he'd told her. At her wide-eyed look, he'd explained, "That's what I do."

Sidney had looked at him with that expressive gaze and said, "You always take care of everyone, don't you?" At his startled look, she'd managed a slight chuckle that had seared its way through his nervous system. "Uncle Philip told me."

He vaguely remembered coughing. "I see."

Sidney tilted her head to one side. "So if you take care of everyone else, who takes care of you?" He'd stared at her, stunned. At his silence, Sidney had looked at him with that probing look that reminded him so much of her uncle. "Everyone needs someone to take care of them," she'd whispered. "Even you."

Her declaration had zeroed in on the secret part of himself he kept firmly hidden in a vault of self-control. Sidney's softly uttered words had thrown open the curtains of his heart and sent light streaming through the window of his soul. He'd had to struggle to restore the internal security system that kept his emotions firmly in their fortress.

Without allowing himself to consider the reasons, Max had changed his plans that night, and taken his date shopping at Tiffany's so he could replace the figurine. The incident with Sidney had rattled him more than he'd thought it should. He still wasn't precisely sure why she'd managed to get to him like that, but he knew that in the handful of times he'd seen her thereafter, he'd felt inexplicably connected to her—as if something mysterious and irrevocable had bonded them together.

He'd made a point, over the next few years, to follow Sidney's life through Philip's reports. With a few phone calls, he'd ensured she had the scholarship money she needed to attend college. She'd graduated summa cum laude, and he'd had nothing at all to do with that. He'd roundly cursed the philandering, weak-spined bastard she'd married soon thereafter, and silently cheered the guts it had taken for her to divorce him. Carter Silas had done a tap dance on Sidney's confidence that would have unraveled most people, but Sidney had impressed the hell out of Max with the courage she'd shown in standing up to him.

Later, he'd learned, she hadn't even begun to impress him. Though Sidney knew nothing of Max's interest, he'd made it his business—compelled at first by the surge of protectiveness he'd felt when he first met her, and later by an odd fascination with wanting to know what she'd accomplish next.

Unknown to Philip, Carter Silas had done more than abuse Sidney's self-esteem. On a snowy February night, Carter had drained their mutual accounts, embezzled a quarter of a million dollars from the brokerage firm where he worked, then left Sidney holding the legal bag while he fled town with his twenty-one-year-old mistress. Max had sent his accountant and his lawyers to Sidney's aid, and hired a private detective to get incriminating pictures of her husband. Max had made absolutely sure that Sidney's lawyers had everything they needed to nail the weasel, but, in the end, Sidney had done most of the fighting on her own. Thanks to Max, her lawyers had shaken the bastard down for enough of a settlement to ensure that Sidney was comfortable. Though the embezzlement charges had never been proven, Silas had floundered for several years until Max finally decided he wasn't worth the bother.

When Sidney had started her temp agency, an effort Philip hinted had taken all the courage Sidney had left, Max had again placed private phone calls. His business associates had suddenly found themselves in desperate need of temporary staff. Sidney had charmed them all with her skill and poise, and he still received Christmas cards thanking him for recommending her to them.

Philip had never asked why Max had taken such a personal interest in his niece, and Max hadn't offered an explanation. If he had his way, neither Philip nor Sidney would ever know that those few seconds in the library, when she'd looked at him with those sad, sympathetic eyes and earnestly asked who took care of him, had opened an aching chasm in his soul that had never healed. No one he cared about, he'd vowed, as long as he had power to stop it, would ever feel as alone as he had at that moment.

Now, she barely resembled the slightly bedraggled, self-conscious girl in his father's library. Her dark hair, thick and luxuriant, framed an expressive face dominated by a pair of intelligent hazel eyes. He'd always liked the way she looked at him. No one else looked at him quite that way—as if she understood some secret part of him that remained hidden to the rest of the world.

And, if he were honest, his thoughts generally ran a more primitive course. With little or no effort, he found himself imagining just how Sidney's eyes would look if he were making love to her. They'd grow misty, he knew, and the color would darken. Emerald green and intense, full of fire and need, they'd steal his breath.

He hadn't bothered to question why he'd insisted she stay for the weekend. There were dozens of practical reasons for the decision, but Max knew none of them explained the knot of hunger that had been steadily growing in his gut since he'd found her in his kitchen that afternoon. His desire to have her on his property had little, if anything, to do with keeping her off the road at a late hour, or his worries about his guests.

He wanted her.

Like a blow to the head, the knowledge had hit him squarely when he'd seen her standing there in the midst of well-ordered chaos. He wanted her.

Hell, he'd probably wanted her for years. Why he hadn't recognized it before, he had no idea. Maybe it was the impossibility of the whole thing. Sidney Grant, and everything she deserved in life, was as out of reach to him as a normal family in a little house with a dog, a picket fence and a two-car garage. So far out of reach, in fact, that he'd never even allowed himself to contemplate what it would be like to have her in his life.

Until today. Until he'd seen her wearing a ridiculously seductive tuxedo and commanding a small army. A surge of adrenaline had raked him, and he recognized it instantly. It was the same feeling he got when he looked at a stock report and *saw* the future; the same feeling that overcame him when he analyzed a financial statement and *knew* the hidden potential of a buried asset or an underutilized resource; the same feeling, he mused, that drove him to gamble millions of dollars on what seemed like bad odds. And with customary dispatch, he'd listened to his gut feeling and not to his head.

With a carefully executed strategy, he'd ensured that he'd have her undivided attention for the next several days. He had her safely in his sphere, where he could watch and listen. He could examine the tension in his gut and sift through the messages screaming through his brain. For three days, he could concentrate on nothing but the hungry need he felt each time he looked at Sidney Grant.

The thought brought a wry smile to his lips. If the heaviness he'd felt in his lower body since earlier that day was any indication, he didn't even need to look at her to feel the effects of her sway over him. He'd retreated here, to his third-story office, to clear his head. It hadn't worked. Evidently, thinking about Sidney worked just as well as watching her. If he survived this weekend, he decided, he'd satisfy several of his more pressing curiosities, and see if this feeling had the kind of payoff he expected.

"I thought I'd find you here."

At the sound of Sidney's voice, Max felt need pour through

his veins like lava. He turned from the window to find her watching him with the same quiet intensity she'd had long ago in his parent's library. His fingers flexed at his sides as he struggled for equilibrium. Easy, he warned himself. Don't overwhelm her. "Hello, Sidney. What brings you up here?"

She held a bottle and two glasses in her hand. "Philip mentioned that if you disappeared up here during the party, you'd probably want this." She set the bottle on his desk.

"Philip thinks of everything," he said quietly, wondering if Philip had thought of the consequences of sending Sidney to him.

"He does." She hesitated. "I didn't mean to disturb you. I just wanted to deliver this. If there's nothing else you want, I need to get back downstairs."

"Do you?" He glanced at the terrace again. "Your staff certainly seem to have everything under control."

She offered him that slight smile, the one that drew his attention straight to her mouth and kept it there. "They do. But it's a large party. Someone has to see to the details."

He wasn't ready for her to leave yet. He was never, he'd long ago admitted, ready for Sidney to leave him. "Do they know where to find you?"

She searched his expression. "Yes."

With a wave of his hand, he indicated the leather chair across from his desk. "Then sit. You've been on your feet all afternoon." At her surprised look, he managed a slight smile. "And don't ask me how I know."

"You're omniscient?" she quipped.

He shook his head at that. "Hardly. But Philip tells me you're maniacal about quality service. I understand what that means. If I were in your place, I'd have checked everything twice, then checked it again."

Surprise flickered in her gaze, but she eased into the chair. "I can spare a few minutes, I guess."

"Thank you." Max studied her for several tension-filled seconds. Her eyes, he admitted with some chagrin, weren't the only things about her that had him struggling for breath. The tailored lines of her uniform did nothing to disguise a lithe figure and the kind of curves designed to catch a man's attention. It skimmed her body in all kinds of interesting ways, yet managed through some tailoring miracle to still appear subdued. After fifteen seconds in her presence, he'd felt his fingers tingling with the urge to thrust one hand into her hair, and snake the other around her waist so he could feel the imprint of her curves against his body.

Sidney began to fidget under his intense stare. She cleared her throat. "I wanted to thank you again for sending Gertie to take care of Philip," she finally said.

"Don't mention it. I was glad to."

"He'll like having her there."

"I hope so." He watched the uneasiness that played across her face. She looked nervous, and, unless he missed his guess, a little heated. It made him feel better to think she was as aware as he of the strange electricity between them.

She shifted uncertainly. "Was there something you wanted?"

You, he wanted to say, just to gauge her reaction. "Philip," he said instead. "I wanted to ask you how much Philip told you about the guest list for this weekend."

A slight smile played at her full lips. "You wanted to strangle him, you mean?"

"Maybe."

She nodded. "I think yes. He suggested that you might be feeling a bit, ah, perturbed by now."

"So he knew that Raymond Lort was bringing Alice Northrup-Bowles as his guest?"

"Yes."

"But he didn't care to enlighten me."

"I suppose not."

"Why the hell not?"

She shrugged. "I wouldn't care to speculate."

He narrowed his gaze. "But you knew."

"I knew she'd be here."

"Did you know it would make me furious?"

"Yes."

"But you didn't tell me either."

She brushed her palm over her jacket sleeve. "I didn't feel—"

"Damn Philip. He should have told me."

"He seemed to feel you'd rescind Mr. Lort's invitation if you knew he intended to bring Ms. Nothrup-Bowles."

"I would have. The bastard. Lort knows exactly how I feel about that woman."

"Uncle Philip felt the crisis could be easily avoided without forcing you to offend Mr. Lort."

Philip would, he thought, his temper kicking up another degree. "I don't give a damn about offending Raymond Lort. Alice is a scheming, conniving leech who happens to make my sister Natalie feel miserable. Alice has a genius for making Natalie forget that she's an exceptionally talented, remarkably gifted woman. Worse, Alice enjoys it." His gaze narrowed. He uttered a dark curse. "And it enrages me."

Sidney visibly stilled. She appeared to be gathering her calm. Slowly, she pushed herself out of her chair, then brushed past him to stand at the window. "Look." Pointing, she drew his attention back to the terrace. "I'd like you to notice that my assistant has your sister fully occupied in solving a crisis which will, no doubt, save your party from certain ruin."

She indicated a darkened corner of the terrace. "Natalie's husband, Paul, is busily distracting Edward Fitzwater's attention from your brother's obvious nervousness, thereby ensuring that Miss Northrup-Bowles has absolutely no chance of attracting Paul's notice." She pointed to the dance floor where Greg and Lauren were enjoying a few moments together. "And Miss Fitzwater is being given every opportunity to wrestle the expected proposal from your brother."

Even as she said it, a waiter intercepted one of Greg's

former girlfriends with a canapé-laden tray. The woman stopped, sampled the confection, then accepted an invitation to dance from one of Max's vice presidents. Max's gaze flicked over the party as he repressed the urge to pull Sidney into his arms. Too soon, he reminded himself. Patience was key. "Nicely done," he murmured.

Her eyes twinkled when she looked at him. "I'm *very* good at what I do."

The statement sent heat skittering along his skin as he wondered, inevitably, just how good she was at other things. "Really?" he said, lifting an eyebrow.

He knew from her expression that she sensed the shift in the conversation. She backed up a step. "Max, is something wrong?"

Max exhaled a deep breath and leaned back against his desk. He had more riding on this weekend than she could possibly know. Philip had understood. And Max had to believe that Philip wouldn't have sent Sidney to him if he didn't think she could help him. It wasn't Philip's fault that Max was having trouble picturing Sidney as his ally when the thoughts he was having weren't nearly so tame. Much as he'd like to concentrate all his energy on her, he couldn't afford the risk. There was too much at stake. "Sidney, look," he began. "I don't know how much Philip told you about this party, but it's extremely important."

She nodded. "Because of the merger with Fitzwater."

He tipped his head toward the window. "Since your staff obviously have my guests completely under control, why don't you sit down and let me explain." He poured himself a drink. "Want one?" he asked.

She shook her head as she hurried around the desk. "No, thank you." Sidney dropped back into the leather chair. "I don't drink on the job."

"You brought two glasses."

"I thought you might have a guest."

He shook his head. "Not up here. I don't entertain guests

in this room.'' He met her gaze, waited to see if she recognized the significance of the statement. Awareness flickered in her gaze. Satisfied, he waved the bottle at her. "Will it change your mind if I tell you this is iced tea?"

Sidney's eyebrows lifted.

"It's a quirk of mine," Max continued. "I don't drink on the job either."

"Aren't you always on the job?"

He gave her a knowing look. "That's why I keep tea instead of bourbon in my decanters." He poured her a glass. "I'm surprised Philip didn't tell you."

"He told me everything he thought I needed to know to help make this a successful weekend for you. He doesn't tell me your personal business."

Max pondered that. Philip had told him certain details about Sidney's life, it was true, but when he thought about it, he really knew very little about her personal habits and preferences. He nodded. "I'm sure he doesn't. That's one of the reasons I like him."

"Uncle Philip is very professional, and he cares for you. You're lucky to have him."

"I know I am. Smart people surround themselves with smart people who are strong where they aren't. I'm sure you've learned that in business."

She nodded. "That's why Kelly's in charge of client relations, and I stick to making chocolates."

Max's gaze narrowed. There was something significant in the statement, but he couldn't put his finger on it. He'd never been particularly gifted at reading the nuances of conversation. Especially not from the female of the species. "Something like that," he admitted.

Shifting slightly in the chair, Sidney waved a hand in the general direction of the party. "The more you tell me, the more I can help you."

A smile played at the corner of his mouth. She was, indeed, Philip's niece. Philip Grant's personal motto was: Knowledge

Is Ammunition. "That's probably true. Are you sure you're willing to help me?"

She looked surprised. "I'm here, aren't I?"

"Against your better judgment?"

"No, of course not."

"How did your staff feel when you told them they'd be working for 'Mad Max'?"

Her lips pressed together in a tight line. "They were pleased."

"I'll bet."

"You pay very well. They were pleased."

Max shrugged. In a burst of restless energy, he slipped open the buttons of his double-breasted tuxedo jacket, then dropped into his desk chair. "Did you tell them I'm prone to fits of brooding and unmanageable temper and that most of my acquaintances are scared to death of me?"

"No." There was firm resolution in her voice. "I did not. I don't indulge in spreading rumors."

Had her expression been any less serious, he might have laughed. She meant it, he realized, and the thought warmed him as little else could. "No, I don't suppose you do."

Sidney watched him for long seconds, then settled back in her chair. "So what else is riding on this besides a merger with Edward Fitzwater?"

Max exhaled. "Just about everything," he told her. "I'm concerned about Greg."

In the next few minutes, Max carefully explained to her how much he wanted his brother's relationship with Lauren Fitzwater to progress. Yes, he admitted, the merger represented a significant gain for Loden Enterprises, but his true concern was for his brother's welfare. Greg needed stability in his life, and Lauren would give it to him. If Philip were there, Max knew, he would have done whatever he could to ensure that Greg's engagement came off without a hitch—Alice Northrup-Bowles notwithstanding.

When he finished his long explanation, he gave Sidney a

cautious look. "Sorry. That's probably more than you bargained for."

"Actually, it's what I expected." Sidney tilted her head to one side in a manner painfully reminiscent of that night in the library. "Max, can I ask you something?"

He sensed danger, but deliberately dismissed it. "Sure." He glanced out the window again.

"Why are you so sure this is right for your brother?"

His hand tightened on his glass. "Family is important to everyone, Sidney."

"By family, you mean marriage."

"For Greg I do."

"Don't you think that's up to him to decide?"

"I know my brother. I know exactly what he needs." He didn't bother to explain that the same instincts that drove him in business told him that his brother's life had reached a crucial turning point. A few more years, and Greg the immature young man was going to become their father—bitter, broke and completely alone.

"I see."

He didn't think he imagined the doubt in her tone and it annoyed him. He turned to face her. "Look, I've spent the last ten years taking care of my brother and my two sisters. Sometimes, I'm in a better position to know what's best for them. In Greg's case, he has trouble committing himself. If he can find a way to screw this up, he will."

"Do you think he'll make Lauren happy?"

"Yes."

She frowned again. "Will he cheat on her?"

Max studied her for a few seconds, cursing the man who'd put that pained look in her eyes. Evidently, the memories of her first marriage still stung. She knew firsthand just how devastating infidelity could be. "No. He won't."

"How can you be so sure?"

"I wouldn't let him." His voice held a note of iron resolve, the same tone he used when he made reckless business decisions and dared his staff to question him.

"You couldn't stop—"

Max shook his head. "That's not what I mean. I mean Greg knows that no one in this family would tolerate it if he cheated on his spouse. We're not that kind of people, Sidney. He'd have hell to pay if he decided to wander, and Greg's not extremely fond of paying consequences."

She studied him. "That's an interesting theory."

He wasn't going to argue with her. She couldn't possibly understand. "It's the way I do things."

As if she sensed the challenge in the words, she gave him a short nod. "I understand."

"Then we're clear on that?"

"Absolutely. I'm here for *you.*"

The slight emphasis nearly undid him. Could she even suspect the effect she was having on him? He searched her expression and found it stubbornly unreadable. Setting his glass on the desk, he leaned toward her. She smelled like chocolate. He found it more arousing than any designer perfume.

Carefully holding her gaze he said, "I'm counting on it."

From the adjacent room, one of Max's maids, who'd spent an hour on the phone with Philip Grant earlier that evening, smiled as she flicked the lamp on and off three times. She watched her contact, the young bartender near the fountain, for a response. He glanced around, then carefully selected a champagne glass to polish with a soft, white cloth. Understanding the message, the maid nodded to the other young woman in the room before she headed off to intercept Max's sister Colleen, who was at that moment, according to the bartender, on her way to find Max in his third-story office. Philip had made it quite clear that Sidney and Max weren't to be interrupted.

The other woman, one of Max's chauffeurs, picked up the

telephone to place a call to Philip Grant. The senior butler had asked for complete information on the weekend's events. He would, no doubt, find this bit of news especially intriguing.

Chapter Three

"I don't know, Philip," Gertie said as she discarded the king of hearts. "If Sidney finds out what you're up to, she'll strangle you."

Philip Grant picked up the king and added it to his hand. "She'll never suspect. Besides, Max needs her." He discarded the three of spades.

Sam Mitchell, Max's groundskeeper, pulled a card from the draw stack. "That's for sure. Last month, I was scared to death he was going to give in and marry the Barlow woman—" He snapped his fingers. "What's her name?"

"Constance," Elena Garcia, who kept the exotic plants blooming in Max's greenhouse, said with disdain.

"Yeah." Sam nodded. "Constance—as in constantly annoying. She's taken on becoming the answer to 'Who Gets To Marry Max?' as a personal project." He tapped his blunt fingers on his fanned cards. "Can you imagine life with her running Max's house?"

Elena clucked her tongue. "I tell you one thing, if he brings home that Barlow woman, I'm going to quit."

Gertie grunted. "You're not the only one. The minute he hints there might be a wedding, I'm giving him my resignation."

"You, and all the rest of us," Sam agreed, tossing the five

of hearts onto the discard pile. "Except maybe Philip. What would it take to make you leave Max, Philip?"

"I don't know," he said blandly. "Are you going to take that card, Elena?"

Elena gave him a dry look. "Don't think you're going to distract me. You may think you're going to force Max and Sidney together, but what will you do if your plan backfires? Greg Loden isn't exactly oblivious to Sidney's obvious charms, you know?"

Sam nodded. "That's true. And with Max breathing down his brother's neck about an engagement to Miss Fitzwater, I suspect Greg'll be looking for some diversion this weekend."

"He won't find it with Sidney," Philip assured them. "I've already told her what Max is expecting from Greg. She'll see that it happens."

"He's a charmer, that one," Gertie mused. "I've seen him turn heads before."

"Not Sidney's. She's immune to him."

"But not to Max," Elena prompted.

Philip shook his head. "Sidney and Max—" he searched for the right word "—communicate." He glanced at Elena. "If you're not going to take that card, I am."

She clucked her tongue as she reached for the card. "You can't expect to win every game, Philip."

While she studied her hand, Philip decided not to ask what she meant by that. Instead, he wondered how Max and Sidney were faring at the estate. He'd seen Max grow from a lonely young boy, who gracefully bore the pressures of the world on his shoulders, to an even lonelier man whose friends and family expected him to solve all their problems. Isolated in a tower of emotional distance, Max Loden was in serious danger of losing his heart. To hear some tell it, he was already past saving. Philip didn't believe it.

Elena dropped a card onto the discard pile. Gertie reached for it. "No matter what you say, Philip, if Sidney finds out you're not really sick, she'll kill you for this."

Philip suppressed a smile. Long ago, he'd given up trying to understand the strange connection between his niece and his employer. But of one thing he was certain: Max needed rescuing. Always the savior, always the one his family relied on in a crisis, always the hero, Max had learned to depend on no one—for support, for help, or even for love. While Sidney, his brave, talented, headstrong niece, had learned to keep the world at arm's length. Hurt one time too many, Sidney allowed no one to penetrate her inner world.

As Gertie studied her cards, Philip considered the niece he loved like a daughter, and the employer he considered a close friend. Only Philip had breached their collective defenses. And while he didn't begin to understand why he'd been blessed with such a role, he took the responsibility seriously. They needed each other. And since the two of them were too thickheaded to know it, he had no choice but to take matters into his own hands.

Gertie discarded the jack of diamonds. Philip picked it up with a feeling of satisfaction. Eventually, he reasoned, Max and Sidney would understand that he was acting in their best interest and forgive him for meddling. He discarded, then set his cards down on the table. "Gin."

Sam grumbled as he began tabulating the score. "One day, I'm going to figure out how you manage to cheat."

Elena dropped her cards to the table with a sigh of disgust. "He marks the cards. He has to. Nobody has his luck."

As Philip piled the cards into a neat stack, the phone rang. Gertie frowned as she reached for the receiver. "Well, let's hope his luck is holding. Sidney already called once this morning. I hope she's not suspicious."

"She's not," Philip assured her.

"Hello?" Gertie answered the phone. Philip carefully watched her expression change from polite inquiry to unabashed delight. She covered the receiver with her hand. "It's Mary Beth," she said, identifying the young woman who'd called last night with news of Max's third-floor rendezvous with Sidney. "She says Max is teaching Bailey how to dive this morning."

Philip lifted an eyebrow—an affectation he'd passed on to his employer. "There's nothing unusual about that. Max is very fond of his niece."

Gertie asked Mary Beth a few more questions, then hung up. "Nothing unusual," she told the small group, satisfaction evident in her tone, "except that Sidney is watching, and Max is watching her watch him."

SIDNEY WAS still questioning her sanity as she methodically made her way around Max's pool, discreetly checking on his guests. Drinks were filled, towels replaced. At a waved command to one of her staff, an ashtray materialized near the elbow of Raymond Lort. Momentarily satisfied, she continued to scan the scene, looking for flaws and, more consciously, trying to ignore the way Max looked sitting on the edge of the pool, patiently teaching one of his nieces how to dive.

She still wasn't sure what had possessed her to agree to stay at the estate for the weekend. She should have known what prolonged exposure to the man was going to do to her. She'd slept poorly last night, and, as much as she'd like to believe her restless slumber owed itself to the strange bed, she knew better. She'd been consumed with thoughts of the way Max had looked at her when he'd delivered that final announcement in his office. "I'm counting on it," he'd said, and her stomach had started dancing the Macarena.

The odd feeling had continued through the evening's festivities, and left her feeling unsettled when Greg Loden had cornered her near a secluded area of the terrace.

"Sidney," he'd said, his voice a little too controlled. "How are you?"

She had searched his expression for signs of inebriation, but other than unnaturally bright eyes, he seemed in control. "I'm fine, Mr. Loden. How are you?"

With his elegantly casual shrug, the one she'd long ago

summed up as his philosophy on life, he'd explained that Max was annoyed that he'd continued to drag his feet on his engagement to Lauren Fitzwater. "You know Max," Greg had told her, "he thinks what's good for business is good for the family."

Sidney frowned. "You don't think your brother is pushing you simply because he wants the business merger with Fitzwater, do you?"

"No. He's pushing me because he thinks Lauren can have a positive influence on my more, er, autarkic tendencies."

"Is that a nice way of saying libertine?"

To her relief, he had laughed, and the strange tension shattered. "No, it's a Harvard economics major's way of saying I enjoy the benefits of being a Loden without bearing much of the responsibility." He shrugged again. "Max likes running the business. He wouldn't consider relinquishing control to any of us."

Thoughtfully, Sidney studied Greg's handsome features. "Have you asked him?"

Greg shook his head as he finished his glass of champagne. "No need. What Max wants is to see all of us safely settled in nice, stable marriages. Natalie and Colleen succumbed without a fight. I like to give Max a challenge every now and then." He leaned closer to her and dropped his voice several decibels. "It builds character, you know?" He'd raised his hand, then, to cup her shoulder. "And speaking of characters, why have you been hiding from us, Sidney? I miss having you around here."

His fingers slid over the fabric of her jacket. Sidney took a careful step away. "I work for a living, Greg."

His amused laugh carried on the night breeze. "Unlike me, you mean?"

She shook her head. "No. I just mean that I have a lot of responsibilities with my business. I don't have as much time to visit with Uncle Philip as I used to."

Greg's hazel eyes searched her face. "Do you have time for other things?"

She sensed the suggestive undertone in the question, and carefully headed it off. "Not really." She set her water glass down with a decisive clink. "It's been nice talking with you, Greg, but I think I should call it a night. The party's winding down, and Max seems to think I might be needed early tomorrow morning. He's probably right."

"Ah, Max," Greg said. "He's always right, isn't he?"

Sidney chose not to answer. "Good night, Greg."

He had hesitated, then gave her a brief nod. "I'll see you tomorrow."

Now, as Sidney glanced around the pool deck, she carefully considered the note she'd received from Max that morning requesting her presence. How much, she had to wonder, did he know about her conversation with his brother, and how much would he want to know? She pushed aside the unsettling thought and told herself, for the umpteenth time that morning, to get a grip. It wasn't working. When she'd spoken to her uncle, he'd assured her that he was much better—so much better that he'd encouraged her not to make the trip out to see him that morning. Reluctantly, if not gracefully, Sidney had agreed.

Fool, fool, fool, she now thought as she looked at Max. She could have used the break, and the chance to think things over. Clad in black swim trunks, he looked—she searched for the word Kelly had used the night before—dishy. That was it. Kelly had informed her that Max's advertising gurus used the word to describe the Max doll and his supposed effect on the female doll population. At the time, Sidney had thought the word a corny advertising gimmick. Now, she merely found it inadequate.

Max Loden wasn't merely dishy, he was devastating. Well, he was devastating her, anyway. Except for the barely veiled looks of Constance Barlow, the same woman Sidney had observed clinging to Max's arm during last night's party, no one else at poolside seemed to realize they were in the presence of Adonis.

Suddenly, as if he sensed her scrutiny, Max turned to meet her gaze. Embarrassed that he'd caught her watching him, she struggled not to look away. He watched her for long seconds, then tilted his head in an invitation to join him.

Sidney glanced around the deck once more, before she threaded her way through the clutter of lounge chairs to stand near Max's shoulder. "Did you need something?" she asked him.

"Watch me, Uncle Max," his seven-year-old niece urged.

"I'm watching, Bailey," he assured her. He remained steadily focused as the child bent nearly in two, then tumbled into the water. She surfaced with a broad grin. "Did I get it right?"

Max nodded. "Absolutely. You can work on keeping your feet pointed if you want to go in with less splash. Otherwise, it's perfect."

"Does splash count?"

"Only in the Olympics."

"Good divers don't splash?"

Max shook his head. "Nope."

"Okay. I'll try." Bailey swam toward him. "But can I try the diving board even if I splash?"

"You have to ask your mother."

Bailey frowned. "She won't let me."

Max plucked her from the pool and seated her on the deck next to him. "I'll tell her I taught you how to dive. Then you can ask her."

He earned a toothless grin. "Thanks, Uncle Max." The child turned inquisitive eyes to Sidney. "Who is that lady?"

Max still didn't look at her. "A friend of mine."

"A *good* friend?"

He paused. "Yes."

Bailey studied her. "I'm Bailey."

Sidney smiled. "I'm Sidney."

Bailey watched her with open curiosity. "How come you aren't wearing a swimsuit?"

"Because I'm not here to swim. I'm here to work."

"Oh. Like Uncle Max."

"He's swimming," Sidney pointed out.

Bailey jumped up and reached for a towel. "Only for me. He promised to teach me how to dive so I could use the diving board. He woulda worked instead if he hadn't promised."

As Bailey vigorously dried her mop of red curls, Max finally turned to look at Sidney. His eyes gleamed in the morning light—like a predator's, she thought. "Good morning," he said quietly.

"Good morning." She plucked a piece of paper from her trouser pocket. "I got your note. You wanted to see me about something?"

"It wasn't a summons."

"It sounded like it."

Max frowned. "I didn't mean—"

"Uncle Max?" Bailey tapped him on the shoulder.

His frown deepened before he looked at his niece. "What, Sprout?"

"*When* are you gonna tell Mama?"

"This morning."

Bailey's gaze slid to Sidney. "Promise?"

"I promise," he said.

"You might get distracted."

Max rolled his eyes. "I will not get distracted."

Bailey continued looking at Sidney. "Uncle Greg would."

"I'm not your uncle Greg."

"No." Bailey shook her head, then shrugged. "I want to dive off the board this afternoon. I told Kristina we would."

"This morning," Max said again, giving his niece a gentle shove. "I'll take care of it."

"Okay."

"Now say goodbye."

Bailey grinned at Sidney. "Nice to meet you, Sidney."

Max ruffled her curls. "It's Miss Grant."

"But she said—"

"It's *Miss Grant*."

Sidney held up a hand, "Max, really—"

He shook his head. "Bailey?"

Bailey capitulated. "Nice to meet you, Miss Grant."

Max and Sidney watched as the child hurried off across the deck. "She's a great kid," Sidney said.

"Natalie is a great mother." Max pinned her with his gaze. "How was your night?"

The question couldn't possibly be as provocative as it sounded. "Fine. You?"

He shrugged, then surged to his feet. Sidney forced herself not to take a step backward as he stood dripping and imposing above her. "It was fine. I wanted to ask you about your plans for this evening. Can you take a break?"

She visually scanned the deck. "Everything seems to be under control. Your guests are apparently content. Except maybe Mr. Lort. He looks a little the worse for wear."

His mouth twitched at the corner. "Yeah, well, if I'd spent the night with Alice Northrup-Bowles, I'd look that way, too."

Sidney ruthlessly pushed aside an image of Constance Barlow, wearing a sparkling designer dress, clinging to Max's tuxedo-clad arm, looking like a "do" example in *Town and Country Magazine*.

Max snatched a towel from a nearby lounge chair, then slung it casually around his shoulders. "I'll tell you what," he said. "Let me change, and I'll meet you in my office in five minutes. Will that be okay?"

She deliberately ignored the warning bells in her head. More time alone with Max. Great. At this rate, she'd be a basket case by noon. The man raised her body heat into the red zone. "That'll be fine."

As SIDNEY waited for Max to join her in his third-story office, she replayed her conversation with Greg Loden in her head. She couldn't put her finger on why the incident had disturbed her so much. Philip had told her, often and in detail, the stories of Greg's misdeeds. It seemed Max was constantly bailing him out of one scrape or another. Generally, the younger Loden brother stayed out of serious trouble. To her knowledge, he'd had no encounters with the law. He'd managed to dredge up some negative publicity a time or two—generally related to his affinity for fast women and fast cars—but, according to Philip, Greg Loden was a decent enough character who lacked any serious direction in life.

Lauren Fitzwater, on the other hand, came from old money and an even older family tradition. Since Greg had begun dating her, he'd calmed down considerably, and it was certainly easy to see why Max felt the relationship was good for his younger brother. Still, the tension between the two men bothered Sidney for reasons she didn't begin to understand. Worse, she felt somehow trapped in the middle.

"Good morning." Max strode into the room wearing khaki trousers and a denim shirt that somehow looked elegant. Philip's scrupulous care of his wardrobe, no doubt. "I'm sorry I kept you waiting."

Sidney shook her head. "No problem. You're the boss."

He frowned at her as he seated himself behind his desk. "I wish you'd quit saying that."

She blinked. "I'm sorry?"

"I don't consider you my employee, you know. I consider you—" he paused, "my partner."

Her stomach started its lurching rhythm again. "I see."

"I doubt it." He shook his head. "I'll explain later. Right now, I want to talk to you about tonight. Greg is waffling."

She blinked at the rapid change in topic. "What?"

"I spoke with him this morning. He's having second thoughts about his engagement to Lauren."

Sidney considered the information relative to last night's

conversation. "He's an adult, Max. He can make his own choices."

"He needs her."

"Max...." She hesitated. "Has it ever occurred to you that maybe Greg needs some purpose in his life?"

"Of course. That's why I want him to marry Lauren. She's good for him. She's stable."

"And she's Edward Fitzwater's daughter."

"What the hell does that mean?" His voice had dropped to a deceptively quiet level.

"Are you absolutely certain that Lauren's, ah, familial credentials don't have something to do with why you're pushing Greg so hard?"

He bit off a curse. "That was a rotten thing to say, Sidney. You may not have the highest opinion of me, but what kind of bastard do you think I am?"

His vehemence took her back. "I didn't mean it like that."

He ignored her. "It's got nothing to do with Edward Fitzwater. The man would be a fool to merge with anyone else. He dotes on Lauren, it's true, and her engagement to Greg will make the deal easier for him to swallow, but he doesn't have much of a choice. He's overfinanced and undercapitalized. If he doesn't merge with me, then someone else will take him over. He left himself vulnerable to this."

"And the vultures are circling?"

"Yes."

"Then if the merger is a foregone conclusion, why push so hard for the engagement?"

"I told you. Greg needs Lauren. It's that simple."

With a sad smile, Sidney leaned forward in her chair to place a hand on his desk. "There's nothing simple about relationships, Max."

He looked down at her hand, stared at it for long seconds. She sensed a struggle in him. "No, I don't suppose there is."

"If you push Greg into a corner, he'll fight you."

He visibly tensed. "If he does, I'll win."

"Probably. But if the price is alienating your brother, is it worth it?"

"It's the right thing for Greg's future. In time, he'll understand that."

"Max—"

He surged out of his chair, rounded the desk, and towered over her. She had to tilt her head back to hold his gaze. His expression looked harder than usual. "I realize this probably sounds ruthless to you, but I've spent my life taking care of my family." He raked a hand over his face. "Sometimes, that means I have to decide what I think is best and make sure it happens. And I'm good at it."

"And do you always get what you want?"

He studied her for long seconds, that same unnerving gleam in his eyes. Then he carefully took her hand in his larger one. In less than a millisecond, the center of his focus had shifted from his brother's engagement to rest squarely on her. She sensed it as surely as she had sensed the tension thrumming through him last night. "As of today," he said quietly, "I'm batting a thousand."

Having the full force of that indomitable concentration directed at her sent goosebumps skittering along her flesh. Anticipatory goosebumps, she realized as she forced herself not to look away. "Max, I—"

He turned her hand to study her palm. "In fact, I think we should just clear this up right now. It's been on my mind since last night."

"It has?"

He nodded. "Very much so. And unless I'm completely off my game, you've been thinking about it too."

"We're not talking about Greg and Lauren anymore. Are we?"

"No."

Sidney shivered. "I didn't think so."

"I've been told that I lack a certain, ah, finesse in situations like this."

"Really?"

"Yes. But it's like a business venture—once I know what I want, I don't see any point in hedging about it."

"Wastes time."

"Precisely." His fingers tightened on her hand. "So do you know why I really asked you to stay out at the estate for the weekend?"

Her brain short-circuited. He didn't give her a chance to recover. "I want you, Sidney."

The soft declaration made her ears ring. Her fingers quivered in his warm grasp.

"And you want me."

Sidney pulled in a ragged breath. "Max—"

He squeezed her hand. "Don't you?"

"I—"

"Look, I'm not trying to rush you. I know small talk generally eludes me."

"You could say that."

"I wouldn't have told you last night—I *should* have told you last night, but I was afraid you'd leave. I wanted you here. With me."

Sidney concentrated on breathing normally. "It wouldn't work. We're too different."

"I thought so, too." He cast a swift glance at the door. "For a long time, I thought so. But I changed my mind."

"If that gets out," she managed to quip, "it could cause the value of the dollar to plunge in the foreign currency markets."

His soft chuckle rumbled along her nerve endings. "You have an overinflated sense of my importance, I assure you."

"As long as we're laying our cards on the table, is this a good time for me to tell you that you scare me to death?"

His eyebrows rose. "I'd never hurt you, Sidney."

"I know that. That's not what I mean."

"Explain it to me."

She searched for words. "I guess—I don't want to feel like another corporate takeover."

He blinked. "Excuse me?"

She pulled her hand from his. "It's hard to explain. After Carter—after my divorce—I swore I'd never do that to myself again."

"Are you comparing me to your ex-husband?" His tone had turned flat—and sounded somehow more dangerous.

"No." She shook her head. "No, you're nothing like Carter. He was weak and selfish, and I was a fool to marry him."

"Sidney—"

"Don't say it," she said with a slight smile. "There's no point in arguing with me. What kind of idiot gets involved with a jerk like that?"

"It wasn't your fault."

She inwardly cringed. He could never understand the flood of self-condemnation that had engulfed her when her marriage dissolved. Max didn't make colossal mistakes. It was beyond his scope of experience. "Whatever. The point is, I had a really hard time putting myself back together after he—after it was over."

"I know." His gray eyes studied her. "Philip told me."

"He tells you a lot, doesn't he?"

"He loves you."

"I know he does." She managed a slight smile. "He loves you, too."

With incredibly gentle fingers, Max tucked a strand of her hair behind her ear. "Sidney, no more stalling." He seated himself on the edge of his desk. "Talk to me."

"I'm afraid of what might happen to me if I get involved with you," she admitted.

"I'll take care of you."

"Oh, Max. Don't you see? I don't want you to take care of me. I've just started to feel like I'm pretty good at taking care of myself. I'm not ready to turn the job over to someone else."

That made him frown. "I didn't mean—"

"I know. It's not you. It's me." She couldn't hold his gaze any longer. "This is all moving a little fast for me."

"I've known you for ten years."

She laughed a little. "You've barely spoken to me, and now, suddenly, you want…" She couldn't continue.

"It's not sudden. I've wanted you for a long time, but things were never right for us."

Her gaze flew to his. "Max—"

"It's true." He leaned closer. "It's complicated, and I'm not sure I understand it. I'm not very good at explaining myself. I don't have to do it very often."

"I don't think—"

He cut her off. "We're going to be together all weekend." His gaze narrowed. "If I have my way, *really* together. I want you to understand that. I don't want to play games."

"I'm feeling overwhelmed."

"I tend to have that effect on people." With his fingertips he gently traced the curve of her eyebrows. The touch made her shiver. "I decided last night that I'm tired of waiting. I'd prefer to know exactly where I stand with you."

She was drowning in the intoxicating sensation of his clean scent filling her head and his warmth wrapping her in a sensory cocoon. "Max, please."

"Please what?" His voice had dropped to a seductive whisper. "Please stop? Please don't stop?"

She shook her head, trying to clear it. "I don't know."

His lips turned into a beautiful smile that stole her breath and made her heart skip a beat. "Don't worry." He reached for her hand, then raised it to press a kiss to her wrist. "I've waited this long, and I may not like it, but I can wait a little longer. I can wait until you're ready."

Sidney drew a steadying breath.

"A few more hours won't kill me."

"Hours?" she choked out.

His smile widened. "Did I happen to mention that in addition to 'Mad Max,' my adversaries call me 'Max the Relentless?'"

"I'd heard that."

He tipped his head so his mouth was a hairbreadth from hers. "You're about to experience it firsthand."

Her knees almost buckled. "I might not survive."

He pressed a swift kiss to her lips. "Don't worry," he said again. "You won't get hurt. I promise."

Her lips burned from the slight contact, but the words penetrated the fog in her brain to leave her with an uneasy feeling. "You can't guarantee that."

He evidently decided to ignore her protest. He shrugged. "I'll let you make the choice, Sidney. Just don't wait too long to make it."

Or, she thought, *you'll make it for me.*

Chapter Four

To her utter relief, Sidney barely saw Max for the rest of the day. She had ample time to consider her reaction to the man as she and her staff prepared for the evening's event. Max's guests proved to be relatively undemanding during the daylight hours, which, Sidney considered, was a good thing. In her current muddle, she wasn't certain she could have adequately handled a major crisis.

More than once, she chided herself for an overactive imagination when Max's staff seemed to study her with undue curiosity. For the most part, she'd known these people for years through her relationship with her uncle. They knew of her long history with the Loden family, and surely found nothing odd about her third-floor rendezvous with their boss. After all, Philip had left her in charge for the weekend. Everyone knew it. Guilt alone was making her think everyone knew she harbored thoughts of jumping their boss's bones.

One of the housemaids sauntered by, offering Sidney a jaunty smile. "Cripes," Sidney mumbled to herself. "Two more days of this and they'll have to have me committed." More likely, two more days of close proximity to Max and she'd turn into a complete simpleton. He had that effect on her. He enveloped her. How in the world, she wondered more than once, could anyone fail to notice the way the man sucked up all the available oxygen and space in a room. He was like a human firecracker—he inspired awe when properly handled, and he had the potential to be positively deadly.

Sidney had worked herself into a nervous sweat by the time she put the finishing touches on a tray of handmade chocolates. The combination of stainless steel and granite in Max's ultramodern kitchen did nothing to chill the slight fever on her flesh.

Unmistakably strong, tanned hands came from behind to rest on either side of her, pinning her to the counter. Sidney pulled in a ragged breath and tried not to surrender to the urge to melt into him.

Max whispered against her ear, "I hope you brought something to wear to the party tonight." His breath fanned her face.

Sidney kept her voice light. "My uniform."

He nuzzled her ear. "I'd rather you attended. I'm looking forward to—" he paused almost imperceptibly "—dancing with you."

"I don't let my staff fraternize with guests."

"You're the boss." He twined a curl of her hair around his forefinger. "You get to make your own rules."

"I like to set an example."

"Sidney—"

She turned to face him. "Not now, Max. I'm busy."

He licked a dollop of chocolate from her fingertips. "Soon, Sidney. I'm not a very patient man."

"You told me you'd let me decide."

He looked like he wanted to argue. Instead, he took her hand in his and pressed it to his chest. "Dance with me tonight," he murmured.

The statement was simultaneously seductive and suggestive. It sent a tremor of heat up her spine. "I don't think—"

"One dance," he said. "Just to tide me over."

"Max—"

"Say, yes, Sidney." He leaned closer. "Or I'll kiss you in front of Eddie."

Too late she noticed the man standing patiently near the door of the kitchen, waiting to deliver the chocolates. He had that carefully blank expression she'd come to recognize as Philip's eavesdropping look. She drew a deep breath and leaned back against the counter. "I'll be busy all evening."

Max's mouth kicked up at the corner. "I'll find you."

Of that, at least, she could be sure.

MAX LEANED against the bar, idly listening to the music as he studied Sidney's profile in the warm glow of the Chinese lanterns. Tonight's event was far less formal than last night's festivities. Sidney's staff had transformed his terrace and broad gardens into a charming recreation of a Victorian boardwalk. His guests strolled along the planked walkways, stopping to sample hot pretzels and fluffy cotton candy. Barkers, clad in striped jackets and straw skimmers, enticed customers into gaming booths where everyone, miraculously, won a prize. His sister Natalie sat, deep in conversation with her husband. She wore the cheap rhinestone necklace he'd won for her like it was the rarest treasure on earth.

And Greg, he noted, was busy impressing Lauren with his pitching skills. Only Colleen, the older of Max's sisters, seemed unwilling to join the festive mood. She'd been sullen and frustrated when she'd found him alone in his office last night. Sidney had just left when Colleen had invaded his third-story sanctuary to give him a blistering lecture on his responsibilities to his guests. He had no business, she'd argued, hiding up there while she and Natalie entertained on his behalf.

Max had soundly advised her to mind her own affairs, and he still regretted the harsh tone he'd used. Twice today he'd tried to find her to apologize, but, typical Colleen, she'd deftly avoided him—a ploy she used when she found him particularly vexing.

Of course, he admitted as he took a sip of his mineral water, she'd had an easier time eluding him due to the decidedly distracted state he'd been in since he'd found Sidney running his kitchens and, for the weekend at any rate, his life.

Watching Sidney now, he wondered at the startling effect she was having on him. He never lost sight of his siblings, yet Sidney had managed to wedge herself firmly into his thoughts until he found himself dwelling all too often on thoughts that were having a predictable effect on his body.

Once again, he felt the familiar kick of desire in his gut. With measured care, he set his glass down on the bar. He'd sensed the heat in her that morning in his office. Her ex-husband, damn the bastard, had made her unsure of herself, but with each minute of the day, Max had felt more certain that the timing was finally right.

The thought sent satisfaction flaring through him. He made his way across the terrace with unflappable determination. How in the world, he wondered, had he waited this long?

Sidney started when he slipped up behind her and wrapped an arm around her waist. "I'm ready for that dance now," he whispered in her ear.

She let out a shuddering breath. He liked it. He liked thinking of her a little off balance. It occurred to him that she'd breathe like that while he was making love to her. With measured precision, Sidney shook her head. "I don't think we should. Not now."

Max edged closer to her. "I think we need to. Right now."

"Max—"

He turned her in his arms so he could see her expression. The slight glow in her eyes coiled through him, relentlessly stoking the fire that licked at his belly. "Now, Sidney."

She swallowed. "I distinctly remember you saying that you wouldn't push me."

His lips twitched. "Didn't anyone ever tell you that men bent on seduction say all kinds of things they don't mean?"

"I'm pretty sure I heard that somewhere."

He slid one hand down her back to fit her against him. "Besides, I think I've exercised remarkable patience. I resisted temptation all last night, and I've waited 'til now. What more do you want?''

Her breath caught as she studied his face. Her expression turned suddenly serious. She stroked the line of his jaw with the tip of her index finger. "Oh, Max," she said quietly, "so much more than you could possibly imagine."

His blood turned to lava. For a few, startling seconds, he flailed about, searching for balance. He muttered a soft curse. It wasn't supposed to be this way. He always stayed in control. Control was crucial. But his brain and his heart didn't seem to be cooperating tonight.

Sidney placed one hand on his shoulder. "What's the matter? You look a little rattled."

"I'd like to know why you'd wait until we're standing in the middle of a crowd to say something like that to me?"

"Paybacks are hell. You've had me reeling since early this morning. I thought maybe it was your turn."

He rubbed his hand at the small of her back. "I told you I didn't want to play games," he warned.

At the warm look she gave him, he felt something inside him rattle loose. "I'm not." Sidney brushed her fingers on his shirt sleeve. "I'm really not. I just think it's kind of sad that you're always wondering what someone wants from you." She tilted her head to one side. "Hasn't anyone ever told you that you're an interesting, dynamic individual who's worth knowing just because you're you?"

Max stared at her. "No."

"Then someone blew it," she said firmly. "I've been thinking about this all day."

"That was my plan."

"It was very effective." Her lips tilted into a smile that kicked his body temperature up another notch. Her hand moved along his shoulder, gently caressing him through the fabric of his tuxedo jacket. "But here's the thing. You told me what you wanted this morning. Now I want to tell you what I want."

Images flooded his brain. Images that had his clothes feeling too tight and too warm. The woman was making him crazy. Worse, he was pretty sure he liked it. "Are you trying to drive me to bedlam?"

"I thought your car was already parked in that garage," she teased.

"Two more days of this and it will be," he assured her. "I want you desperately. I didn't realize how much until I got this close to you."

Sidney sighed, a soft exhalation of breath that wended its way into his heart and left him yearning. "Oh, Max."

"Desperately," he said again.

"That's just it. Something tells me we shouldn't, but I want it, too."

With a soft curse, he tugged her toward a secluded arbor, shielded from the party with a curtain of honeysuckle vines. "Why don't you tell me about it while we dance?"

Her soft laugh ricocheted off his nerve endings. "Because we'd never finish the dance, and you'd probably embarrass yourself, and me, in front of your guests."

Max stepped into the arbor, then pulled her tight against him, all the while asking himself how in the world had he waited this long for the incredible feel of Sidney Grant in his arms?

At his earlier request, the band had begun playing a slow, jazzy song that allowed him to move against her in a way meant to entice. Instead, he found himself caught in his own snare. "You're trying to kill me, aren't you?" he said.

"No, although I seriously thought about it this afternoon when you tried to seduce me in front of Eddie."

"Was I successful?"

"We're having this conversation, aren't we?"

Max sucked in a breath. "Damn, Sidney." The way she flowed into his embrace gave him a shaky feeling that he was going to have serious trouble letting her go. "Have you always had this talent for mental demolition?"

"Is it affecting you?" An enticing tremor laced her voice. The sound intoxicated him. "Absolutely."

"I'm glad."

Max wasn't about to question what had brought on her sudden reckless mood—not when he was within hours, *minutes,* maybe, of getting something he now craved like an addict. She'd tied him into a neat bundle of knots, and at this moment, he realized, she could ask him for just about anything and he'd get it for her. For the first time in his life, he understood how men managed to ruin their lives over women.

He inhaled a deep breath of her scent. Clean and womanly and with the slightest touch of chocolate, it sent his blood pressure to the moon. "Oh, Sidney, I want—"

A sudden clatter at the edge of the terrace arrested his attention. He parted the honeysuckle with a deft swipe, then swiftly scanned his guests to find Lauren and Greg having a heated argument and rapidly drawing a crowd. He muttered a dark curse.

Sidney tensed in his arms. Her attention traveled first to the argument, then to one of her assistants who was already swooping down on the pair, then finally to Max. "You take Lauren," she urged him. "I'll handle Greg."

He frowned. "*I'll* handle Greg."

"No, Max. Trust me. You'll make matters worse if you strong-arm him right now. Lauren is going to need the kind of reassurance only you can give her. I'll take care of Greg."

He hesitated. The argument grew louder. His body was still clamoring for attention, and he felt torn. Shaking his head to clear it, he pressed a hard kiss to Sidney's lips. "Later," he said. "We'll finish later."

Without comment, she broke free of his embrace and headed for the arguing couple. Max followed close on her heels. Seconds before they reached them, Lauren peeled away from Greg and fled across the lawn. Max shot Sidney a resigned look before he set off in pursuit.

Sidney breathed a quiet sigh as she eased to a stop near

Greg. She snatched a glass of champagne from a passing waiter and shoved it into his hand. "Looks bad," she said quietly.

Greg frowned at her. "Damn Max," he muttered. "This is all his fault."

Sidney scanned the crowd, found her staff, and gave them a signal to get the party back on track. In seconds, the band was playing a swing number, each guest found a glass of champagne in their hand, and Sidney's staff had the party back in full swing. She exhaled a slow breath, then turned to Greg. "Do you want to talk about it, or would you rather I left you alone?"

His tense expression eased. "You've been taking lessons from Philip, I see."

She shrugged. "I just find that sometimes, problems don't seem so large once I've talked through them. If you want someone to listen—" she looked meaningfully at Natalie, then Colleen. Greg's gaze followed hers. "Someone," she continued, "who is a little more objective about the whole thing, I'll be glad to be that person. I'm sure this is very stressful for you."

He studied her for long seconds, then his lips moved into the easy, charming smile she remembered. "You know, Sidney, you're an amazing person."

She laughed at that. "No, I'm not."

"Sure you are. You just defused a potential atom bomb. I don't know how you do it, but you're incredible."

"I like what I do. I like knowing that my clients trust me to give them a seamless event. It feels good to me."

His gaze turned speculative. "I'm sure it does." Slowly, he set his champagne glass down on a small table. "If the offer's still open, I think I would like to talk to you."

Sidney nodded. "Of course."

"Meet me in the gazebo," he prompted with a quick look at his watch, "in, say, ten minutes?"

MAX GRABBED his brother's sleeve in a tight-fingered grip. "I need to see you."

Greg glanced nervously at his watch. "Now? I, uh, have an appointment."

"Now." He jerked Greg into the library where a weeping Lauren Fitzwater, her scowling father, and her simpering mother were grating Max's already too-tight nerves. Greg assessed the small group with a slight wince. "Hello, Lauren."

She raised tear-filled eyes to his. "Greg."

Edward swore as he lurched from his chair. "You bastard." He would have stalked forward, but Max quelled him by shoving Greg into a chair. Edward started to pace. Lauren continued to cry.

Max reached for the shredded remains of his formidable calm. "All right. Lauren, you start."

She hiccuped. "I thought—I thought everything was going so well." Her sodden gaze found Greg's. "This wasn't my idea, you know."

To his credit, Greg had the decency to squirm. "I know."

Edward glared at him. "We had an agreement."

"Daddy—"

He held up a hand to interrupt his daughter. "Let me handle this, Lauren."

Max gritted his teeth. "Calm down, Edward."

The older man faced him with a dark scowl on his already flushed features. "Calm down? You're as bad as he is. You're pushing them because you want Fitzwater Electronics."

Max refused to take the bait. "I have tried to persuade Greg that I think he's fortunate to have a woman like Lauren in his life. It's got nothing to do with business."

Edward gasped. Lauren shot Max a watery smile. "Thanks."

He nodded. "It's true." His gaze swung to her father. "And you know it. Fitzwater is ripe for takeover. If I didn't do it, someone else would."

If possible, Edward's face turned redder. His wife held out a beseeching hand. "Darling, sit down. Please."

Edward stalked toward Max. "You greedy son of a bitch."

Max lost his slender hold on his patience. Greg, he noted, kept glancing out the window with a wistful expression Max recognized as his preflight look. "Sit down, Edward," he commanded.

With a stunned expression on his face, the older man dropped into his chair. Max cleared his throat. "Now. I want all of you to shut up and let Lauren tell me what's going on."

Edward sputtered, "But she—"

"Shut *up*, Edward." He glanced at Lauren. "What happened?"

She looked nervous, but, he noticed to his great relief, calmer. She raised her gaze to his. "I'm sorry, Max. I didn't mean to make a scene."

"I doubt it's your fault," Max said quietly. His brother shot him a mutinous look. "What's going on?"

"Greg—" she glanced at him, "Greg thinks maybe we should wait a while longer before we announce our engagement."

Max's eyebrows lifted. "I wasn't aware there was an engagement."

Edward's breath came out in a hiss. "You son of a—"

"Darling, please." His wife laid a hand on his sleeve. "Let Lauren finish."

Lauren was still looking at Greg. Greg was still gazing out the window. "We hadn't told anyone. He asked me a month ago."

A wave of relief crashed through Max. He struggled to suppress a triumphant smile and merely nodded. "And you said yes."

"Yes. I did."

"Why?"

Greg jerked his gaze from the window. The look he gave Max was glacial. "Thanks for your support."

Max shrugged. "I was curious, not critical."

"Could have fooled me."

Lauren brushed a hand over her silk dress. "Because," she said quietly, "fool that I am, I'm in love with your brother."

Greg finally looked at her. "Lauren."

She nodded. "It's true, Greg. I know you thought I was doing it for Daddy. I wasn't." She looked at her father. "I wouldn't."

His brother, Max noted, had paled. Lauren drew a shuddering breath. "I did it because I'm in love with you." Her voice faltered on the last. "But if you've changed your mind—"

"I haven't changed my mind," he asserted.

Max impaled him with a sharp look. "Are you sure?"

Greg swallowed. "I'm sure."

Edward growled. "Then what the hell was going on out there, just now?"

All eyes turned to Greg. He tugged at his collar. "I don't know. It's the pressure." He looked at Max. "You're pushing too hard."

Max said nothing. Greg hesitated, then looked away. "Everyone at this party knows we're supposed to announce our engagement before tomorrow night. And everyone also knows that when we do, Fitzwater Electronics and Loden Enterprises will be well on their way to a merger." He shrugged. "I don't like flaunting my life in front of spectators."

Max snorted. "It's never stopped you before."

"This is different," his brother snapped. "It's personal."

"I'm glad you realize that," Max said.

Greg frowned at him. "You can't make all my choices for me, Max. You don't get to run my life."

"No," he said slowly, "but you certainly enjoy your access to the family finances."

"Are you threatening me?"

"Do I need to?"

Lauren gasped. "Max, please."

He looked at her. "Don't worry, Lauren. I'm not going to cut him off and leave you hanging."

Edward swore again. Lauren looked stung. "That's not what I meant."

Wrestling with an unexpected burst of guilt, he waved his hand in an agitated motion. "This is pointless. All I want to know is, can we expect another scene like this before tomorrow night, or not?"

Greg's mouth twitched in an unpleasant smirk. "You mean, are we going to give in and let you have your way?"

"I didn't say that."

"You didn't have to."

Lauren stood. "Please, both of you. Stop it. If Greg wants to wait, we'll wait."

"How long?" Max pressed.

"As long as he needs," Lauren said quietly.

Max looked at Greg. "Give her a timetable."

His brother's eyes glittered. "Max—"

"Do it," he said quietly. Too quietly.

Greg's jaw visibly clenched. "You can't—"

"Do it." He bit out each word with careful precision.

Greg hesitated a second longer, then finally shot Max a resentful look. "Fine. We'll do it tomorrow night. After dinner."

"Greg—" Lauren held out her hand.

Greg shook his head. "It's all right, Lauren. If you want to marry into this family, you might as well learn this now. Everything's easier when Max gets his way." He levered out of his chair and stalked from the room.

Lauren whispered a soft apology and hurried after him. Edward Fitzwater looked at Max with a slightly menacing expression, while his wife studied the beadwork on her handbag. Max fought with a rare burst of conscience. He felt like a jerk, he realized. And it was disturbing the hell out of him. "Anything else you wanted, Edward?" He couldn't keep the edge from his voice.

The older man glared at him. "Has anyone ever told you how much of a bastard you are?"

"Plenty of times."

"Edward—" his wife reached for his hand. "It's all right. Lauren wouldn't agree if she weren't happy with Greg's decision."

Edward looked unconvinced. "You have no principles at all, do you?"

Max didn't bother to respond. He had no answer. "If we're through, I'd like to get back to my party."

With a grunt, Edward stood. "I'm sure you would." He reached for his wife's hand. "I think we'll retire. Good night."

Max waited until they'd closed the library door behind them to exhale the tight breath that squeezed his lungs. "Damn," he whispered, not entirely sure why his head suddenly pounded and his stomach felt knotted. He'd gotten what he wanted. He should have felt better.

With a sharp flick of his wrist, he switched off the lamp on his desk, throwing the room into near darkness. He could more clearly see the terrace now, where his guests milled about in blissful ignorance of his turmoil. Music filtered into the room, and in the soft glow of the Chinese lanterns, he saw Greg—his white jacket visible even in the shadows— making his way to the gazebo.

Max felt his fingers clench into a fist. He watched Greg's retreating figure for long seconds, then, for the first time in his life, deliberately looked the other way.

Chapter Five

The following morning, Max stood on Philip Grant's front porch and knocked on the door. Gertie jerked it open. Her face registered a mild surprise. "Mr. Loden."

Max peered past her into the dim interior. "How's Philip?"

She held up a warning hand, then slipped outside to join Max on the porch.

"Resting," the older woman said. "He had a bad night."

"Is he worse?"

"I think he's a little better this morning. His fever might have broken."

"How long can it take for the flu to run its course?"

"Days," Gertie assured him. "There's a strain going around that knocks people out for a week."

Max's eyes drifted shut on a sigh of frustration. He was mind-numbingly exhausted. As if that confrontation with his brother hadn't been enough to shred his nerves, now he had a situation at one of his plants to deal with. His attorney had called last night to give him the news—one of Loden Enterprises' manufacturing facilities had suffered an explosion. Max probably had a few dead, or at least seriously injured employees. He was still waiting for a report. He focused bleary eyes on Gertie. "Is he awake? I want to see him."

Gertie wavered. "I'm sure he'd love to visit with you, but I wouldn't stay long. Sam and Elena came by this morning to assure him everything's all right at home.'' She looked at Max. ''You can imagine how worried he is about not being with you this weekend.''

''Everything's under control,'' Max assured her. ''Sidney's taking very good care of me.'' Thank God, he thought. Without Philip on hand, Max didn't think he'd have felt secure leaving the estate—no matter how good the reason—with anyone but Sidney in charge. The company and the employees needed him, but, as usual, he felt pulled in too many directions. Realizing that Gertie was still looking at him from beneath raised eyebrows, he concluded, ''Sidney's very good at what she does.''

Gertie's gaze visibly warmed. ''I'm sure she is.'' She pushed open the door. ''He's resting on the sofa.''

The darkened room felt stifling. Max had to suppress the urge to pull back the curtains and lighten the place up. Wrapped in a cotton throw, Philip lay on the sofa looking exhausted and pale—a shadow of the vibrant man he knew. He strode forward to sit in the chair by the couch. ''How are you feeling, Philip?''

His eyes fluttered open. ''Better than I look, I assure you.''

The quip cheered him. ''I'm glad.''

''Did you bring Sidney?''

''I didn't tell her I was coming. She's at the estate.''

Philip nodded. ''Good. She's needed there.'' He struggled to sit up, but Max placed a restraining hand on his shoulder. ''Don't,'' he told him, ''that's an order.''

Philip gave him a weak smile. ''As if that ever worked. I'm not very good at taking orders.''

''Humor me,'' Max muttered.

Philip coughed. ''How are things at the estate?''

''Fine. Sidney's showing her mettle. There's nothing for you to worry about.''

''Next thing I know—'' a painfully dry cough squeezed from his chest ''—she'll be taking my job.''

"Not likely." He watched Philip through narrowed eyes. "No one could replace you, old man, and you know it."

"That's the way I like it."

Max's nod was short. "I don't doubt it."

"Why are you here?"

"Other than to see you?"

Philip nodded. "It must be serious or you wouldn't have left the estate."

"I've got some business problems I need to handle. Nothing major, I assure you. I'll be home tonight."

"Has young Mr. Loden made his announcement yet?"

"He's promised me he'll do it at tonight's dinner party."

"You need to be there."

"I will."

Philip seemed satisfied. "I've thought of a few things I forgot to tell Sidney. I'll have to call her."

"She's busy," Max said carefully. "Tell me, and I'll let her know."

"She needs to make sure the wine steward doesn't forget that Edward Fitzwater prefers the Chenenceaux claret. There's a case in the cellar."

"All right."

"And see that the kitchen staff regularly replaces the fruit in the guest rooms. I don't want bruised produce in those bowls."

Max suppressed a smile. "I'm sure you don't."

"How is Natalie?"

Max grunted. "She'd be a hell of a lot better if Alice Northrup-Bowles had stayed home, you old coot."

"Is Sidney keeping her busy?"

"Of course. Sidney has made sure that Natalie is completely involved in the party's success. She hasn't had a chance to brood over Alice's malicious nature."

"I knew I could count on Sidney."

Max crossed his arms over his chest. "You should have told me Alice was coming, Philip."

"You would have rescinded Mr. Lort's invitation."

"I would have told Ray Lort he could go to hell."

"My point exactly." Philip lifted an unsteady hand to stroke his chin. "Sometimes, you don't always know that certain things are for your own good."

"But you do?"

"It's my job." Philip gave him an intense look. "Someone has to look after you."

Max resisted the urge to look away. What was it about this family, he wondered, that gave them the ability to zero in on his few vulnerabilities? "You'd be very proud of Sidney. She's got everything running with her usual precision." He exhaled a long breath. "Is there anything else you need, Philip? I've got to get to the office."

"No. Gertie's taking very good care of me. And Sam and Elena came out this morning to check on us. I'll be fine. Just wish I wasn't confined to this blasted couch. You're sure everything's all right out there?"

"I don't want you to worry about anything." Max rose to his feet. "We miss you, of course, but I assure you we'll have Greg safely engaged by tonight."

Philip's eyes drifted shut. "I knew you would. You're in excellent hands."

Max exhaled a soft breath. "And I'm very much looking forward to it." He carefully studied Philip's ashen face. "You picked a hell of a time for this."

Philip met his gaze. "It was bound to happen sooner or later."

The sly old fox knew exactly what he was doing, Max thought. "I'm not complaining, I assure you. In fact, I'd say your timing is going to serve me quite well."

Gertie joined them by the couch. "All that matters," she said firmly, "is that everything is taken care of." She patted Philip's hand. "You're not even to think about going back to work until you're completely well."

Philip lifted his eyes to Max. "This engagement is going to be quite demanding. You know that."

"I've thought of that." Max wiped a hand through his hair. "Greg's engagement to Lauren means my entertaining schedule is about to go haywire. I've never planned a wedding before. Natalie and Colleen handled their own and gave me the bills. As I recall," his eyebrows lifted as he looked at his butler, "you were heavily involved in their plans."

"A society wedding requires an extensive amount of planning. There's nothing like having a professional on your team."

Max shrugged. "I'm sure Lauren will rise to the occasion. Her father wouldn't have it any other way."

Philip shook his head. "Still, the next few months will be extremely demanding on your schedule and your personal life."

"It's Greg's wedding," Max said carefully.

"You know what I mean."

"Not really."

"There'll be an engagement party, a bachelor party, something extravagant to make Edward Fitzwater feel like he hasn't been railroaded into anything—"

"That would take a small miracle."

"You've got a lot to think about." Philip's voice held a warning note.

Max flashed him a wry smile. "You've got to get better soon, old man. I'm not sure how I'll survive without you telling me what to do and how to act."

"You'll need help."

"You've got that right." Max shook his head. "I've got a company to run, a merger to manage, and a brother whose hand is going to need holding until he finally walks down the aisle."

"What you need," Philip said carefully. "Is a professional."

"What I need is a trainer."

"Then I recommend that you talk to Sidney. No one could do a better job of managing your social calendar for the next several months."

Max stilled. "Sidney?"

"Naturally. She's the obvious choice. She knows your family well, will have informed opinions about your brother's preferences and the dynamics of, er, family gatherings. I think you should talk to her about a contract."

Satisfaction flared through Max. A contract. Something binding. Something that meant she was legally his. Something that wasn't subject to mercurial moods and changes of heart. "I'm in need of professional services," he said carefully. "On an exclusive basis."

"As you've said, your schedule will be quite demanding. I don't see how she could manage other events simultaneously. Her assistant will have to take over."

"Kelly Lars."

"Yes," Philip said. "The young woman is quite capable."

He had promised Sidney that he'd let her decide. He had not, however, promised that he wouldn't try to significantly manipulate the outcome—which, after their conversation last night, he was even more determined to do. Max shook his head to clear it as a strange kind of euphoria clouded his thoughts. "I'll have to make it worth her while."

"She might drive a hard bargain," Philip warned him.

Of that, he was sure. "I'm counting on it," Max said. "I'm very much counting on it."

Philip nodded. "Kelly can handle the business. Sidney has already told me that this isn't her busiest season."

Max nodded. "I'll pay her enough to bring on extra staff to cover her other events."

Gertie clucked her tongue. Until then, Max had forgotten her presence. She threaded her plump fingers together and fixed him with a hard stare. "You'd best not push too hard, Mr. Loden. Sidney doesn't like to be pushed."

That much he knew. "I'm aware of that."

Philip gave him a shrewd look. "Talk to her. If necessary, I'll talk to her. I'll feel better knowing everything is in her hands."

"So will I," Max said.

Sidney was powerless to resist Philip, and they both knew it. She might cheerfully kill Max for bringing this up in front of the one man he knew could win her cooperation. At least, though, he'd have her where he wanted her. Mostly. He felt better than he had all day. Since their precipitous parting last night, he'd been preoccupied and frustrated. When he'd been unable to find her late that evening, his mood had turned from sour to rotten. He didn't like feeling unsteady on his feet. But a *contract*— even the word felt good to him. This was familiar territory. He gave Philip a reassuring look. "Don't worry about a thing. I'm sure she'll agree."

Philip's eyes drifted shut on a contented sigh. "So am I," he whispered.

AT SEVEN O'CLOCK Tuesday morning, after an almost sleepless night, Sidney tossed down her pencil with a disgusted sigh. She dropped her head into her palms and fought the urge to hurl the mound of paperwork across the room. Her nerves, she knew, had been wound too tight and stretched too thin before she'd even attempted to begin sorting through her former accountant's cryptic notes. By the time her uncle Philip had arrived at Max's estate, ready to resume his position as head of the household staff, Sidney had wanted to fall at his feet in gratitude.

She had caught only glimpses of Max since Saturday night's fiasco. When Greg met her that night in the gazebo, he'd related the events of the previous few minutes, and vented his frustration over Max's manipulation. While Sidney didn't doubt there was another side to the story, she'd winced at Greg's version of Max's callous remarks. According to the younger Loden brother, Max had virtually blackmailed him into announcing his engagement to Lauren the following night. She'd gone to bed Saturday night feeling confused, and awakened on Sunday frustrated and annoyed.

Max was nowhere to be found. According to his sister Colleen, he'd left the estate early that morning. Colleen had delivered that piece of information with a cool indifference that left Sidney feeling edgy. Max did not return until minutes before the evening's dinner party. Sydney had no chance to talk to him, but his grim countenance bothered her. Something drastic had happened in the past few hours to put that scowl on his face.

Sidney had stood in the shadows of the dining room and watched him when Greg finally rose to make his announcement. Not a flicker of expression had registered on Max's grim countenance.

Later, she'd tried to talk to him, but Colleen had stopped her on her way up the stairs to his third-floor office. "Max," his sister had informed her, "asked not to be disturbed." Frustrated and completely baffled, Sydney had spent a restless night wondering about what had transpired after Max left her the night before. She'd almost expected him to turn up at her room after he'd finished negotiating his latest family crisis. Instead, he'd been detached all day. And, evidently, his desire for privacy extended to his houseguests. He'd left the job of seeing them off on Monday to Natalie—a good thing, Sidney had mused, as Colleen seemed more prone to toss them out on their collective ears.

Early Monday morning, Philip had arrived at the estate. After a brief meeting with Max, he descended from the third floor to hand Sidney an envelope with her name scrawled in Max's firm, spidery writing. She had known better than to press him for details. Philip loved her, she knew, but he would never dream of betraying Max's confidence.

Angry at Max's dismissal, she'd tucked the envelope into her jeans pocket, and set to work. By noon, Sidney's staff had cleared their equipment and personal belongings, returned the rooms to their original state, and finished dismantling any remaining traces of the weekend's festivities from the estate. Philip inspected the grounds and the house and expressed his fulsome appreciation for all she'd done. With a warm hug, she'd assured him that she'd been glad to help. The vans were loaded, her employees were on their way home, and Sidney finally found a moment to herself.

After explaining to her uncle that she had paperwork awaiting her, she'd slipped into her car and opened the envelope.

A check. Twice her normal fee, as promised. And no note. She'd checked the envelope twice, expecting something, anything, that might explain his odd behavior since they'd parted on Saturday night.

In fact, during the long, silent hours of Sunday afternoon, while she'd worked with her staff to prepare for the evening, she'd mentally recounted all the reasons why she shouldn't get too involved with Max Loden. The precipitous end to last night's flirtation, she'd argued, had been the best thing for both of them. It could never work. They came from different worlds. They had nothing in common but an isolated incident in his parents' library. He lived in a palace and she worked in the kitchens. It was as simple as that.

But, try as she might, the argument failed to dim the profound tug on her heartstrings she felt when she thought of the stark loneliness she'd often glimpsed in his expression. That drew her like little else. She remembered feeling that alone, that terrified. When she'd come to live with her uncle, that same sense of fear had overwhelmed her.

What she saw in the depths of Max's soul drew her inexorably into the flame. She couldn't, wouldn't, turn away from him. It wasn't in her to stand by and willingly let another person experience that depth of loneliness. His entire life, Max had felt the pressure of knowing everyone depended on him. To Sidney's knowledge, he'd never felt the pleasure of depending on someone else.

That thought affected her as nothing else could.

But the cheque and the solid evidence it gave her of his

casual dismissal should have taught her *something*. There could never be a future for her and Max. He needed a woman who could serve at his side, be a partner in all his endeavors, in life and in business. She could never be that person. If she learned anything from her failed marriage, it was that she had no business trying to pretend she was something she wasn't. She could, however, prove to him that he was worthy of love and care and compassion, not for what he had, or what he could do, but for who he was. And if she could accomplish that, then perhaps the scars she'd bear when they parted would be well worth the opportunity to banish that bleak look from his eyes. By Saturday night, when he'd asked her to dance, she'd been ready to leap off the bridge with him.

Then, he'd disappeared. And, evidently, she'd thought as she studied the empty envelope, hadn't felt the need to offer an explanation.

Now, in the stark light of the morning after, Sidney looked at the check and frowned. Something about it made her feel distinctly unpleasant. For easily the hundredth time she reminded herself that she'd known Max was unpredictable and inscrutable, and refused to let herself dwell on it. Her taxes were demanding her attention, and she didn't have the time, or energy, to dwell on the age-old mystery of Max Loden.

If she had half a brain, she'd consider herself lucky for having escaped the weekend with her heart intact. She had less than two days before this damned audit hearing, and if she didn't somehow, someway, make sense of all this, there was no telling what Uncle Sam might do to her.

The commanding knock on her door startled her. Her gaze fled to the wall clock. With a slight groan, she realized that Kelly must have encountered a problem of monumental proportions in the charity luncheon they were working that day. Nothing else would have brought her to Sidney's door at seven o'clock in the morning when she knew Sidney was waging war with the IRS. And no one, she mused as she padded toward the door, who knew her well, would even think of trying to see her before nine. So-called morning people, she firmly believed, were a plague on society.

She wiped a hand through her mussed hair and jerked open the door. "Kelly—" Her heart stopped beating at the same instant her voice died.

Max stood there, frowning at her. He looked intense, and some distant part of her brain registered, disgustingly attractive in charcoal-gray trousers and a deep blue shirt. He raked her appearance with a sharp glance. "You look like hell."

Sidney blinked. "What are you—"

He brushed her aside and strode into her apartment, followed by a brainy-looking young man in a pristine navy suit. "Good morning," the man muttered.

Sidney sucked breath into her lungs as she turned to face him. "Max—"

He was staring at the paperwork that lay on her table and, in all fairness, was strewn across her floor. "Are these your accounts?"

The experience was beginning to feel surreal. "What?"

He picked up a tax form. "Good Lord. You're doing this by hand. Don't you own a computer?"

"It's a worksheet," she mumbled, unsure why.

"George," Max looked at the other man, "what do you think?"

George carefully cleared a spot on Sidney's dining room table for his briefcase. "I'm sure it's not a problem, Max."

Sidney leaned back against the door, feeling the need for support. "Excuse me?"

"Do you have everything you need?" Max asked.

George visually scanned the piles of ledgers and receipts. Behind his wire-framed glasses, his gray eyes looked alert and, unless she missed her guess, challenged. "Oh, I think so. Her hearing isn't until Thursday morning. I'm sure we can get this straightened out by then."

Max's nod was short. "Do whatever you have to, George. If you need more people, get them." He looked at Sidney.

"Why don't you take a shower? You look like you're about to fall over."

"I'm exhausted," she said before she could stop herself. Damn the man. She owed him nothing, and certainly not explanations.

He indicated her bedroom with a jerk of his head. "Go get ready. I'll wait."

That snapped her from the relative stupor she'd experienced since she'd found him on her doorstep. "Wait just one damn minute, Max. What do you think you're doing?"

He blinked. "You're annoyed."

Good Lord, he sounded shocked. Her fingers curled into fists. "That surprises you? You march in here at 7:00 a.m. and start barking orders like a field general, and it shocks you that I might be the tiniest bit testy about it?"

"You're not a morning person," he said blandly. He seemed to factor the information into some mental file cabinet. "Sorry it's so early, but I wanted to give George and his staff enough time."

George, she noted, had picked up her phone and was giving quiet instructions to someone on the other end. Sidney struggled for several seconds to regain her equilibrium. Her apartment had begun to spin. She took three deep breaths. "What are you doing?"

"Philip, er, mentioned that you were here preparing for an audit, and that your former accountant is no longer—" he paused "—available."

"My accountant is in Brazil with half a million dollars of someone else's money."

"Well, yes."

"Philip told you?" Good grief, her uncle evidently didn't share the same sense of commitment to *her* privacy that he felt for his employer's.

"I beat it out of him," he said without batting an eyelash.

"Oh, cripes."

Max crossed his arms over his chest. "Don't be angry at

him, Sidney. He mentioned it in passing, and I pulled a few strings to find out the rest.''

''You spied on me?''

''No, of course not. I—''

''Max?'' George held the receiver in one hand.

''What?''

''I've got Eleanor on the phone. Pat and Leslie are on their way. She wants to know if you need anything else?''

Max glanced at his watch. ''No. Tell her thanks.''

George nodded and went back to his phone call. Max's gaze returned to Sidney. ''As I said, I asked a few questions of a few people I know. That's all.''

''On their way over?'' Sidney said quietly, still focused on George's comments. ''Who's on their way over?''

''Oh, that. George's staff. Don't worry about a thing. They're great, excellent in fact. I wouldn't keep them on retainer if they weren't. They'll have all this straightened out for you in no time.''

She had to grind her teeth to keep from shouting at him. ''This is—''

He glanced at his watch again. ''Look, how much time do you think you need to get ready? I told the hotel manager we'd be there by eleven. We'll need a couple of hours to get into the city at this time of day.''

''Hotel—'' Sidney shook her head to clear it. ''Stop it,'' she said sharply.

His gaze abruptly met hers. ''What?''

It felt good to have the reins of the conversation again. ''You're being deliberately evasive, and don't think I don't know it.''

George's eyebrows lifted as he watched her from his vantage point by the telephone. Max frowned. ''I don't know what you're talking about.''

''Yes, you do. You're trying to take over my life, and you don't want me to notice.''

''That's absurd. If I wanted to take over your life I'd have done something a lot more effective than bring you an accountant.'' He looked at George. ''No offense, George.''

''None taken.''

Sidney stalked across the room. ''I'm not going to fall for it, you know. Everyone else in your life may find this too-busy-to-explain-myself act of yours intimidating but I don't.'' She glared at him. ''I find it annoying.''

Max's expression turned nonplussed. ''Now, Sidney—''

She waved a hand to cut him off. ''You haven't spoken to me since Saturday, then you turn up here at the crack of dawn and expect me to fall into your clutches.''

''You're being melodramatic.''

''Am I?''

He wiggled his hands at her. ''I don't have clutches.''

''Ha,'' she said, because nothing else came to mind. ''You know exactly what I mean.''

''Is this a good time for me to tell you I don't have the slightest idea what you're talking about?''

''Where were you all day Sunday?''

His eyebrows knitted in confusion. ''I was called out of town on business. Didn't Colleen tell you?''

''Why didn't *you* tell me?''

''I couldn't find you on Saturday night. I looked for an hour. Then I went to bed. I had to leave before six on Sunday, and I didn't think you'd want me to wake you. I asked Colleen to convey my regrets.''

Sidney felt some of her irritation drain away. On Saturday night, she'd spent an hour and a half talking to Greg Loden in the gazebo. ''Why did you have to work on Sunday?'' she asked quietly.

He tilted his head to one side. ''Colleen didn't tell you, did she?'' Sidney shook her head. Max swore beneath his breath. ''Just after I finished talking with Greg and the Fitzwaters, I got a call from one of my attorneys. There was an accident at one of our smaller manufacturing facilities, and a couple of workers died. I flew out to the site on Sunday to check on things and do what I could for their families. I didn't get back until Sunday night. I stayed through dinner so I could be there for Greg's announcement, and then had several more meetings to make sure everything was taken care of.''

She felt wrung out. "Oh."

Max was frowning. "Colleen was supposed to tell you."

"She didn't."

"I don't understand that."

Sidney remembered the frosty look in his sister's eyes and let out a slow breath. It scraped her nerves to think of him handling what had, no doubt, been an extremely unpleasant task on his own. Whatever Colleen's motivation, it clearly hadn't been concern for Max. "Is everything all right?"

"What?"

"The families of those workers. Is everything all right?"

Something flickered in his gaze—something that made Sidney have to tamp down the urge to go to him, and wrap her arms around his waist. He nodded. "Yes. I took care of them."

Just like always, she mused. "I'm sorry."

He looked confused. "You couldn't have done anything."

"I could have been your friend. I'm sorry you had to do it by yourself. I'm sure it was very difficult for you."

Visibly nonplused, Max stared at her. "So are you mad or not?"

The corner of her mouth twitched. "Direct as usual."

Max lifted one shoulder in a pale imitation of a shrug. "In case you haven't noticed, subtle conversation generally eludes me. Especially the female variety."

She frowned at him. "I'm not mad."

"Good," he said, but he continued to watch her with a narrow-lidded gaze.

Sidney slid a hand through her hair and looked at George. He'd hung up the phone, and was studying a photograph of her and her uncle Philip with undue interest. "Thanks for coming on such short notice, George.'' She walked to him with an outstretched hand. ''I'm Sidney Grant.''

George set the picture down. ''Uh, George Hampton.'' He shook her hand. ''Nice to meet you, Miss Grant.''

''Oh, good grief. Please call me Sidney. What time did you get summoned out of bed this morning?''

He tugged at his tie. ''I'm normally a very early riser.''

A smile played at the corner of her mouth. ''I see.''

''Max pays me extremely well,'' he muttered.

''I'm sure he does.'' Sidney indicated the mound of paperwork with a sweep of her arm. ''Still, by the time you finish going through this, you'll be wanting a bonus.''

Max, she noted, stood rooted to the floor, staring at her with a wary look in his eyes. She smiled at him and quipped, ''That'll be all right, won't it, Max? The bonus, I mean.''

He merely nodded. She picked up the thick packet of information from the IRS and handed it to George. ''Here's what they sent me. I have to confess, it might as well be Greek.''

George scanned the letter, then flashed her a bright smile. ''Oh, this is actually quite good news, Miss Grant, er, Sidney. Max was under the impression that you were being audited.''

''I'm not?''

George shook his head. ''This is an information request. We'll have this settled in no time.''

''Good,'' Max said, ''then Sidney is free for the day.''

George nodded. ''Absolutely. I'm sure everything we need is here in her, uh, files.''

That made her laugh. She supposed there was something vaguely resembling a manila folder somewhere in the clutter of her table. ''Very tactful, George.''

He pushed the wire-framed glasses up the bridge of his nose. ''If we need anything, we can always call you.''

Sidney looked at Max. ''Am I going somewhere?''

He looked relieved to have the conversation back on concrete terms. "I told you, the manager of the hotel is expecting you at eleven."

"What hotel?"

"The Carlisle." When she said nothing, he added, "Greg's engagement party. I'm thinking of having it there."

"Oh. It's a nice place. What do you need me for?"

His expression turned strangely piercing. "That's something I'd like to discuss with you," he said carefully. "If you have time today."

Her eyebrows lifted. "You pretty much made sure I would."

Max nodded. "We can discuss it in the car."

He had, she noted, neatly ducked the issue. "I have some errands I have to run this morning, and I need to stop by the charity luncheon Kelly is handling for me and make sure she has everything she needs."

"No problem," he said. "I'll go with you."

"*You're* going to run errands?" Good Lord, could this day grow any stranger?

"No," he said with careful patience, "I'm going to accompany you. You're going to run errands."

"I see."

Max nodded. "When can you be ready?"

Sidney thought of resisting him, then an image of his strained expression at Sunday night's dinner party popped into her head. Poor Max. When had someone taught him that every problem was his alone to bear? She felt her heart open a little wider toward him. "Give me thirty minutes."

He looked relieved. "Whatever you need."

Sidney shook her head and padded toward her bedroom. She was kicking off her shoes when Max stepped through the door. Startled, she glanced at him. "Max, this is my bedroom."

His gaze traveled to the bed, then back to her. "I'm painfully aware of that."

"Was there something else you wanted?"

He hesitated, then nodded. In two quick strides, he reached her, placed his hands on her shoulders and pulled her to him. "I just wanted to make sure we're clear on this," he murmured, then covered her mouth in a kiss full of hunger and need.

Stunned, Sidney stood still for a second, then yielded to his firm persuasion. With a slight groan of triumph, Max wrapped his arms around her, locking her to him in a firm embrace. She eased her hands up his chest, twined them around his neck. The intensity of the kiss enveloped her. Cast adrift in a sea of sensation, she clung to his shoulders for support. Kissing Max Loden, she decided, was a little like drowning—she felt simultaneously disoriented and weightless. As abruptly as it began, he ended it. When he lifted his head, she had to blink several times before he snapped into focus.

He wore the same fierce expression. "I didn't want you to be confused," he said softly. "Not about this, at least."

"Oh." She was dimly aware that she sounded like an idiot, but couldn't seem to form a coherent thought.

Max, however, seemed satisfied. He studied her face, then released her. "I'll let you dress." And he strode from the room.

Sidney dropped to her bed. She pressed her fingertips to her still-sensitive lips and met her gaze in the mirror. "Cripes." The flushed face and oddly sparkling eyes bore little resemblance to the weary reflection she'd seen moments ago. She had a vague feeling that she'd just survived a hurricane.

Sucking in a breath, she thought about Saturday night, when he'd asked her to dance—when she'd stepped into his arms knowing she was making an irrevocable decision. Since her divorce, she'd carefully guarded her heart, unwilling to make the same mistakes she'd made with her ex-husband. Kelly stayed on her case about her too conservative approach to life. For years, Sidney had used the demands of her business as an outlet for her passion. But something in the way Max looked at her, something about who he was, made her feel uncharacteristically reckless.

And, she decided as she studied herself in the mirror, she had the distinct feeling that the odd craving licking at her belly was no longer going to satisfy itself. Shaking off a slight tremor of foreboding, she grabbed her robe and headed for the bathroom. Dear Lord, the man was going to be the death of her.

Chapter Six

When she joined Max in the living room a half hour later, George was still issuing quiet orders on the phone. Max stood, hands in his trouser pockets, with his back to the room, staring out her window. Sidney crossed to him and laid her hand on his shoulder. He glanced at her with the same odd look he'd worn when he'd left her bedroom. "Ready?" he asked.

She nodded. He reached for her hand and enclosed it in a fierce grip. "Thank you."

Sidney hesitated. "Max—are you sure you're all right?"

"Yes, why?"

"I don't know. You seem—intense."

That won her a slight smile. "More than usual, you mean?"

She nodded. "Yes."

He pulled her toward the door. "I'm fine now," he said softly. "I was afraid you wouldn't come."

He issued a final few commands to George, then pulled the door shut with a soft click. Sidney paused at the landing. "What are you talking about?"

"This weekend—" He shook his head. "I handled it badly."

Sidney shook her head. "I'm sure it was very difficult for you." At his confused look, she added, "Helping those families at the plant."

His gaze narrowed. "It was."

"You were distracted. I understand."

"You do?"

There it was again—that bleak loneliness that turned his silver gaze a colorless gray. With a soft sigh, she rose on her tiptoes to press a soft kiss to his cheek. "I'm sorry you couldn't find me on Saturday night, but for the record, you could have gotten me up on Sunday morning."

"I left the estate at five-thirty in the morning."

"You were on your way to an extremely difficult situation. I'm sorry you felt like you had to go alone."

He blinked. She shook her head. "That's what friends do, Max. Wouldn't you have done the same for me?"

"That's different. I'm often up very early."

She rolled her eyes. "Stop taking everything so literally. All I meant was that I have no doubt you would have inconvenienced yourself a little just to make me feel better. I would have done the same thing for you."

When he didn't answer, merely continued to watch her with that strange look in his eyes, she tugged on his hand. "Don't worry about it," she assured him. "I'll show you later."

When they emerged onto the busy street, Max's limousine was parked at the curb. Sidney shot him an accusatory look. "I thought you said the thing was pretentious."

He shrugged. "It is."

"Then why are you using it?"

"I'm trying to impress you."

She stared at him. "Are you actually trying to tease me?"

He tipped his head to one side. "If you think I have the fortitude to tease you right now, you've grossly overestimated me."

Giving the car a dubious look, she shook her head. "This really wasn't necessary, you know."

"I know. But the space in the back gives me a chance to get some work done. With rumors of the merger floating around, things are a little crazy right now. I'm trying to keep our stockholders calm without tipping my hand.''

Yet, he'd made time to call his accountant and spend the morning with her. ''You should be at the office today.''

''This is the next best thing,'' he assured her.

Sidney gave him a warm look. ''Have I told you that I think you're adorable?''

''Lord, I hope so.''

Sidney laughed. ''Poor Max. I can see I have a lot to teach you.''

''I'm very much looking forward to it.'' The look he gave her curled her toes.

Charlie had rounded the car and opened the door for them. Max indicated it with a sweep of his hand. ''After you.''

Inside, Sidney saw Lois Stein, the older woman who had been Max's secretary for as long as Sidney remembered. The mobile office in Max's limo was complete with a laptop computer and portable fax machine. Sidney waved. ''Hello, Lois.''

''Hello, Sidney. Nice to see you again.''

Max cleared his throat. ''We should get going.''

Sidney nodded. ''Why don't I sit up front with Charlie? Then you can work, and I can tell him where I need to go.''

''No.'' The resolute note in Max's voice gave her momentary pause.

''But—''

''I want you in the back,'' he said firmly. ''With me.''

''But don't you think—''

He placed his hand at the small of her back. ''I can see I have some things to teach you, too, Sidney. I want you in the back.''

She gave him a disgruntled look. ''You can work better if you don't have to listen to me chatting with Charlie.''

''In the back,'' he said again.

''That seems silly.''

''With me,'' Max insisted.

She shook her head. "Geez, Max, do you always have to act like such a tyrant? You can't always have your way, you know."

"Today I can." He guided her into the car, then looked at Charlie. "Take Miss Grant wherever she wants to go, Charlie. We don't have to be at the Carlisle until eleven. If we're running late, I'll call."

"Sure thing, Max." Charlie shot her a grin. "Where to, Miss Grant?"

Her eyebrows lifted. Miss Grant. He'd never called her Miss Grant. Charlie was her uncle Philip's poker pal and the only other member of Max's staff who'd been with the Loden family since before Max's birth. "Charlie, if you start calling me Miss Grant, I'll forget to answer."

The older man slid a casual look at Max, then met her gaze again. "Okay," he said quietly. "Where do you need to go?"

She didn't miss his careful omission of her name. With a slight frown, she gave him directions to her bank. There was something odd, she thought moments later, about writing out a deposit slip for the check Max had given her while beside her, Max transacted a quarter of a million dollars worth of international currency purchases.

And the rest of her day unfolded in a similarly bizarre fashion. When his limo drew stares in the small parking lot of her local bank, Sidney decided to save the rest of her errands for later, and gave Charlie directions to the site of the charity luncheon.

When they entered the chaotic ballroom at the hotel, Kelly's eyebrows lifted so high they disappeared behind her bangs when she saw Max standing near the door, intently watching the activity.

"We're going to talk about this," Kelly said firmly.

Sidney didn't doubt that. Kelly would hound her mercilessly. "I wouldn't dream otherwise."

"Soon," her friend added.

"Tomorrow." Sidney handed Kelly back her indispensable

clipboard. "We'll have lunch. You can debrief me about today, and I'll spill my guts."

Kelly glanced at Max, who stood near the entrance of the ballroom, talking on his cell phone. "Did he happen to explain why he went missing on Saturday?"

"It's a long story."

"I'll look forward to hearing it. How did he tear you away from your private hell with the IRS?"

"He gave me a team of accountants who are, even as we speak, sorting my files."

"God—I love a man with flair. Some guys just bring flowers. Where did he learn to be so romantic?"

"Believe me, at seven o'clock this morning, I was thinking an accountant in a navy blue suit was enough to make me swoon."

"I wasn't kidding," Kelly assured her. "You gotta admit, the man has a certain, ah, panache."

"You could say that."

"Definitely. You're sure that Fitzwater woman is going to marry the brother?"

"That remains to be seen."

"Yeah, well," Kelly shook her head, "if she backs out, I think I'll get in line. You promise you'll give me a full report tomorrow?"

"If this day turns out to be as bizarre as I think it will, I'll be dying to talk to you."

"If you're that desperate, you could always call me tonight—unless you, uh, think you might have other plans."

Sidney laughed. "You're so subtle, Kel."

"It's my forte."

"Well, the only plans I have tonight are for an early bedtime and a good night's sleep. I was up all night trying to make sense of Tick's notes."

"Serves you right for hiring an accountant named Tick."

"Thanks for your support."

Kelly looked at Max again. "Believe me, you've got me

totally in your corner." Her expression turned serious. "It's about time you decided to quit letting that jerk you married have control over the rest of your life."

"Kel—"

Kelly gave her a gentle shove. "Tomorrow. Right now, you've got the great toy tycoon wistfully longing for you."

"Wistfully longing?"

"Just look at that expression."

"I hate to break this to you," Sidney chided, "but that particular expression is annoyance."

"Let me tell you something, babe. I got a lot more experience in that department than you do, and the only thing that man is annoyed about is that it's taking him so long to get between your sheets."

"Kelly." Her voice held a warning note.

Kelly prodded her toward Max. "Tomorrow," she said. "We'll talk about the whole thing tomorrow. I have a feeling the phrase 'Who Gets To Marry Max?' is about to take on a whole new meaning."

Hours later, Sidney leaned back against the leather seat of Max's limo. Nervous energy had gotten her through the interview with the hotel manager, but her sleepless night and the latent anxiety of the weekend were catching up to her. Beside her, Max talked on the phone, his feet propped on the opposite seat. His secretary had taken a cab back to Max's office when they'd arrived at the Carlisle. For the first time since that moment in her bedroom, she was alone with Max.

He didn't look at her, but he seemed to sense her fatigue. He eased his arm around her shoulders and guided her head to his chest. With a soft sigh, she closed her eyes to enjoy the sensation of listening to his voice with her ear pressed to his chest.

It seemed like seconds later that Max prodded her awake with a soft kiss. "Sidney?"

She blinked. "Hmm."

"Sidney, wake up. You're home."

She had to shake her head to clear it. "What?"

He smiled at her as he smoothed her hair off her forehead. "Home. You've been asleep."

"I was?"

"You were."

She glanced out the window. They were in front of her apartment building. "I've been asleep for two hours?"

"About."

"I'm sorry."

"Did you stay up all night working on your taxes?"

"Yes."

Max shook his head. "You should have told me."

"It wasn't just that," she said before she thought better of it. "I haven't slept very well since Saturday."

In the slightly shadowy interior of the car, his eyes sparkled. "Neither have I." Sidney blushed, which won her another soft kiss. "Rest assured, I'm going to talk to my sister about that."

"That's not necessary, Max. I'm sure it was just a misunderstanding."

"Maybe."

She squeezed his forearm. "Forget it. It's okay."

Max shrugged. "I called George and told him to have his people out of your apartment by the time we got home."

"That wasn't necessary, either."

"It was. I want you to get some rest."

She gave him a slight smile. "Judging from this afternoon, you didn't have to run him off. You notice I didn't have any trouble sleeping through the ride home."

"I didn't run him off. He assured me he has everything he needs from you. They'll finish up tomorrow at his office."

"I'm pretty sure I forgot to thank you for doing this. In case you didn't notice, I was drowning before you and George came to the rescue."

He lifted one shoulder in a casual shrug. "I was glad to

do it. I just wish I'd known about it sooner. Philip should have told me."

"It wasn't your problem." He looked like he wanted to argue, so she cut him off with a slight wave of her hand. "Never mind. Just consider yourself eternally thanked for your help. I'm sorry I was such lousy company this afternoon."

He gave a tendril of her hair a slight tug. "You weren't."

"Most men would find it offensive to have their, uh, companion conk out on them."

"Most men are jerks." His expression was dead serious.

Sidney laughed. "I see your opinion of yourself is still intact."

"Absolutely."

"We could have used the ride home to discuss the layout of the Carlisle."

"We could have. We can also do it later. I asked Lois to reschedule our appointments at the other two hotels to this weekend."

"Um, about that—"

"Yes?"

"What exactly is it that you want from me?"

"Exactly?" he asked carefully.

Sidney swallowed. "Regarding the hotels. I mean, I don't need to tour them to tell you which one will work best for you. I've staffed and managed events in all three."

"I wanted to see the layout myself."

"That's understandable. Still, what do you need me for?"

He gave her a probing look that made her blush. Max reached for her hand. "I wanted to talk to you about that on the way home, but you were exhausted. I spoke with Philip on Sunday morning."

"You did?"

"Yes. And he suggested that Greg's engagement is going to significantly broaden my social calendar for the next several months."

"I don't doubt it."

"I'd like you to help me."

She looked at him closely. "What do you mean help you?"

Max leaned back against the black leather seat. "Philip suggested that perhaps your professional expertise could be beneficial in this."

"Excuse me?"

"I'd like to have you under exclusive contract until after the wedding."

Sidney blinked. Maybe the fatigue of the last couple of nights was dimming her concentration. "Max—"

"I'm going to have the engagement party, the wedding, and, considering the merger, an extensive number of professional obligations to fulfill. And I'd like your help."

Sidney's eyebrows drew together as she studied his inscrutable expression. "Let me get this straight, Max. You're feeling a little stressed about your social life, so you want me to manage it for you?"

Frustration marred his features. "I'm not handling this well."

"You could say that."

He drew a deep breath. "What I'd like is a business arrangement that guarantees your professional assistance through the next few months."

"And you want to pay me for this?"

"Of course." He looked genuinely baffled.

Sidney scowled at him. "Did anyone ever tell you that you're a real jerk, Max?"

"I didn't realize you'd be offended by a lucrative business deal."

She reached for her door handle. "I'm offended that you'd offer me something entirely different over the weekend and then show up here and offer to pay for my company."

He had the grace to wince. "I'm not offering to pay for your company. I'm offering to pay for your services."

"Color me flattered."

"I'm screwing this up, aren't I?"

"Yep."

He drew a deep breath as he reached for her hand. "Okay, look, let's start this over. I'm not trying to offend you."

Sidney shook her head. "Just tell me what you want."

He searched her face. "I want to acquire you."

If she hadn't known him as well as she did, she might have laughed. Instead, she shook her head and laid her hand against his face. "Oh, Max. How did life get to be so hard for you?"

"Sidney—"

She pressed a kiss to the corner of his mouth. "Why yes, Max, I'll be happy to help you manage your social life. For free. That's what friends do."

"That's not a sound business decision."

"Bummer."

"I'd feel better if I had you under contract."

"I don't doubt it, but you're going to have to trust me on this one."

He searched her face. "I don't want to take advantage of you. I'm more than willing to pay for your professional expertise."

"So noted, and gratefully acknowledged. Don't worry about it. I can take care of myself, and if you get out of hand, I'll let you know."

Relief filled his eyes. "I'm sorry I offended you."

Amusement made the corner of her mouth twitch. "Don't mention it."

"If I'd known you were so exhausted, I never would have taken you into town today."

"I'm sure you were anxious to get this settled."

"No, I wasn't."

"Then why the siege at my apartment this morning?"

His lips twitched. "I didn't want to wait any longer to see you. It didn't have a damned thing to do with Greg's wedding."

Sidney laughed. "You could have just asked me, you know. You didn't have to go to all this trouble."

Max nodded. "Next time, I'll know." He swept her hair from her forehead. "You're beat, Sidney. Are you sure you don't want me to carry you to bed?" he whispered.

With a slight shake of her head, Sidney pushed open her door. "And you said you didn't have the fortitude to tease me today."

"I'm not teasing."

Pushing open the door, she said, "I think I can make it on my own steam."

She would have exited the car then, but Max grabbed her hand. "Wait."

She glanced at him. "Yes?"

"I've got to go. Lois has been begging me since this morning to go into the office and handle some of this merger mess. But I want to take you to dinner tomorrow night. What time should I pick you up?"

"Is this another command performance?"

He frowned. "What?"

She smoothed the fierce expression from his forehead with her forefinger. "Don't worry. You'll get the hang of it. Won't it be easier if I meet you downtown at your office?"

"Do you have to come into the city anyway?"

"Yes."

"All right. What time?"

"What time suits you?" she asked.

"Oh, hell," he muttered, and pulled her to him for a kiss that thoroughly muddled her brain. "Right now," he said, when he finally raised his head. "Right now suits me."

"Lois needs you."

"And I need you," he growled.

She placed her fingertips on his lips. "Duty calls, Max."

"Doesn't it always?"

There was something very sad about that statement. She

pressed a kiss to the corner of his mouth. "What time do you want me tomorrow?"

His eyes drifted momentarily shut. When he looked at her again, she saw the banked fire in his gaze. "Six-thirty."

"I'll be there." She stepped onto the curb, then ducked her head back into the car to smile at him. "Have a nice day at the office, honey," she chided.

Only Max could make the name he called her sound so affectionate.

Chapter Seven

"Then what happened?" Gertie leaned across the table in the kitchen of Max's Manhattan penthouse suite and pinned Charlie with a shrewd look. "Exactly."

Charlie frowned at her. "I couldn't say. Exactly."

Philip chuckled. Charlie was one of his closest friends, and, he had no doubt, felt as strongly about Max and Sidney as he did. "Come on, Charlie. Had Max closed the window between the seats or not?"

Charlie's eyes twinkled. "He closed it on the way home. As far as I could tell, Sidney was asleep, and Max was on the phone."

Sam frowned. "That's it? He had her alone in the back of the car, and he stayed on the phone? What the hell's the matter with that man?"

Elena laughed. "Give him a break, Sam. He's a little new at this."

"At women?" Sam asked. "Where have you been?"

"At chasing women," Elena corrected. "They normally chase him."

Charlie nodded. "That's true enough."

Gertie clucked her tongue in the manner Philip found oddly endearing. "He is going to need a little help with the romance."

Elena concurred. Sam grunted. Philip regarded them all with an amused smile. "I think you're underestimating him."

"Philip," Gertie said, her voice slightly strained, "he took her an accountant."

"She needed an accountant."

"Women need lots of things," Elena interjected. "When I was first married, I needed an iron. But when Paulo gave me one for my birthday, I was furious with him. Men have trouble with this."

Gertie nodded. "And Max has more trouble than most." She looked at Philip. "If you want this to work, you'd better help him."

"What do you suggest?"

"Well, for one thing," Charlie said, "keep Max's sister, Colleen out of the picture."

Elena uttered a frustrated oath. "That Colleen. She is determined to keep Max to herself."

"I don't think she likes the idea of Max getting involved with someone," Gertie said.

"Someone," Philip asked, "or someone like Sidney?"

The small group fell silent. Sam spoke first. "I don't think it's Sidney, exactly. I think Colleen is worried that Max could be serious about her. Colleen doesn't like the idea of things changing around here."

"Shows what you know." Elena rapped her fingers on the table. "Colleen, she's completely different from Natalie. She's selfish. Like her mother was. She's got an unhappy marriage, and she wants everyone else to be unhappy, too. Even Max."

"Especially Max," Philip said quietly. They all looked at him for an explanation. He shrugged. "It's just a feeling I have. Colleen blames Max for her problems with her husband."

"That's true," Charlie concurred. "I drove her out to the Hamptons the other day, and I heard her telling someone on the phone that Max would never understand how miserable she is.''

"Colleen was miserable long before she married Mr. Wells," Gertie said quietly.

The small group nodded. Philip released a slow breath. He didn't like the turn of the conversation. Generally, he tried to avoid gossiping about Max and his private life. He'd made the decision to draw his friends into his confidence about Sidney simply because he knew he'd need their help. Max was many things, and Philip loved him like a son, but they were right: he had no idea how to court a woman. He took a sip of his coffee and studied them all over the rim. "All right," he finally said, "we'll help. I'll suggest something at the first opportunity."

"Flowers," Elena said emphatically. "Suggest flowers."

Sam nodded. "Sidney wouldn't respond well to something extravagant. If you just tell Max that he might want to give her something a little more personal than George Hampton, he'll buy her a refrigerator."

"Or an iron," Gertie quipped.

Philip set his cup down with measured precision. "This may be harder than I thought," he admitted.

AT THREE O'CLOCK the following afternoon, Max was thinking the same thing. He glanced at the clock on his office desk as he slowly rotated a pencil between his thumb and forefinger. Paul Wells, his brother-in-law and vice president of administration for AppleTree Toys, was briefing him on a labor problem at their southeast facility. Max hadn't heard a word he'd said. Belatedly, he realized Paul had stopped talking. He seemed to be waiting for an answer. So Max nodded and said, "Sure, Paul. If that's what you think is best."

Paul's eyebrows lifted. "Max, I just recommended that we burn the Georgia plant to the ground and relocate the operation to Liberia."

Max frowned. "Why the hell would you want to do that?"

"I don't. I was just pretty sure you hadn't heard a word I said."

"Oh." Max shook his head. "Sorry. I'm a little distracted."

"You're kidding."

Max ignored his sarcasm, carefully placing the pencil on his desk. "You were saying?"

"Uh-uh." Paul dropped the file he was holding on Max's desk. "I'd rather talk about you."

"I wouldn't."

"I don't doubt that." His eyes danced with amusement. "What's going on, Max?"

"It's not going to do me any good to say, 'nothing.' Is it?" Afternoon sunlight streamed through the window of his seventy-third-floor office. The amber glow that slanted across his desk gilded the polished cherry.

"No."

Max genuinely liked Paul. He especially liked that the man had had the good sense to fall wildly in love with his sister, Natalie, and the even better sense to marry her. Paul was one of the few people in Max's acquaintance who had the nerve to stand up to him. Paul, Max mused, and Sidney Grant. He leaned back in his chair. "When you first wanted Natalie," he said carefully, "What did you do?"

Paul sat down. "Well, I wrote out my letter of resignation. I figured you'd fire me for hitting on your sister."

"I'm serious."

"So am I."

Max shook his head. "I have better sense than that, you know."

"You fired Ed Lasen when he dated her."

"Ed Lasen was a bastard. He didn't want Natalie. He wanted to ingratiate himself with me."

"Yeah, well, you can see why maybe I was a little concerned."

"Not really. I don't fire competent people. I already knew

Lasen was a fool. The only reason he had a job is because I inherited him when we acquired Toy Land.''

''And you wanted an excuse to fire him?''

''I didn't need one. But after Natalie, well, let's just say I knew that any man stupid enough not to see that my sister is an incredibly gifted, remarkable woman, wouldn't have much of a future at my company.''

Paul laughed. ''You're not going to get any arguments out of me.''

''That's just one of the things I like about you. But you still haven't answered my question.''

''What question?''

''About Natalie.''

''Oh.'' Paul regarded him with a curious look. ''Why are you so interested in this all of a sudden?''

''I've never chased a woman before,'' Max admitted. ''I'm not exactly sure how it's done.''

Paul let out a low whistle. ''I see.''

''I'm not kidding.''

''I didn't think you were. Natalie told me this weekend that she thought maybe there was something going on between you and Sidney Grant. I didn't believe her.''

''My sister is a little too observant sometimes.''

''Evidently. So I take it the lady is resisting?''

''Not exactly.''

''Then what's the problem? Exactly?''

''I told you. I've never chased a woman. I don't want to screw it up.''

''Poor Max. Always had the girls falling at your feet, have you?''

Max stifled a frustrated oath. ''Look, forget I mentioned it. It's not important.''

''You're serious about this, aren't you?''

He hesitated, then nodded. ''Yes.''

The teasing glint left Paul's eyes. ''Okay. What do you want to know?''

"I don't know," Max admitted. "I want to know the seven habits of highly effective romances."

"It's a little more complicated than that."

"That's what I was afraid of."

"Does Sidney know you're, uh, interested?"

"Yes."

"What did you tell her, exactly?"

"I told her I've wanted her for years, and I think the timing is finally right for us. And that I don't see any reason to wait any longer."

"I see."

Max frowned. "What's that supposed to mean?"

"Well, sometimes it helps not to be quite so blunt."

"I don't see why I should lie to her about it."

"It's not *lying*. It's being tactful," Paul said.

"I hate that word."

"I know."

Max leaned back in his leather desk chair. "Damn. I didn't think it would be this hard."

"Maybe it's not. Is Sidney putting up a fight?"

That brought a slight smile to his face. "No."

"She doesn't argue with you?"

"Are you kidding? She'd take me down in a second if she wanted to."

Paul studied him, his expression thoughtful. "Is that so?"

"Absolutely. What I like about Sidney is that she doesn't play games. I know exactly where I stand with her."

"So what did she say when you indicated your, ah, readiness?"

Max felt a surge of satisfaction. "She said yes."

Paul blinked. "Why are you arguing with a yes?"

"I don't know. It's different this time. It matters more. Not only do I have the utmost respect for her uncle, but I respect her, too. I don't want her to get hurt."

Paul nodded. "I see."

"And you still haven't answered my question."

"About chasing women?"

"Yes."

"Something extravagant usually works."

"I gave her an accountant."

Paul blinked. "Excuse me?"

"George," Max said. "She was having tax problems. So I gave her George for a few days."

"How romantic."

Max frowned. "I realize that it must seem a little practical—"

"A little?"

"Okay, a lot practical, but according to Philip, she was completely stressed out. I wanted George to help her."

"It could have been worse," Paula conceded. "You could have given her a calculator."

Max winced. "I bought her a laptop this afternoon."

"Oh, Lord."

"I didn't give it to her yet," he hastened to explain. "Geez, Paul, she was doing her taxes by hand."

"A computer?" Paul's expression looked pained.

"It's a top-of-the-line machine."

"Max, didn't Natalie tell you about the time I bought her a blender for our anniversary."

"No."

"She almost killed me."

"What the hell's wrong with a blender?"

"Women have a thing about that. You don't buy them practical gifts when you're supposed to be romantic."

Max's gave narrowed. "Is there a manual?"

"I wish. Look," Paul leaned forward in his chair, "here's the best advice I can give you. Don't mention the computer. Don't even let her see the box."

"I don't see—"

"I've been married for seven years, Max. I'm telling you, anything that plugs in is not the way to a woman's heart."

"Then what should I have done, bought her lingerie? I was afraid she'd kill me."

"Probably. And if she didn't, Philip would." Paul rubbed his hands on his trouser legs. "Sweep her off her feet, Max. And if you're smart, you'll make it look like you went to a lot of trouble."

"I spent four hours picking out the laptop."

"She'd rather have a daisy."

"That's ridiculous."

"Do you want the woman or not?"

A knot of anxiety clenched in his gut. "You can't imagine how much."

"Then think of it like a business merger—like Fitzwater. What was the first thing you did when you decided you wanted Fitzwater Electronics?"

Max started to relax. This was familiar territory. "Learned his weaknesses."

"There you are. Winning a woman is the same as negotiating a peaceful merger."

"Sounds ruthless."

"Don't think of them as her weaknesses, think of them as her soft spots."

That, he thought wryly, he could do. He'd been spending an inordinate amount of time considering all of Sidney Grant's soft spots. "I see," he said quietly.

"Are you sure?"

"I think so. What you're telling me is that I should do my research."

"Uh-huh. Nothing flatters a woman like knowing a man is paying attention to her idiosyncrasies." He fiddled with his tie. "Let me give you an example. Last year for Natalie's birthday, I wanted to do something really nice. We were having some problems."

Max frowned. "She didn't tell me."

"They weren't *that* serious, just the kind of things married couples go through every now and then. Anyway, I just wanted her to know how much I loved her. So I racked my brain for weeks trying to come up with the perfect gift.''

''What did you give her?''

''I took her out to lunch.''

Max waited for the punch line. It never came. ''That's it?''

''Well, sort of. If you remember, we were really busy then. We had the Monster Mash launch and were having trouble with the X2 prototypes.''

Max's gaze strayed to the Max doll he kept on the bookshelf of his office. It served as a reminder of how far he'd come. At the moment, he wished he felt the doll's reputed self-confidence. ''I remember,'' he told Paul.

''I was scheduled to go to the sales conference in Seattle.''

Max slowly nodded. ''You sent Roger instead.''

''Right. I took two days off just to spend with my wife. It couldn't have been more inconvenient, and if you hadn't been my brother-in-law, and an all-around fair guy, I might have even been afraid I'd lose my job.''

''Natalie got the point?''

''Clearly. She was so overwhelmed that I was willing to put her, and her birthday, over the demands of my job that she, we, well—I'm not going to tell you the rest.''

Max rolled his eyes. ''Thanks for that, at least.''

''Anyway, my point is, you're probably not going to get very far by throwing money at her.''

''She seemed impressed enough with George.''

''You were meeting a need she had. You got lucky on that one. Just don't make practicality a habit.''

''I have never seen the purpose in deliberate impracticality.''

''You're not a woman.''

''For which I give thanks almost daily.''

Paul shot him a wry smile. ''Romance her a little, Max. It's not going to kill you.''

''Are you sure?''

''Positive.''

Max picked up his pencil again. "You know, this is a hell of a lot easier when the women do the chasing."

"Sure, but then you end up with a woman like Constance Barlow to keep you company."

At the sudden bad taste in his mouth, Max grunted. "Point well taken."

Paul fiddled with his tie. "So, uh, in case my wife asks, can I tell her that you're maybe taking the question of who gets to marry Max a little seriously?"

Max frowned at him. "Who said anything about marriage?"

"Natalie," Paul said. "You know how the woman loves weddings."

"And you know how much I hate that slogan."

"Sure. Uh. So can we get back to the merger now?"

"In a second. One more thing."

"Yeah?"

"If you tell Natalie we had this conversation, I'll fire you."

"ROMANCE HER," Max told his reflection in the mirror three hours later. He'd showered and changed in the private bathroom off his downtown office. "This is going to be a disaster." Though he couldn't remember the occasion clearly, he was fairly certain he hadn't felt this nervous since the night of his sixth-grade graduation. Then, his father had given him an incoherent lecture on the importance of honor, integrity and commitment. Of course, the lecture had been delivered via ship-to-shore phone line. Max's father had been on a Caribbean cruise with his latest mistress at the time.

Now Max took careful note of his too fierce expression and frowned. For the love of—he bit off the curse. Whatever Paul had meant, he was fairly certain he wasn't supposed to scowl at Sidney all evening. Charlie had delivered his tuxedo an hour earlier. Philip had attached a note to his suspenders wishing him a pleasant evening. The note, somehow, had a

far greater effect than any lecture he'd ever received from his
father.

"Hi, Max."

At the sound of her voice, his shoulders tensed. He turned
to find her watching him from the doorway to his office. The
broad expanse of Oriental carpeting suddenly seemed a mile
long. He forced himself to smile. "Hi. You're on time."

Her eyebrows lifted. "Did you think I wouldn't be?"

He clenched his back teeth in frustration. This was going
to be a disaster, he told himself again. With his deplorable
lack of tact, he had as much chance of romancing Sidney
Grant as he did of buying the moon. He drew a deep breath.
"Of course. I see you, ah, got my message." He'd asked his
secretary to call her and let her know the evening would be
formal. She wore a simple black sheath that effectively
knocked his designer socks off.

"Yes." She glanced down at her dress. "I hope this is all
right."

Max nearly choked. The dress skimmed her figure in all
sorts of interesting ways, ending a couple of inches above her
knees. Heretofore, he'd never considered himself a leg-man,
but Sidney Grant was changing him. Smooth legs, sheathed
in sheer black stockings, tapered to slim ankles. She wore a
pair of sensibly heeled shoes that probably should have
looked practical, but somehow managed to tantalize him. Max
squelched the direction of his thoughts before he went stark
raving mad. "You look great."

"Thanks."

He nodded and started the long trek across the carpet. His
hands, he realized, were tingling. The sensation heightened as
he drew closer. He was beginning to recognize the feeling as
the odd need he had to touch her. She leaned against the
doorjamb as she watched his measured stride. Several feet
from her, Max stopped. "Don't you want to come in?" he
said. To his own ears, his voice sounded husky.

A smile played at the corner of her lips. "Come into my parlor said the spider to the fly?"

"I don't want to devour you," he lied.

Sidney laughed, then crossed the few steps to him. She slid a hand up his lapel, and he almost toppled to the carpet. "Funny. I was thinking maybe I'd devour you."

His head swam. Max crushed her to him with a low groan and covered her mouth with his. The taste of her was heady and daring. She smelled spicy and clean, and blood roared in his ears as he kissed her. When his lungs screamed for air, he wrenched his mouth from hers and lifted his head.

Sidney made an intoxicating little sound and dropped her forehead to his shoulder. "I missed you, too," she muttered.

He should have gotten an Oscar for the low chuckle he managed. Lord, she was going to be the death of him. "How is George?" he said quietly, and was absurdly pleased when she blinked in obvious confusion. "The accountant."

At the slight prompt, understanding dawned in her gaze. "Oh. George. He's fine. He's, uh, through actually. He straightened everything out for me. Thanks to you."

"Good." Max swept a few tendrils of hair from her cheek. "I'd be jealous if you thought about him tonight while you were with me."

Humor made her eyes sparkle. "Not much chance of that, is there?" She wiped the traces of her lipstick from his mouth with the tip of her index finger. "You sort of suck up all the space in my brain when I'm around you."

Easing a hand down her spine, he nudged her closer to him. "The feeling is mutual."

"Really?"

"Absolutely." He studied her a minute, then eased his fingers to her elbow. "We'd better go."

"What time are our reservations?"

"Eight."

"Oh." She stepped away from him. "It's just a quarter to seven. What's the hurry?"

"We've got a ways to go before we get there," he said softly and led her to the door.

Chapter Eight

Three and a half hours later, as Sidney glanced up at him, her eyes shining, her lips curved into an inviting smile, Max decided he definitely needed to give his brother-in-law, and his butler, a bonus. At the Swing Easy ballroom in Cincinnati, the Glen Miller Orchestra was playing "In the Mood," and Sidney Grant had Max completely under her spell.

Vaguely, he remembered thinking it was supposed to be the other way around. He had been the one doing the chasing. Still, there was no denying that Sidney had caught him. He spun her in another deft move, then caught her close again. Lord, he felt good. Euphoria didn't begin to describe the emotion roaring through him.

Sure, Sidney had given him a censorious look when they'd arrived at the airstrip where his private plane awaited them. She'd chastised him for the extravagance, needled him to tell her where they were headed, then plagued him with questions all the way to the Swing Easy. But her suspicion had turned to undisguised pleasure when they'd entered the room. She'd turned the full force of her smile on him, and he'd practically collapsed at her feet. "How did you know?" she'd asked, breathless and enchanting.

"That you like swing dancing?" He captured her hand in his, "Philip told me."

She laughed. "He taught me."

"That's what he said."

"Who taught you?"

"Some dance instructor my mother found." Max had led her to the floor.

"But, Max, why did you bring me all the way out here? There are swing clubs in New York."

"It's Glen Miller," he said blandly. "I thought you should have the best."

The sound of her laughter had seared its way down his spine. The orchestra played "Stardust," Sidney turned into his arms, and Max went straight to heaven.

Now, as he stood watching her taste the various desserts on the sampler platter he wondered just how the hell he'd waited this long for her. Her eyes closed in quiet rapture when she bit into a raspberry tart. His entire body reacted. "Good?" he said, his voice harsher than he'd intended.

Sidney nodded. "Divine."

He plucked a piece of chocolate dipped shortbread from the tray. "Is the chocolate as good as yours?"

"It's not bad," she said, meeting his gaze. "But mine's better. Remind me, and I'll make you a batch."

"I'd like that." He swallowed the confection without really tasting it. He still remembered the way Sidney's hair had smelled faintly of chocolate, and the way he'd longed to bury his face in it and absorb her.

"Most candy chefs use too much paraffin," she was explaining. "It makes the chocolate easier to work with, but it's not as rich." She was licking her fingers where the tart had oozed from its shell.

Max swallowed hard. "You don't use paraffin?"

"Just enough to make it hold its shape." Her eyes twinkled. "I am not a candy chef, I am a chocolate artist." She studied the dessert tray, then selected a tiny pecan pastry. "Here," she told him. "Try this one." She popped the tart between his lips.

He barely resisted the urge to suck on her fingers. The

brown sugar and pecans melted in his mouth. Just like she would, he thought wryly. What was the matter with him? He could never in his life remember being this thoroughly seduced over a plate full of sugar—over anything, for that matter. And she wasn't even trying. If she really set her mind to it, she'd probably kill him. Max swallowed the pecan treat, then reached for her hand. "Enough for now," he said. "I'd like to dance." He was dying to hold her.

She smiled at him. "I would, too. I'm having a wonderful time."

He turned her into his arms. "So am I."

And the rest of the evening passed in similar bliss. He was, he admitted, completely addicted to her. When he could think about something other than the indescribable feel of her pressed against him, he'd take the time to consider why Sidney affected him like this. He'd known plenty of women who'd wanted him—for one thing or another. But he'd never seen such a sweet combination of desire and longing in a woman's eyes—at least not in the eyes of a woman who was looking straight at him.

By the time they were settled back on his plane, Max felt as high as their cruising altitude. He'd instructed his pilot to take his time with the return flight. He wanted to draw out the sheer sense of energy he felt just watching Sidney smile at him.

For the first time in longer than he could remember, he felt at ease and sanguine, and even better, he knew exactly why. Sidney sat across from him, that same lustrous smile on her lips that had been tempting him all evening. "You look happy," he told her.

She laughed. The throaty sound sent heat coursing through him. "I am," she said softly. "I can't remember the last time I enjoyed myself more."

"I'm glad."

She tipped her head to one side as she looked at him. "You went to an awful lot of trouble tonight."

"It's been a while since I had a first date with a woman who—" he shook his head. "It's been a while."

Sidney pursed her lips. "I can safely say I've never had a man work quite this hard to dazzle me on a first date."

"Good."

Sidney hesitated for a moment. "I—I'm not sure I understand what this was all about."

"No?" he asked.

She shook her head. Max studied her through narrowed eyes. "It was about showing you how much I want you. I wanted you to know there can be more for us than what I think will be fantastic sex."

Color flooded her face. "Oh," she said, and licked her lips.

The blood started to roar in his ears. "I wanted you to know," he said softly, "that I think things will be incredible between us, and I'm willing to work for it."

"Why?"

The innocent question made his eyes widen. "Why? Hell, Sidney, you know why."

She rested her hands in her lap. "Actually, I haven't got a clue." Her voice was so soft, he could barely hear her above the roar of the jet engines.

Max frowned. "My God. You're serious."

She didn't look at him. "It's just that I wouldn't say, generally, that I'm the kind of woman who inspires men to, er, grand passion."

"Oh, hell." He closed his eyes and dropped his head back against the seat. "You know, there are times when I could cheerfully kill your ex-husband." He used his thumb to nudge her chin up so she could feel the full force of his gaze. "How did that bastard convince you that men wouldn't want you?"

Her gaze turned wary. "I think you're giving him too much credit."

Max chose not to argue. "Do you know," he said, "that when I hear you laugh it makes me want you?"

"No."

He leaned closer. "You have the most incredible scent." He nuzzled the bend of her neck. She stiffened, but didn't pull away. "Sometimes, I dream about it."

Her breathing had turned shallow. He saw the lambent heat in her gaze and pressed his advantage. "When I imagine," he deliberately kept his voice low, "what it's going to be like between us, it makes me feel a little crazy."

"Max, I don't think—"

He slid his hands along her forearms. "My concentration is shot to hell. Paul was trying to brief me today, and I couldn't stop thinking about you."

"Oh." Her voice had turned husky.

He twined a tendril of her hair around his index finger. "When I think about how soft your hair is, it makes me wonder what it's going to feel like when I'm with you and your hair is spread across my pillows." Lifting his eyelids, he pinned her with a meaningful look. "But mostly, I think about what it's going to be like when we're so close that our heartbeats match."

Sidney's eyes turned cloudy. "So do I," she admitted quietly.

The breath left his lungs in a whoosh. "So do you think you could give me a rough estimate of just how long this is going to take?"

"How long what's going to take?" The flush on her skin spiked his temperature several notches. Did she turn that delicious shade of rosy pink all over?

"Can you tell me how long you'd like me to wait for you?"

"Max—" Sidney framed his face in both her hands. Searching his gaze for answers, she asked, "Is that what this is about? You want to know how long I'm going to dangle you on my hook until I let you go to bed with me?"

The question sounded crass. He cursed himself for that. Once again, with his usual skill for tact, he'd managed to screw up. What he felt for Sidney wasn't some kind of sordid, purely physical drive for gratification, and he sure as hell didn't like knowing that she thought it was. "No." He clenched his teeth. "Sort of." He dropped his head back against the seat and uttered a dark curse. "Sorry. I'm not handling this well."

"I wouldn't say that, exactly."

Max spent several long seconds in emotional turmoil, then scraped himself together. "Look, Sidney. I want you to be very clear on this, if nothing else. I want to make love to you, but I also want to be your lover. It's not the same thing. We're both old enough to know the difference."

Her eyelids fluttered as she glanced away from him. "Yes."

When she didn't speak again, he tightened his grip on her hand. "Please tell me what you're thinking."

She raised her eyes to his, and it took every ounce of control he possessed not to pull her onto his lap and kiss the daylights out of her. She looked so incredibly adorable with that glint of determination in her eyes, and the firm set of her chin. Sidney reached over and loosened his tie. "All right," she said. "Here are the hard facts." The tip of her tongue flicked out to wet the corner of her mouth. That sent his blood pressure to the moon. "First, you didn't have to work this hard to impress me."

He wondered what she'd say if he told her he was contemplating asking her to go to Milan with him. He owned a villa there—a very private, very well-staffed, very accommodating home where he could have her to himself for weeks on end. "No?" he asked.

"Uh-uh." She shook her head. "I was already pretty impressed."

"You were?" What would she do if he simply pulled her onto his lap, he wondered?

"Yep." she shifted in her seat. "And second," her eyes turned cloudy with passion, "in case you doubted it, I'm completely under your spell. I think I have been since I was fifteen years old.''

Because he thought he might die if he didn't, he leaned over and kissed her then, a light teasing kiss that left him desperate for more. If he could, he realized, he'd devour her, and then, maybe, this gnawing hunger would abate. ''Sidney,'' he whispered against her mouth. ''You're tearing me to pieces. I've got to have you.''

''You've got me,'' she said as she threaded her fingers in his hair. ''You—ah—'' her voice shredded as he nipped at her earlobe ''—believe me. You've got me.''

He swept his hand over her hip. He couldn't wait any longer to give her mouth the kind of leisurely exploration he'd been craving all night. At that moment, he could easily picture himself drowning in the sheer sensation of holding her. Her hands gripped his head. Her lips moved in time with his. Her head tilted back against the seat to give him unrestricted access. ''Sidney,'' he tore his mouth from hers to run it along her jaw, ''baby, you can't imagine what you're doing to me.''

She pressed on his chest until he loosened his grip. The bewitching smile she gave him made his heart miss its next beat. ''Yes, I can,'' she said. ''Because you're doing the same thing to me. It's a little—overwhelming.''

''Don't be afraid of it.''

A perceptible pause. ''I'm not.''

''You're sure?''

She nodded. ''Yes. Do you—do you know why?''

Of course he knew why. She could trust him because he was the most trustworthy person on earth. He took care of everything, always. Just like he'd take care of her. Belatedly, he realized she was waiting for an answer. He shook his head to clear it. ''Why?''

''Because you make me feel really good.''

The unexpected admission had his heart racing. Her expression turned so serious that he tightened his hand on her hip. ''I want to.''

"You make me feel—desirable." She fiddled with his collar. "I haven't felt that way in a long time. Not since—" she looked away "—not since Carter."

His back teeth clenched so hard they hurt. He uttered a harsh, two-word expletive that summed up his thoughts on Carter Silas.

"Thanks for the vote of confidence."

"Sidney—"

She pressed her fingers to his mouth. "Sorry. Self-deprecation is an old habit."

"I hate what he did to you."

"Your loyalty is appreciated."

He studied her for a minute, disliking the suddenly reticent look in her eyes. With his index finger, he nudged her chin until she looked at him. "Honey, listen to me. No matter what that SOB said to you, or did to you, or didn't do for you, you are an incredibly desirable woman." His mouth kicked up at the corner. "Hell, half the women's magazines in the world have named me the catch of the century, and you've got me hooked."

Sidney managed a slight laugh. "Wonders will never cease."

He kissed her eyebrow. "Believe me, Sid, you've practically got me panting."

Her fingers played a nervous rhythm on his shoulder. "That's what I'm trying to tell you."

The husky note in her voice set off a warning bell in his head. "Why do I have the feeling this is going to have something to do with delayed gratification?"

A smile played at the corner of her mouth. "Because you're an expert at strategy. I've heard that."

"Sidney—"

"Max, really. I—" she slipped away from him and back into her previous seat before he could stop her. "I want you to listen to me for a minute."

Years of business negotiations had taught him the wisdom

of selective silence. He forced himself to wait until she continued. She leaned back in her seat. "You went to all this trouble." She indicated the plane with a wave of her hand. "You pulled out every stop, and even invented a few that no one had thought of before. No one has ever worked that hard for me."

"Then the men you've dated are fools."

She flashed him a smile. "Thanks. But—I don't want you to think you have to do that for me. I don't want you to think that I'm just one more woman who wants Max Loden because he's the catch of the century." Her half smile bewitched him. "You moved heaven and earth for me, and it's not that I don't appreciate it. I'm flattered and dazzled and a little overwhelmed. But it's important to me that you know you could have gotten just as far if you'd brought me a daisy."

He frowned. "Have you been talking to Paul?"

"Who?"

"Natalie's husband. He said the same thing to me today."

"He told you to bring me a daisy?"

"He told me not to give you the laptop computer I bought for you."

Sidney laughed. "Oh, Max. What am I going to do with you?"

"That's the operative question, isn't it?"

She nodded. "I've been thinking about this all day. About us, I mean."

The sudden pain in his fingers made him realize he'd gripped the arms of his chair. Forcing his fingers to relax, he asked, "Reach any conclusions?"

"I think so." She brushed her hair back with an elegant sweep of her hand. In some ways, he mused, Sidney was the most elegant woman he'd ever known. Her every move captivated him. "I think that you were right about some things," she said quietly. "Maybe you're right. Maybe it's time for us. I—" her eyes drifted shut. "I could fall in love with you."

Relief poured through him in a torrent, knocking him mentally off guard. Vaguely, he realized that the simple statement shouldn't mean so much to him, but euphoria was momentarily clouding his brain. "I hope so." His voice had turned husky.

Her eyes lifted again, and he saw the resolution in them. "But it's risky, you know. I don't want to be another one of your conquests."

His gaze narrowed. "You aren't."

"I believe you." She looked around the plane. "Trouble is, I don't think you want to be another conquest either."

"What the hell are you talking about?" He felt the vibration as his pilot lowered the landing gear.

"I know a lot about you, but I don't feel like I really know you. And you don't really know me. I don't know what kinds of food you like, or what your favorite color is. I don't know what kind of music you like, or which baseball team you root for."

"I hate baseball."

"Or that you hate baseball." Sidney leaned forward and put her hand on his knee. "But I do know that I couldn't bear it if you thought I wanted to be with you for any reason other than the fact that, well, you're you."

Would she ever stop surprising him, he wondered? "Lord, Sidney."

She drew a deep breath as the plane glided onto the runway. "It's like I told you on Saturday night. I know that a lot of people depend on you, Max. You're kind of used to that. I don't want to be one more person on that list."

"But—"

She held up her hand. "If we, when we—make love…" her slight blush twisted around his heart and squeezed. She gave him a self-effacing smile. "I don't want any doubts between us. I don't want you to think I'm with you because you're the guy with the jet and the big house and the limousine who swept me off my feet."

Max stared at her. He could feel the bonds of reality sliding away from him. Nothing had prepared him for this. "Sidney—" his voice sounded garbled.

The plane had taxied to a stop. Sidney's lips turned into a slight smile. "I want to make sure you know I'll be just as happy with the guy who brings me a daisy."

Max made a mental note to tell his gardener to plant an acre of the damned things at the first opportunity. "I'm not sure I like this."

She grinned at him. "You will. Are you free tomorrow night?"

"I don't know." At that particular moment, he wasn't sure of his own name.

"Have your secretary call me tomorrow if you are," she told him. "Come over, and I'll fix you dinner."

"Dinner?"

"Yeah, you know. That meal you eat when you aren't working until midnight."

"Right. I have a vague recollection."

"And if you can't make it tomorrow, we'll do it another night. Okay?"

He nodded. He could be scheduled for dinner at Buckingham Palace, he realized, and he'd cancel in less than a heartbeat. His pilot opened the cockpit door. "We're here folks," he announced. Max looked at him. "Thanks, Dave."

"Sure, Max." He nodded at Sidney. "Miss Grant. Nice to see you again." Dave exited the plane through the main door.

Sidney glanced at Max. "You know, I've been meaning to ask you about that. I've known these people most of my life. Why do you have them all calling me Miss Grant all of a sudden?"

Max pinned her with a piercing look. "Evidently," he said quietly, "there are certain things you want to accomplish. And there are things I want to accomplish." He surged to his feet. "Let's just say I think it's past time you knew how much you're worth." At her startled expression, he offered her a slight smile. "See? You're not the only one with an ace up your sleeve, Sid. I've got a few surprises of my own."

"OH MY LORD!" Kelly closed her eyes and leaned back in her chair. "You're kidding. Tell me you're kidding."

Sidney jabbed at her Mandarin chicken salad with her fork. "Nope. That's what he said."

"And you walked away from him? Geez, Sid, if some man dragged me off to Cincinnati—hell, if he took me to *Paramus,* and then told me he thought I needed to realize how much I was worth to him, I think I'd fall at his feet."

Sidney laughed. "No, you wouldn't. You'd come back with some pithy comment about admiring the man's excellent taste in women."

Kelly shook her head. "I'm good on my feet, Sid, but not that good. This guy is dynamite. Besides, you've wanted him forever." Kelly took a bite of her overladen burger.

"I have not." She frowned.

Her friends eyebrows lifted. "Oh, come on, Sidney. You don't have to play games with me."

"I'm not. I never even thought of Max in that—like that, until last weekend at his house."

Kelly stared at her. "You really don't know, do you?"

"Kelly—"

"You don't. You have no idea how that man affects you."

Sidney resisted the urge to squirm. "I'm very attracted to him."

"Attrac—Sidney, you're in love with him."

"You're being ridiculous. I hardly know him."

"You know enough. You've been in love with him since you were fifteen years old."

"I had an adolescent crush. What girl wouldn't? He's very compelling. That was a vulnerable time in my life."

Kelly snorted. "No doubt. After what your mother did to you, I'm sure you were starving for compassion."

"I was. The first time I met Max—" she shrugged "—he made a big impression on me."

"I'm sure he did."

Sidney toyed with her salad again. "But I never once entertained the idea that there could be anything between me and Max."

Kelly shook her head. "I saw the way he looked at you. That man is hooked."

"So he says."

"But you're afraid to reel him in."

"He's not a trout, you know. He's a financial tycoon who happens to be a little out of my league. You said it yourself—the question on everyone's lips is 'Who Gets To Marry Max?' I don't think his circle of friends and business associates is ready for the answer to be, 'Sidney Grant, unwanted illegitimate child and divorcée.'"

"Sidney—" Kelly braced her hands on the table and leaned toward her "—is this about Carter?"

"Of course not."

Kelly looked dubious. "Are you sure?"

"Of course I'm sure." When Kelly still looked unconvinced, Sidney nodded. "Carter did a lot of rotten things to me, but I'm not going to let him ruin the rest of my life. I'm not going to give him that much power."

Her friend's expression softened. "I'm glad. When I think about—" she shook her head. "It makes me want to slug the jerk."

"Me, too," Sidney said with a soft smile.

"Dibs on the first punch."

"Sorry, uncle Philip already claimed it."

"It would serve that creep right to get his lights dimmed by an old man."

"Don't underestimate my uncle. He throws a mean right hook."

"Are you serious?"

"Sure. I never told you?"

"No. Is that where you learned? I thought you took a self-defense class."

"Nope. When I first moved here, I had a lot of anxiety. Uncle Philip wasn't exactly experienced in dealing with angst-ridden teenage girls. So he did the only thing he could think of. He took me to the gym, and taught me to box. I worked off a lot of aggression beating the crud out of a sandbag."

"You know, the more you tell me about your uncle, the more I like the guy."

Sidney laughed. In the three years that Kelly had worked for her, she'd grown extremely fond of the other woman's candor and quick wit. "He likes you, too. He says you're good for me."

"I am. Without me, you'd sink into a sea of introspection. You depend on me to keep you appropriately shallow."

"So *that's* why you keep telling me to jump Max."

"Well, I have to admit, I have a certain preoccupation with what that man would look like in the buff. I figured a firsthand report from you would be the closest I could get."

Sidney laughed. "You're impossible."

"I'm telling you, Sid, after I saw that man in a swimsuit last week, well, let's just say I have a new definition of muscle tone. What's he do? Work out, like, fifteen hours a day?"

"I don't know. I'll have to ask uncle Philip."

"Why don't you ask Max instead?"

"I'm sure that would go over quite well. You know, Max," she said in a mocking tone, "Kelly's been wondering just what you do to maintain those washboard abs."

"Don't forget to ask about his rear end. I'd like to know how many leg lifts a person has to do to have a butt like that."

The image of Max doing leg lifts sent Sidney into a fit of laughter. "I'll try to remember that. I'm glad to know your concerns about this relationship have to do with Max's personal fitness routine."

Kelly's expression turned serious. "Noooo. That's not true. I just think it's past time you found out what it could be like between you and a guy like him. They're not all like Carter you know."

"I know."

"Good." Kelly nodded. "By the way, all we have on the calendar is the Geyerson affair tonight, which I'm covering, and the Heart Association reception."

"Have you inspected that hotel? The ballroom layout is a little strange."

"Yes. I sited the place last week while you were tied up with the Drysdale wedding. Chip has already started on the buffet."

"So the coordinator approved the suggestion for chilled hors d'oeuvres?"

"Yep. She loved your idea of putting the shrimp on an ice pyramid. I think the candles will really set it off."

"Good. I was afraid she'd think it was too clinical looking."

"I told her you wanted to use green-and-red linens and purple flowers. She bit."

"Smart woman."

"Brilliant." Kelly tipped her head to one side. "So, since everything is under control here at your empire, do you want to knock off and go shopping this afternoon?"

"What?"

"Shopping." Kelly waved her hand in an absent fashion. "I thought you might like something new to wear tonight."

"He's just coming for dinner."

Kelly ignored her. "You, ah, might want to consider something lacy and black. Men like that."

"Kelly—"

"Or, I've heard green can be nice. Takes 'em off guard."

"I was leaning toward jeans and a sweatshirt."

Kelly groaned. "Tell me you're kidding."

"It's an informal dinner, Kel. Not a well-planned seduction."

"That's what I was afraid of. At least tell me you're planning to serve oysters."

"Pesto fettucini."

"Oh, ugh. Take my advice and give the poor man something with some fat in it. I have a rule about that. Never have a dinner party with less than forty grams of fat per serving. It's bad form."

"You'll be relieved to know that I was thinking of chocolate amaretto cheesecake for dessert."

"Good plan." She pursed her lips. "Serve that first."

Sidney's lips twitched. "You're so subtle."

"It's my middle name." Kelly narrowed her gaze. "So about the shopping."

"I'm not going shopping."

Kelly's sigh rustled the baby's breath in the centerpiece. "I was afraid of that. Okay, promise me one thing—"

"I'm not calling you to tell you what happens."

"Not that." Kelly gave her a stern look. "I have some tact, you know."

"I hadn't guessed."

"Very funny. As it happens, I was going to ask you to swear you won't wear that ratty yellow sweatshirt with the parrot on it."

"It's a condor."

"Whatever. Don't wear it." Kelly rapped her fingers on the table. "I have a personal rule about that."

"Another one?" Sidney teased.

"Yes. Never wear something on a date that looks like you used to paint in it."

"I like that sweatshirt."

"Did you, or did you not, paint your living room while wearing that."

"Guilty."

"I rest my case."

Sidney tossed down her napkin with a soft laugh. "Okay, okay. I'll give in on the sweatshirt, but I'm standing my ground on the pesto."

"More's the pity."

Chapter Nine

"This is great." Max twirled another forkful of the fettucini. His eyes gleamed with appreciation. "What is it?"

She watched him with barely concealed amusement. "Pesto fettucini. I'm glad you like it."

"I was starving." Still wearing the white shirt and suit trousers he'd worn to work, he looked relaxed and comfortable at her table—remarkably so, she mused, for a man who'd dined with royalty.

"I noticed." He was on his second serving of the heavy dish. "Did you eat lunch today?"

Max shook his head as he swallowed his mouthful. "Too busy." He leaned back in his chair where he'd casually slung his double-breasted jacket and silk tie.

"You shouldn't skip meals, you know."

"Trying to take care of me, Sidney?" The teasing light in his eyes turned them an extraordinary color.

"No. That's Uncle Philip's job. I just nag." She idly toyed with one of the daisies in the huge bouquet Max had brought her that evening. No telling where he'd gotten them. They weren't in season. He'd probably had them flown in from Holland.

Max laughed. She liked the sound. "Actually," he said, "don't let Philip fool you. He nags worse than an old woman."

"I can believe that." She rose to clear the dishes. Max scooped up his plate and followed her to the sink.

"But today, I don't think even your uncle could have saved me. Fitzwater is making my life hell."

"Edward or Lauren?"

"Edward. Lauren's a peach."

"How's Greg?"

Max shrugged. "Brooding. He'll get over it." Sidney decided not to argue. Max handed her his plate. "You want me to load the dishwasher?"

"Depends," she said, rolling back the cuffs of her green silk blouse—the one concession she'd made to Kelly's badgering. She began stacking the rinsed plates on the counter.

"On what?"

"Are you a dishwasher despot or not?"

"Excuse me?"

"If you promise not to rearrange the dishes in my dishwasher, then yes, you may load. If you're going to give me a lecture on the space efficiency of stacking things in certain places, then you can sit down and wait for your dessert."

Max titled his head to one side. "Can't we just throw them away and buy new ones?"

She flicked him with a towel. "No. I like these plates."

He wrapped his arms around her waist and buried his lips in her hair. "Then I have a confession to make."

"I knew it." A shiver traveled down her spine as his fingers traced the line of her ribcage. Sidney swallowed. "You *are* a dishwasher despot."

"Actually," he muttered, turning her to face him, "I was going to tell you that I don't think I've loaded a dishwasher in fifteen years."

With a laugh, she turned in his arms. Placing her hands on his shoulders, she rose on tiptoes to drop a soft kiss on his mouth. "You're very cute. Did you know that?"

"I'm awfully glad you think so." His hands traveled up her spine, smoothing the silk over her flesh.

Max dipped his head to kiss her again. Sidney leaned into him with a soft sigh of capitulation. As his lips moved over hers and his hands continued their exploration of her angles and curves, Sidney started to sink into the sheer sensation. She was seconds from drowning when a sharp knock at her door intruded on their private world. Max groaned as he released her. "Who is it?"

Frowning, Sidney headed for the door. "I don't know." she opened it to find her uncle on the landing. "Uncle Philip. Hi."

"Hello, Sidney." He looked grave. "I'm sorry to bother you."

"Is something wrong?" She beckoned him inside.

"I need to speak with Max. Is he here?"

Max strolled out of the kitchen. "Of course I'm here. What's wrong, Philip."

"I'm sorry to interrupt." Philip glanced at Sidney. "Your phone isn't working."

She gave Max an apologetic look. "It's off the hook."

Max's eyes widened appreciatively. Her uncle didn't comment as he looked back at his employer. "And you didn't answer my page."

"I'm not wearing my pager."

At Philip's frown, Sidney stifled a giggle. He was dying to lecture them both, but wouldn't dream of breaching his own rigid rules of service etiquette. He cleared his throat and looked at Max. "Under the circumstances," he said quietly, "I thought it best not to let this wait until you, er, returned."

Sidney frowned. "Uncle Philip, is something wrong?"

Philip shook his head. "It's not serious, I assure you, but I would like to speak with Mr. Loden alone for a moment."

Max grunted. "Spit it out, Philip. Whatever you have to tell me, Sidney can hear."

"Very well. It's your sister, sir."

Max frowned. "Which one?"

"Mrs. Blake."

"Colleen. What's wrong?"

"She's left Mr. Blake. She's in town at your penthouse and wants to see you right away."

Max uttered a harsh curse, then dragged his hand over his face. "Oh, hell."

Sidney released the breath she'd been holding. "I'm sorry, Max."

When he looked at her, his expression was haggard. "I have to go."

"I know."

"I'm sorry."

"It's okay. I understand."

He hesitated, visibly torn. "She needs me."

"I know, Max. It's really all right." When he still didn't move, Sidney looked at her uncle. He was watching Max with an expression of concern and curiosity. On impulse, Sidney took a step closer to Max. "Do you want me to go with you?"

The look he gave her was unfathomable. She could have drowned in it. "Would you?"

"Of course." She gave his hand a slight squeeze. "That's what friends do."

His fingers closed on hers in a bruising grip. "Philip, did you drive out here, or did you bring the limo?"

"I have my own car."

Max nodded. "You go ahead, then. We'll be right behind you."

THEY MADE the long trip to Max's penthouse in relative silence. Without the midday traffic, it took just over an hour. Max's mind spun through a dozen different lectures he intended to deliver to his sister, but they were overshadowed by self-recriminations. Colleen had been brooding for weeks, and he'd ignored the signs. He'd allowed Greg's engagement to distract him, and, if he were honest, since last weekend, he'd spared little thought for anything beyond the seduction of Sidney Grant.

He pulled into his reserved parking space, then looked at Sidney. "Thanks for coming with me."

She offered him that slight smile that tied his guts in knots. "I was glad to."

"Rain check on dessert?"

"Of course."

"And everything that comes after it?" he asked in a tantalizing whisper.

Amusement danced in her eyes. "Have you always had this one-track mind?"

"Lately, anyway."

"Did anyone ever tell you that too much tacky thinking can permanently damage your brain cells?"

With a nod, he leaned across the console to press her into her leather bucket seat. "If the general state of mush my brain has been in the past few days is any indication, I don't doubt it," he whispered, and covered her lips with his.

The kiss lingered for countless seconds. He wanted to disappear in it, drown in it. If he could lose himself in the wondrous feel of kissing Sidney, he might forget the confrontation that awaited him upstairs. When she softly moaned, he wrapped his hands around her shoulders. "Soon," he whispered. "It's got to be soon."

Sidney's hand wended around his neck. Her fingers buried themselves in his hair. "Yes, Max."

The capitulation had a potent effect on him. He felt the heaviness in his body, the roaring intensity in his blood. With a conscious effort of will, he ripped his mouth from hers. His soft curse filled the air between them.

Sidney smoothed her index finger over his lips. "We should go upstairs," she whispered.

His breathing remained harsh, but he managed a slight smile. "This wasn't what I had in mind when I imagined you saying those words to me."

"I know. Me either." Her hand caressed the line of his jaw. "It'll be all right. You'll see."

He nodded, then pushed open his door. They rode up in the elevator together. Max held Sidney's hand in a firm grasp. Philip had arrived moments before them and swung open the door to the spacious penthouse suite. "Mrs. Blake is in the den," he said quietly.

Max nodded and started across the plush navy carpet, still holding Sidney's hand. When they entered the book-lined room he used as an office, Colleen Blake, elegantly clad in an ivory silk suit, paced before the marble fireplace. When the door swung open, she turned to face them, her expression full of malice. "Max. God, I'm sorry Philip disturbed you. I told him not to."

Max led Sidney into the room, then shut the door with a decisive click. "What's going on, Colleen."

Her gaze flicked to Sidney. "It's a family matter," she hedged.

Max nodded. "Philip told us you've left Warren."

His sister's scowl deepened, marring her normally attractive features. Sidney had always felt that Colleen lacked the inner beauty of her sister, Natalie. "I have."

"Are you out of your mind?" he challenged. "What in hell are you thinking?"

Colleen's hands fisted at her sides. "I see you've decided that it's *my* fault. Don't you even want to hear the facts first?"

"Where is Warren?"

"I don't know."

Max scowled. "What do you mean you don't know?"

"I haven't seen him since this morning."

"So have you left him or not?"

She dropped into a leather armchair with a theatrical sigh. "I have. I can't take it anymore, Max. I just can't."

"Can't take what?" Max strode to the beverage cart where he poured himself a glass of what Sidney now knew was filtered water. He glanced at her, raising the glass in silent query. She nodded, and he filled a second tumbler. "Colleen, do you want something to drink?"

She sniffed. "Do you have anything stronger than lemonade?"

"You know the answer to that."

"Thanks, I'll pass." She studied the tips of her manicured nails.

Max handed Sidney her glass. "All right, Colleen, tell me what this is about."

His sister turned her angry gaze on him. "If you ever paid attention to what was going on under your nose, Max, you'd know what this was about. Warren is driving me crazy, and I can't live with him anymore."

"Is he cheating on you?"

"Who are you kidding?" she challenged. "You'd probably know that before I would. You're the one who follows our every move."

Max's jaw tightened. "Quit acting melodramatic. Is he, or isn't he?"

"I don't know. I doubt it."

"Are you cheating on him?" Max asked.

Colleen's laugh was unpleasant. "And risk your wrath? Not likely. Though I'll admit, I've thought about it. At times, I think I'd do just about anything to put an end to the interminable hell I'm in."

Max took a long drink of his water. "You could try charity work."

"Like sweet little Natalie, you mean? Sorry, soup kitchens aren't my forte."

Max's frown deepened. "What do you want me to do?"

"I want to divorce Warren, and I want you to promise you won't cut me off."

"Divorce? On what grounds?"

"Irreconcilable differences."

"I wasn't aware that boredom was considered legal grounds for dissolving a marriage."

Colleen shrugged. "You can't imagine what it's like, Max. You've never had to live like this."

Max set his glass on the beverage cart with measured calm. "Look, I don't want to argue with you. And I never intended for you to be unhappy. But I'd like to talk to Warren before I—"

"I'm sure you would." Colleen's frown deepened. "That's just like you. You'd take his word over mine as long as it suited you."

"Damn it, Colleen. If you'd think about this for a minute—"

"I've been thinking about it for three years."

"I can't believe—" A soft knock on the door interrupted him. "Enter," Max barked.

Philip Grant gently opened the door. "Mr. Blake is on his way up." He glanced at Sidney. She couldn't interpret the look he gave her.

"I don't want to see him," Colleen said.

Max swore. "Will you be reasonable for once in your life?"

She glared at him. "By reasonable, you mean, give you your way?"

"I mean stop acting like a spoiled brat."

Colleen's face flushed. "You don't have to be such a bastard, Max. I'm fully aware that if I make you angry enough, you'll retaliate by shutting the family purse. You don't have to resort to name-calling."

Sidney sucked in a pained breath. She had no doubt that the barb had hit its mark, but Max's expression didn't flicker. On impulse, she crossed the room to stand next to him and slip her hand into his. The only sign he gave that his sister's remark had affected him was the way he clenched her fingers. The tense silence thickened until the door burst open and Warren Blake, looking harried and frustrated raced into the room. He didn't spare Max and Sidney a second glance. Focused on his wife, he hurried toward her. "Colleen! My

God, I've been so worried. Why didn't you tell Estelle where you were?'' His trench coat hung loosely at his sides. His uncombed hair and day's worth of beard stubble contributed to his dishevelment.

When Colleen wouldn't look at him, Warren glanced at Max. "What's going on?"

"I don't know, Warren. Maybe you can tell us."

He shook his head. "I don't know. I got home from work around seven, and Estelle—our housekeeper—told me she hadn't seen Colleen since eight o'clock this morning." He thrust a hand into his coat pocket and produced a note. "I found this in our bedroom." Warren looked at Colleen. "Honey—"

She finally faced him. "Oh, stop it, Warren. No one is impressed by this dramatic show of concern. Except maybe my brother, who has a habit of seeing only what he wants to."

Sidney shifted her hand to lace her fingers through Max's. The subtle change in his breathing belied his calm facade. He said firmly, "I'd like to hear what Warren has to say."

"I'm sure you would," she snapped. "And whatever it is, you'll believe him."

Warren frowned. "Max doesn't deserve that."

Sidney had to bite her lip to keep from agreeing. Max released her hand and strode into the center of the room. "Warren, sit down." He indicated the chair next to Colleen. "I want to hear your side of the story first."

Warren dropped into the chair with a dull thud. "I don't know what to tell you."

"This couldn't have taken you by surprise," Max said quietly. "Colleen's been unhappy for months."

Sidney saw the startled look Max's sister sent his way. Max, however, kept his eyes trained on his brother-in-law. "What's going on?"

Warren squirmed in his chair. "We've had some disagreements, like all married couples, but nothing I didn't think we could work out.''

"Disagreements?'' Max's voice had dropped to a low rumble.

Warren studied the tassels on his loafers with avid fascination. "It's personal, Max.''

"It's obviously not so personal that the two of you aren't sitting in my library telling me about it.''

Colleen made a delicate sound of disgust. "As if you'd give us a choice.''

Warren sent her a quelling look. "Colleen—''

"You don't have to be afraid of him,'' she bit out. "He's not God, you know. No matter what he thinks.''

Sidney clenched her teeth against a growing need to liberally distribute her opinion. From discussions with her uncle, and the few chances she'd had to observe Max's family together, she had a fairly clear picture of Colleen's animosity toward her brother, her family and her husband. Even though Philip rarely shared intimate details of Max's life with her, Sidney had read between the lines often enough to develop a strong impression of Colleen's bitterness. Unhappy even before her marriage to Warren Blake, the oldest of Max's siblings resented everyone and everything around her—especially her oldest brother, who she seemed to blame for her discontent.

Sidney had fully suspected that Colleen's failure to deliver Max's message about his emergency trip that weekend of the house party owed more to her resentment of her brother than a miscommunication.

Max was pacing now, his face an expressionless mask. Warren finally broke the silence. "Look, this is all very uncomfortable.'' He glanced at Sidney. "I see you were, uh, engaged for the evening. Maybe Colleen and I can go home and—''

"No.'' Colleen rose from her chair. "I'm not going back to that apartment, Warren.''

Warren reached out a hand to her. "Honey—"

"Stop it." She stalked away from him. "Stop being so damned agreeable. It's why we're in this mess to begin with."

"What mess?" Max faced his sister. "Tell me what's going on."

"And what?" Her expression turned distinctly unpleasant. "You'll write a memo detailing your response to the matter?"

Sidney ground her teeth. As if he sensed her frustration, Max flashed her a bleak smile. "I haven't always been such a jerk, have I?"

Warren rose to his feet. "This has nothing to do with you, Max. I'm the one she's angry at."

Colleen muttered something under her breath and started toward the door. "This is going nowhere."

Max curled his fingers around her forearm and halted her progress. "You wouldn't have come here if you didn't want something from me. Now that Warren's here, I want answers."

Warren looked nervous. "Here's the thing," he said. "Colleen has been regretting, lately, that she didn't marry a man like Paul Wells—a man with ambition."

His wife sent him a cutting glance. "At least you admit that."

"That I have no ambition?" Warren shrugged. "I like what I do." He looked at Max. "Paul is the high-achiever type. No one was surprised when you made him a vice president."

"Least of all Natalie," Colleen said.

Max's fingers tightened on her arm. "Stop that."

"What?" She jerked her arm away. "Stop criticizing your precious little sister? Give me a break, Max. There's not a soul who knows you who isn't aware that you think Natalie walks on water. I wonder what you'd do if you knew just how Natalie and Paul played you for a fool. Didn't you ever wonder why Paul, an extremely ambitious member of your acquisitions team, suddenly found himself swooning over your sister? Give me a break, Max.''

Abruptly, Max released her arm. "That's enough."

Warren nodded. "That's not fair, Colleen. Just because you resent me for not being more like Paul doesn't mean you can attack Natalie."

"Oh, God forbid anyone attack poor, defenseless Natalie."

Sidney's dislike was growing thicker by the second. She took a step forward, a blistering retort ready on her lips. Only Max's cautioning glance stopped her. He shook his head slightly before he looked again at Warren. "Warren, you want to tell me what this is all about? I'm losing my patience."

"It's about the fact that Paul is one of your vice presidents, and he's very good at what he does. He likes what he does. Consequently, you pay him well and he and Natalie live the kind of life she grew up with. They have a condo on the upper West Side. They have a home in the Hamptons. They have an investment portfolio and a house full of staff, and a social life that lands them in the pages of *Town and Country Magazine*.

"I, on the other hand," he gave his wife a rueful glance, "am a drafting engineer. I like what I do. I *love* what I do, but drafting engineers don't make the kind of money that executive vice presidents make, and because I wasn't about to let you give me some fabricated executive position simply because I'd had the good sense to marry your sister—"

"That's not why I offered you a job, Warren," Max said.

Colleen swung her gaze to Max. "You did?"

"He did," Warren said. "And I turned it down." His expression turned sorrowful. "I like my colleagues. I like my company. It's not that I think I would have been miserable working for you, Max, it's just that I like the idea of having built the reputation and career that I have at a company I've worked for since I got my graduate degree."

Max nodded. "I understood that, Warren. I wanted you

onboard because I respected and admired your abilities and your integrity.''

"Thanks." Warren nodded. "But the truth is, because I chose this path, Colleen and I live in an apartment, and we don't have closets full of designer clothes. The only Caribbean holiday we've had is the cruise you gave us as a wedding gift. Our social life is dinner and a movie every other week. We appear in *Town and Country Magazine* only when one of us gets caught in a picture with you or Natalie. Colleen doesn't like it. She thinks if I had more ambition, we'd have a better life. She's probably right." He dropped into his chair with a dejected sigh. "The thing is, I love Colleen." He looked at her. "I know you don't believe that, but it's true. I love you. I just can't be the person you want me to be."

Max looked at Warren for long, tense seconds. Colleen kept her gaze fixed on a spot somewhere beyond her brother's shoulder. "Colleen?" Max finally said. "Do you have anything to say?"

She turned her angry eyes on him. "You wouldn't believe me anyway."

"Try me."

Her facade of anger finally began to crumble. Sidney decided that Colleen had either missed an opportunity for a lucrative and successful stage career, or that she genuinely possessed the heart they'd all thought missing. "Max," Colleen said quietly, "you can't imagine what it's like to know that you and Natalie and Greg never worry about the future."

Max's lips twitched. "I worry about the future every second I'm awake."

"You know what I mean." She dropped into a chair. "Natalie and Greg were so young when Mother and Father died—they don't remember. But I do. I heard the arguments. I knew that Father had run the company into the ground. And I knew that by the time you finished wrestling with the shareholders after Father's death, you barely had two pennies to scrape together."

Max's frown deepened. "I had no idea."

Colleen dabbed her eyes. "Yes, well, I'm not the idiot you all thought."

Warren nodded. "That's true enough. If it weren't for Colleen, God knows what would have happened to our household finances."

His wife gave him a bland smile, that, at least lacked its earlier malice. "Thanks, Warren."

Her husband squeezed her hand. Colleen shrugged as she looked at Max once more. "Things were awful, and I knew it. You tried so hard to keep us from knowing what kind of stress you were under, but if it hadn't been for the success of those damned dolls—" with an elegant wave of her hand she indicated the Max doll on the bookcase "—we'd have lost everything."

"It's true," Max said gravely. "I risked everything on AppleTree Toys, and rebuilt the rest of Loden Enterprises with the capital I earned from the Real Men collection. As corny as I think it is," he continued ruefully, "Who Gets To Marry Max was more than just a slogan. It was a lifesaver."

Warren shook his head. "Who would have thought that the family fortune was riding on plastic dolls?"

Max shrugged. "I just knew. I can't explain it. I knew it would work, and it did. But I never wanted Colleen and Natalie and Greg to have any inkling how close we came. Our father had bled the company dry. I didn't want you to remember him that way."

"I didn't," Colleen insisted. "Father was a good man, and he was good to us. I knew that. But I heard him arguing with Mother, with the lawyers, with everyone. I knew how bad things were. For a while, I wondered if maybe the accident that killed them wasn't an accident."

Sidney looked at Max, startled. The flash of pain in his eyes told her that he'd entertained the same suspicions. Colleen seemed lost in her memories. "There was enough insurance money to stake your risk on the Real Men collection. Isn't that right, Max?''

"Yes," he said gravely.

"It was our last chance and I knew it." She wiped a hand through her hair. "God, you can't imagine what those weeks were like for me. I was terrified. You were an adult—out of college—but what was going to happen to the rest of us? Where would they send us? What would the creditors do if the whole thing went under?"

"I wouldn't have let anything happen to any of you." Max jammed his hands in his trouser pockets. "You have to know that."

"I do now, but I was nineteen and scared to death." She paused. "And I swore to myself that I'd never live like that again."

"Until she married me," Warren said miserably.

Max shook his head. "My God, Colleen, if you were having money problems, why didn't you tell me? I knew Warren wasn't pulling down an enormous salary, but I didn't think—''

"We don't have money problems," Colleen said firmly. Sidney looked at her in surprise. Max's sister straightened in her chair. "We have a perfectly normal middle-class existence. We don't have debt. Warren makes a decent living doing what he's doing. He works hard." She gave her husband a slight smile. "I never meant to infer that I doubted that."

"That's not what it looked like earlier," Max said tightly.

Colleen shook her head. "You don't understand. I told you that you wouldn't."

"I'm trying—''

"I know," she said curtly. "The point is that while we don't have money problems, I don't exactly feel safe. If Warren lost his job, if something were to happen to him, I'm not sure what I'd do. I don't have any training. It's not as if I could get a decent job anywhere. And I couldn't stand to sit around and let you take care of me. I'd turn out just like Mother." She sighed. "When I look at Natalie—at Paul—damn! It's not that I'm jealous, Max, it's that I'm terrified. Perpetually. And I can't take it anymore. Warren doesn't understand why I need a house, with a yard that I own that no one can take away from me. He doesn't understand why I want enough insurance to make sure I'm not going to end up living off you. I need to know that we have a stock portfolio, and a series of mutual funds that are earning interest above the prime lending rate. It doesn't have a damned thing to do with Natalie's baby shower being featured in *Town and Country Magazine,* and everything to do with the way I saw my mother stashing loose change in her lingerie drawer the week before she died."

Warren looked shocked. "I didn't know."

"Neither did I," Max said, his voice somber.

"Well, I can't take it anymore. While Natalie lives out her fairy tale and meets every one of your expectations, I can't do it. Face it, Max—you may have Natalie and Greg under your thumb, but you've never had me. I cannot live like this anymore, and if you hate me for it, well, tough."

"Hell." Max scrubbed a hand over his face. "Warren, who's handling your financial portfolio?" Warren blushed. Max shook his head. "No one apparently. Damn it, I cannot believe no one told me this was going on."

Colleen frowned at him. "You don't have a right to know every detail of our lives, you know."

"I could have helped you," Max insisted. "I would have." Warren flinched. "I can take care of my wife, Max."

"No one is saying you can't, but even I don't try to manage my own investments without help." Max drew a calming breath. "All right. Here's what we're going to do." He walked to the desk in long, ground-eating strides. Sidney stepped out of his way. Max rounded the desk and jerked open the top drawer. He pulled out a business-size checkbook. "You probably don't know this, Colleen, but Loden Enterprises recently hired Warren's firm to consult for us on construction of a major processing facility we're building in St. Thomas.''

"You did?" Warren said.

"Are you serious?" Colleen asked.

Max's nod was short. "Yes. Paul managed the bid process. If you have questions about it, you'll have to ask him. I didn't even know until yesterday."

"You didn't tell me," Colleen said to Warren.

"I didn't know."

"Anyway," Max started making out a check. "As part of the arrangement, we're sending a drafting engineer down to the site to preview it and report on its suitability. It may be advisable to relocate to San Quentin depending on our goals and the general topographic needs."

"That could be true," Warren added. "If you're doing processing, you'll need maximum square footage."

"Precisely." Max continued writing the check. "Naturally, when Paul informed me that we'd chosen Warren's company for the job, I requested Warren as the head of the project."

"I'm flattered." In actuality, Warren looked shocked. "You could have had someone a lot higher up the ladder. Hell, for what you're paying, you probably could have had the owner of my firm."

Max raised one shoulder in casual disregard. "I told you. I've always had enormous respect for professional expertise. Your boss informed us that you could handle the project load. I believe he was supposed to give you the news this afternoon or tomorrow."

"He hasn't talked to me yet."

"I'm sure he'll make the announcement soon. Probably tomorrow morning." Max scrawled his signature on the bottom of the check, then looked at his sister and brother-in-law. "So, I'd like the two of you to travel down there together— at my expense."

"Max—" Colleen frowned.

"Consider it an anniversary present, Colleen. Your twelfth anniversary is next week, isn't it?"

"Yes," Warren said. "The fifth."

"That's what I thought. Take a cruise down there, survey the site and report what you find." He extended the check. "Normally, I would have had Paul handle the signing bonus and expense advance, but since you're here, I might as well do it tonight."

Warren accepted the check, then gave Max a shocked look. "This is for twenty-five thousand dollars!"

"It's a standard five percent bonus plus five percent expense advance."

Colleen gave her brother a shrewd look. "Max—"

He held up both hands. "You can check it out with Paul if you want. Or with Warren's boss for that matter."

"There's no way we'll spend this much money," Warren insisted.

"That's why it's called a bonus," Max said blandly. "So what I suggest you do is take a week or so to go down there, spend some time together, and when you get back, come see me and we'll set up your stock portfolio."

Colleen studied Max through narrowed eyes. "This isn't going to change things, you know."

Max's expression turned conciliatory. "Will the two of you at least agree to spend the next few weeks talking about this, and then we'll see where it gets us."

"I'm willing if Colleen is." Warren pocketed the check, then looked at his wife. "I'm sure we can work this out, Colleen. Please, just give it a chance."

She visibly wavered. "I don't know—"

"If nothing else," Max said smoothly, "you can have the satisfaction of knowing that Natalie has never been to St. Thomas."

"Natalie," Colleen interjected, "is afraid to fly and afraid to sail. She'd have a tough time getting to any island."

"My point exactly," Max said. Sidney searched his expression, but learned nothing. This, she imagined, was the man who reportedly brought corporate giants to their knees by sheer force of will.

Colleen hesitated a minute longer. "All right," she finally said. "We'll try it."

Warren looked noticeably relieved. "And I'll get the report to you as soon as possible. You won't regret this, Max."

Max looked at his sister. "Are you all right?"

"It's not a simple problem, you know. You can't send me off with a pat on the head and expect it to go away. Not even a twenty-five-thousand-dollar pat."

"I'm not trying to patronize you."

"I'm glad to hear it." She studied Warren for several seconds. "I'm willing to talk about it."

He nodded. "That's all I ask."

"But I'm calling Paul," Colleen warned. "If you're making this up, Max, I'm going to be furious."

"You do that," Max said. "Whatever you need to feel reassured."

Warren took Colleen's hand. "Can we go home now?"

She hesitated, then laced her fingers through his. "Yes."

"Thanks. Good night, Max." He led his wife to the door.

When the library door shut behind them, Max fell back in his chair with a low curse. "That woman is going to be the death of me."

"She's, uh, volatile. Isn't she?"

"You could say that." He slid the checkbook back in the drawer. "Natalie is as calm as a breezeless day on the ocean. Colleen is more like a tropical storm front. You never know what the hell she's going to do."

Sidney smiled at him as she rounded the desk. "That was a very nice thing you did."

"What?"

"That little story about the contract and the check." She sat on the edge of his desk and put her hands on his shoulders. "I had no idea you were so good on your feet."

"Sidney—"

She leaned forward and kissed him soundly. "It kind of makes me wonder if you're good in other positions, too."

"Hell." In one swift move he dragged her off the desk and pulled her onto his lap. "When did you develop this talent for conversational grenades?"

She laughed. "I'm hoping to make it up to you that you never got to try my dessert." She bit his earlobe.

"I'll send someone over to get it out of your refrigerator."

"It'll keep until tomorrow."

"I won't." He covered her mouth in a ravishing kiss.

His hand was working at the hem of her blouse, tugging it free from the waistband of her black pants when she pulled her lips from his and whispered. "Don't you need to make a phone call?"

He raised his head, his expression blank. "What?"

"A phone call."

"What the hell are you talking about?"

She trailed one finger along the line of his mouth. "Well, it occurs to me that Colleen is probably going to call Natalie as soon as she gets home tonight. And Natalie will ask Paul what Colleen's talking about. And if Paul has to work out the details of a major contract and a proposed processing plant by tomorrow morning when Warren gets to work, you might want to tell him now."

His eyes focused. His lips twitched into a slight smile, and he slid one hand from under her blouse to reach for the telephone on his desk. "Give me five minutes."

With a slight laugh, she buried her face in the curve of his neck. "I have a feeling even you are going to need more than five minutes for this one."

He grumbled. She smoothed the crease from his forehead. "It's okay, Max. I understand."

"You shouldn't. You should be furious."

"Why? Because you're a nice man who feels a strong sense of responsibility toward your family?"

He smoothed a hand down her back. "You're a remarkable woman, Sidney Grant."

"Not really," she said as she eased off his lap. "I just remember what it's like to be unhappy." She glanced away from him. "I wasn't always this easy to get along with."

"You'd never convince me."

She laughed. "Ask Uncle Philip. So, as much as I hate to say it, I think this is good night."

He frowned. "I don't want you to leave."

"I know. But you need to talk to Paul. You've got a lot to do before tomorrow."

"Sidney—"

She tucked her blouse back into her waistband. "It's late. I should go. I've got work to do."

"Doing what?"

She gave him a censorious look. "Running my business, just like you."

"I wish you'd let me pay you."

"Why? So you could have me at your beck and call?"

"Yes."

That made her laugh. "Oh, Max, you're hopeless."

"At least let me give you the laptop. It's still in the box."

"I don't need it."

He closed his eyes. "Of course you need it."

"Can it make chocolates?"

"No, but it can do a hell of a lot better job at keeping your books than you do now."

"But wouldn't it require me to actually *enter* stuff into it?"

"That's not—"

She waved her hand. "That's why I pay an accountant."

"Look how well that turned out."

"Okay, so that wasn't the best decision I ever made. I lived and I learned. I have George now. Which, by the way, I've been meaning to ask you. Can I afford George?"

"Of course."

"Because you're paying his fees?"

"Yes."

"At least you're honest."

"Consider it a benefit of doing business with Loden Enterprises."

"Do you supply any of your other service providers with free accounting services?"

"No one else needs them."

"How flattering."

Max shook his head. "Quit trying to distract me. It won't work."

"I know. You're never distracted."

"You'd be surprised. Lately, I'm distracted all the time. It's just that I'm distracted *by* you, not with you."

"Oh." She felt absurdly pleased.

He gave her a pointed look as he drummed his fingers on the desk. "Yeah. And right now, I'm distracted by the fact that I want you to stay the night. All night."

Sidney shook her head. "I can't. It's too—awkward."

"Excuse me?"

"Max," she said patiently, "my uncle *works* here."

"He sleeps downstairs. We're alone."

"He also wakes you up and brings you your paper and coffee."

"I'll call him and tell him to take tomorrow off."

Sidney rolled her eyes. "Never mind. Just believe me when I say it's not going to be tonight."

"When is it going to be?"

"Very tacky, Loden."

"Yeah, I guess." He studied her in the dim light. "But I still want to know."

Sidney thought it over. It was, indeed, a very good question. Until now, they seemed like the most ill-fated pair on the planet. She looked at his rugged features, remembered, for an instant, the look of hurt she'd seen in his eyes when Colleen had hurled her accusations at him, and decided the time had come to leap off the bridge. Sidney drew a deep breath and plunged. "Didn't you say that you'd asked Lois to rearrange our appointments at the two hotels you wanted to site for this weekend?"

"Yes."

"Tomorrow is Friday. We can see the one in the city tomorrow morning, then drive out to the one on Long Island tomorrow afternoon. We can site the hotel on Saturday, spend a day around the beach, and er, come back on Sunday."

His eyes glittered. "Are you telling me that you're willing to give me three uninterrupted days?"

Butterflies did the Rumba in her belly. "Yes."

"No intruders?"

"Not unless they're your intruders."

"They won't be. I assure you."

"I'll take your word for it. And I'll go home now so you can get some work done."

"I'll drive you," he offered.

"No, that's silly."

"Sidney, it's a two hour drive back to your place."

She shook her head. "I have an apartment behind my office. I keep the extra room for this reason."

"For when you run out on desperate men in the middle of the night and leave them aching for you in the small hours of the morning?"

Her lips twitched. "For when it's too late to go home, and I have to be back in the city for an early appointment. I have several changes of clothes there. It's not a problem."

"Are you sure? I don't mind driving you."

"You're not fooling me, Max. This is a ploy to get me alone again."

"We're alone now."

"You know what I mean."

"Unfortunately. I don't suppose it would do me any good to suggest that I have Charlie drive you in the limo."

"Lord, no. It's the middle of the night. Don't get that poor man out of bed."

Max dug in his pocket for the keys to the car. "Any chance you'd let me drive you to your office, then?"

"Nope. You've got work to do. You have to completely rearrange your schedule, and Warren Blake's life, before tomorrow morning."

"You win," he said as he tossed her the keys. "At least take my car and not the damned subway. I'll be up all night worrying that you got mugged."

"I've been taking care of myself for a very long time."

"Humor me."

She pocketed the keys. "Okay."

"And call me when you get there."

"I will."

"Are you sure you won't let Charlie drive you?"

"I'm sure. It's too late. I don't want you to bother him."

"Hell, Sidney, I pay him for this."

She shrugged. "I know, but I don't. It wouldn't feel right to me."

Max shook his head. "Fine. Just promise you'll be careful."

"Absolutely. I'll bring your car when I meet you at the hotel tomorrow morning."

"Fine." He reached for the phone. She turned to go, but he stopped her. "Sidney?"

"Yes?"

"I'm not going to let anything get in the way of this weekend. I want you to know that."

She winked at him. "You'll impress me no end if you pull it off, Max."

He started punching buttons.

Chapter Ten

Philip Grant picked up the phone and dialed the number from memory. On the other end, a smooth, well-modulated voice answered, "Thank you for calling The Keswick."

Philip smiled. "How are you, Hector? It's been a while since I've heard from you.

Hector Jarvis, general manager of the historic Keswick Inn on Long Island, exhaled a pleased sigh. "Philip Grant. What a delightful surprise."

"I doubt it, you wily old fox. You know precisely why I'm calling."

"I assume this has something to do with Mr. Loden's scheduled visit this afternoon?"

It came as no surprise to Philip that Hector knew Max was on his way to the inn. Hector had a way of knowing everything that went on in his small empire. "It does. I wanted to discuss something with you."

"I understand that Mr. Loden is bringing a guest."

"He is," Philip told his old friend. "A special guest."

"My banquet manager informed me that Mr. Loden's guest is an event planner who is helping with the younger Mr. Loden's wedding arrangements."

"Did he now?"

"He did."

"Did he tell you that Mr. Loden's guest also happens to be my niece?"

"Sidney?" Hector said in delight. "Really?"

"Really."

"Well, this is a pleasant surprise."

"I'm assuming that Mr. Loden is booked into a suite."

"He is. I have him staying in the Commodore. You remember. That's the two-story suite with the master bedroom and the second bedroom upstairs, and the sitting area and dining area downstairs."

"Yes. I remember."

"I, uh, assume you know that Mr. Loden has booked only the one room."

"I do."

"Then may I assume that Sidney will not be staying the weekend?"

"You may assume nothing of the sort." Philip smiled.

"You don't say?" Hector sounded both pleased and amazed.

"I do," Philip assured him. "I consider it a most fortunate turn of events."

"Indeed. I thought you'd told me that Ms. Barlow was currently holding Mr. Loden's attention."

"The winds have shifted."

"Quite favorably it seems."

"That's how I feel about it."

Hector laughed. "And I'm certain that you played no role in any of this. You have such a talent for minding your own affairs."

"I played an enormous role in it, I'll have you know. The entire thing was my idea."

"I might have known."

"Yes, you might have." Philip glanced at the clock. "They should be arriving sometime early this afternoon, and I wanted to make certain you understood the situation."

"Quite well."

"I'd like them to have a very good time."

"You may count on me, Philip. You know that."

"And I'd like them to have an uninterrupted good time, if you know what I mean."

"Naturally. Emergencies only. Anything else?"

"I'd like to be kept informed of anything extraordinary."

"I have your telephone number programmed on my speed dial."

Philip nodded, satisfied that he'd done what he could. "Thank you, Hector. I deliberately recommended the Keswick to Mr. Loden because I felt I could count on you."

"I'll do everything I can."

"The press may be a problem. Thus far, Sidney hasn't been with Mr. Loden often enough for word to leak of a relationship, but you know how these things can go. I'm certain Max wouldn't appreciate having a society reporter yelling 'Who Gets To Marry Max?' over the hedgerow. Do you have any reason to believe you'll be hounded by the paparazzi this weekend?"

"We have no celebrities in residence at the moment. Everything should be quite peaceful then, unless Mr. Loden decides to make a spectacle of himself."

"Always a possibility," Philip conceded.

Hector chuckled. "Indeed. But I'll alert the staff."

"I'd appreciate it."

"I think she'll be good for him, Philip."

"As do I," Philip concurred. "As do I."

MAX WATCHED Sidney walk toward him across the lobby of the hotel and had to jam his hands into his trouser pockets to keep from pulling her into his arms. She'd looked at him with such sweet longing when she'd left his apartment last night, it had taken every ounce of control he possessed not to beg her to stay with him. This morning, she looked fresh and captivating in navy trousers and a crisp white blouse. Her luxuriant hair was piled on her head in a froth of waves that seemed to beg for his fingers.

She glided to a stop two feet in front of him. "Good morning."

Max looked at her, felt the tug of desire racing through him, then decided caution was a sucker's game. He toppled her into his arms and kissed her. Hard. After her initial gasp, Sidney stumbled the final two steps toward him, wrapped her arms around his waist, and kissed him back. Max felt euphoric. When he lifted his head, he grinned at her. "Good morning."

She reached up to wipe the lipstick from his lips with her index finger. He was coming to adore the way she did that. "I missed you, too," she said quietly.

"You look like you slept."

"Why, thank you. You're looking very fit yourself."

Ignoring her sarcasm, he wrapped one arm around her shoulders and headed toward the banquet manager's office. "My point is, if you missed me half as much as I missed you, you wouldn't have slept at all. I didn't."

Sidney slanted him a flirtatious look that had him seriously considering blowing off the morning's appointment. "Is this a good time for me to advise that chilled cucumber slices do wonders for eliminating bags under the eyes?"

"Order me a gross," he said as they stepped onto the elevator. "I have a feeling I'm going to need them."

Sidney laughed. The sound simultaneously delighted and bewitched him. "I'm sort of counting on it," she said quietly.

Max made a conscious decision to get through the morning's business with all possible haste.

AN HOUR LATER, they were settled in his car, heading out of Manhattan toward the Keswick Inn. Her hand was nestled in his, and Max's only regret was that he hadn't had the foresight to ask Charlie to drive them.

"What would he do all weekend?" Sidney asked.

Max hadn't realized he'd voiced the sentiment out loud. "He could have come back into the city."

"It'll be easier if we have the car."

He slanted her a dry look. "I'm aware of that. I'm also aware that if Charlie were driving, I'd be free for—other things."

"Oh."

He squeezed her hand. "I adore you. Have I mentioned that this morning?"

"No."

"Well, I do. Thank you for giving me this weekend."

"You're welcome."

"Did it put too much of a strain on your schedule?"

Sidney shook her head and several more tendrils of her hair cascaded to her shoulders. "Kelly is extremely capable. We only had two events scheduled, and one is relatively minor. She can handle it."

"You're lucky to have her."

"Incredibly."

"And she's lucky to have you."

She gave him a surprised look. "Why do you say that?"

"Because good business people like Kelly are relatively easy to find. Creative geniuses like you are rare. Without you, she couldn't do what she does."

"I never thought of it that way."

"It's symbiotic. I have that same relationship with several members of my staff. They need me, and I need them. Knowing that is what makes a good leader a great leader."

"You know, Max, you're really a remarkable man."

He raised their joined hands to press a kiss to the back of her fingers. "I'm awfully glad you think so."

HECTOR JARVIS met them on the front steps of the Keswick Inn. Designed in the charming style of an English country home, the large inn catered to a decidedly sophisticated clientele. Hector had served, during his long tenure, in almost every position at the inn. He was now one of the most respected concierges in the business because of his hallmark service and the almost fanatic loyalty of his customers.

He shook Max's hand with open affection. "It's so very nice to see you, Mr. Loden. I was delighted when my banquet manager told me you were considering the Keswick for your brother's reception."

Max nodded. "I've got great memories here, Hector. You run an excellent operation."

Hector beamed. "We certainly try." His gaze shifted to Sidney. "It's a pleasure to see you again, Miss Grant. How is your uncle?"

"He's well," she assured him, trying not to squirm as she realized that Hector Jarvis knew precisely why she was here.

Hector signaled a bellhop to retrieve their bags from the trunk of Max's car. "I've booked you into the Commodore," he told Max. "I trust that will be satisfactory."

"Of course." Max looped his fingers beneath Sidney's elbow and began walking up the stairs. "I knew I could count on you, Hector."

"I'm pleased you thought so." The older man waited while a doorman swung open the impressive brass-trimmed door. "You'll also be happy to know that I expect things to be relatively quiet here this weekend. You should be able to enjoy a very refreshing couple of days."

Sidney stifled a groan. For his part, Max seemed oblivious to her discomfort. "Thank you."

"We aim to please, Mr. Loden."

Once inside, Max paused beneath one of the massive crystal chandeliers. "We were scheduled to meet with your banquet manager this afternoon. Do you think it would possible to postpone that meeting until tomorrow? We've had a long trip."

"Absolutely no problem," Hector assured him. "If Kathleen isn't available to show you around the facility tomorrow,

I'll do it myself.'' His gaze slid to Sidney. ''What time would you prefer?''

She started praying that the floor would swallow her whole. How she could have forgotten that her uncle and Hector Jarvis were fast friends, she'd never know, except that Max had turned her brain to mush. ''Whatever time you wish,'' she managed to say, though her voice sounded slightly breathless.

''Not too early,'' Max said abruptly. ''Let's make it ten o'clock.'' He looked at her. ''Is that all right with you?''

''Fine,'' she choked out.

Hector beamed at them. ''Excellent. I'll see you then. Your bags have been taken to your room. Please call me if you need anything else.'' He extended his business card to Max. ''Here's my private extension. I'll be here until seven this evening, then you'll be able to call on my assistant, Felix, if you need anything after that.''

Max pocketed the card with a short nod. ''Thank you, Hector. As usual, you've taken care of everything.''

''My pleasure, Mr. Loden.'' Hector indicated the elevator with a sweep of his elegant hand. ''Billy has the elevator waiting. I trust you'll enjoy your stay.''

Max began tugging her toward the elevator. ''I'm sure we will,'' he assured him.

Sidney lost her battle with her blush. She felt the tell-tale heating of her skin as Max guided her into the lift.

As the elevator made its painfully slow ascent, Max kept his firm hold on her hand. Sidney's nerves started to win their silent war with her confidence. Agreeing to this weekend had been one thing. Actually going through with it, well, she wasn't sure she had the guts for that.

Anxiety had begun tying her stomach in knots the moment she'd met him that morning. She had thought, hoped even, that she'd be able to overcome the fear this time. Surely it had been long enough—enough time had passed since Carter, she'd told herself. And she trusted Max. He was her friend.

But from the instant he'd taken her hand in the hotel lobby, waves of panic began building. She couldn't stop them.

And she cursed herself a thousand times a fool for not foreseeing it. She had known that having the full force of Max's indomitable focus directed at her would be an amazing experience, but as the bell rang with the passing of each floor, her stomach did another somersault.

Beside her, Max's body emanated raw energy. When the elevator doors slid silently open at the third floor luxury suite, Max handed Billy a twenty dollar bill and guided Sidney into the room. His eyes glittering he stared at the elevator until the doors glided shut.

With a low growl, he pulled Sidney into his arms. "Thank you," he whispered before he covered her lips with his own.

It was every bit as overwhelming as she'd thought. "Max," she said softly. He hungrily devoured her. His hands molded her closer, his mouth glided over hers with intoxicating thoroughness.

When he finally lifted his head, Sidney's knees nearly buckled. "Max, I need to talk to you."

Max's low chuckle skittered along her nerves, making her shiver. "Say whatever you want, baby. You have my complete attention."

The panic rose. Sidney drew several deep breaths. Max swept a hand up her spine. "I knew it would be like this for us," he muttered. "I've never wanted a woman like I want you."

"Oh, my." A sense of foreboding poured through her. Sidney moved one hand from his shoulder to his chest, where his heart pounded a steady cadence. "Max, I—"

"I might never get enough of you."

"Wait, I—"

"Sidney." His heated gaze threatened to scorch her. "I'm on fire."

If the sheer heat of his body pressed so closely to hers were any indication, he was right about that. She wavered a second longer, studying his expression while she did battle with her insecurities. The intense concentration, the fierce wanting, the banked heat were all there. Everything that threatened to overwhelm her. Everything she feared would steal her identity. But she also saw the hint of vulnerability—that terrible loneliness that lurked just beneath the surface. And it swayed her like nothing else could. Somehow, this was all moving faster than she'd planned. Now that the moment was finally here, with no interruptions in sight, she battled a fit of nerves.

With a soft sigh, she took firm hold of herself. This was Max—one of the most generous, caring men she'd ever known. She could trust him. "Max, before we—before we go too far, here, there's—there's something I want to tell you."

His hands cradled her face. So strong, but so gentle. He would never hurt her, Sidney reminded herself. "Sidney," he said, his voice a purr, "is something wrong?"

"No." She firmly shook her head. "No."

"Are you afraid of me?"

"Lord, no! I couldn't stand it if you thought that."

"Am I pushing you too hard?"

"Not really."

He kissed her again. "I really hadn't planned on pouncing on you the minute we got behind a locked door."

That made her smile. "Really?"

He looked slightly sheepish. "Okay, I thought about it, I just didn't plan it."

"It's all right." She rubbed her palms on the backs of his hands. "I just—I have something I want to tell you first."

His fingertips caressed the whorls of her ears. "I'm listening."

She drew a deep breath. "I need to be on top."

He blinked. He looked like he was having the devil's own time trying not to laugh. "Excuse me?"

"Don't laugh." The heat in her blood was beginning to

give way to embarrassment. "Oh, please don't laugh." She'd die if he did.

His expression turned somber. "Honey—"

"I couldn't stand it if you laughed at me. Not about this."

Max gathered her to him. "I'm not laughing. I promise. Tell me what's going on."

She swallowed. "I, it's just that I have this, this phobia. Oh, cripes! I should have told you before. It's just that I didn't think we would—I mean, this is so planned. I thought I'd have more time to—"

"Shh." His hand began to make a soothing journey from the crown of her head to the small of her back. He repeated the caress in slow, tender strokes. "Shh. Tell me now."

"I can't stand to be crowded when I—when I make love. I need to be on top." Her voice quaked with embarrassment.

Max tipped her away from him to study her face. "Why were you afraid to tell me that?"

"You don't mind?" she said softly.

"No." He studied her through narrowed eyes. "Does this have something to do with your ex-husband?"

She didn't want to talk about that, not now. Maybe not ever. "Does it matter?"

"Maybe."

"I'd really rather not think about Carter right now."

He hesitated a second longer, then kissed her again. "Me either," he said when he raised his head, but he continued to watch her with a speculative gleam in his eye.

Simultaneously relieved and embarrassed, Sidney deliberately pushed aside her anxiety. He said he understood. And she would believe him. Laying her hand against his face, she whispered, "Why are you looking at me like that?"

His eyebrows lifted. "Like what?" His voice had that rumbling quality that turned her bones to butter.

"Like I'm an undercapitalized business with significant resale potential."

Max chuckled, and the sound warmed her. "I assure you,

I haven't thought about stock acquisitions in the last—'' he checked his watch ''—five hours.''

''I'm flattered.''

He started unbuttoning her shirt. ''You should be.'' Max studied her as he worked open the buttons. ''My head doesn't turn easily, you know.'' He spread open her blouse and took several seconds to simply stare at her. ''Did you know,'' he said, his voice hoarse, ''that you're the most beautiful thing I've ever seen?''

Her heartbeat quickened. How had he known that here, in the luxurious suite, paid for by his success, where the thick Oriental carpet and antique furnishings served as the perfect foil for Max's unique brand of personal charisma, she would struggle with a sense of inadequacy? ''This feels a little odd to me,'' she admitted softly, reaching to unbutton his shirt as he had hers.

''You didn't think it was odd this morning.''

Her lips twitched. ''Yes, I did. You just made me forget.'' He watched her as she finished opening his shirt. She spread it open to reveal his white T-shirt.

''I think it's my turn to feel flattered,'' he said.

Sidney leaned back against the wall. ''You do that to me, you know? Even in my wildest imagination, I never pictured this. Being here with you.'' She looked around the room. ''Being anywhere with you.''

''I imagined it,'' Max admitted quietly. ''And lately, I've done almost nothing *but* imagine it.''

''You aren't making me feel better.''

''There are a lot of things I want to make you feel.'' He laid one hand on her shoulder. ''And there are a lot of things I want to know.'' He tilted his head to one side. ''Will you let me learn your secrets, Sidney?''

She was lost. With a slight nod, she leaned against him. ''I think I've waited forever.''

Max swept her into his arms and carried her up to the master suite. With a tenderness she could never have imagined, he undressed her, and himself, and then joined her on the bed where he showed her with his words and his hands and his mouth how much he wanted her. He was exquisitely tender, letting her set the pace, never asking for more than she could give. He eased away from her only once—just long enough to pull a foil packet from his wallet to ensure her protection.

When she was nearly mindless with need, he caressed her shoulders and eased her carefully on top of him. He waited, his wonderful eyes searching hers, his face a mask of desire. Sidney sighed and took the final step to seal their union.

The expression on his face, she thought as she felt the storm overtake her, would be forever seared into her brain.

TWENTY MINUTES later, Max was still trying to catch his breath. Damn, she'd nearly killed him. He couldn't remember a time when a woman had come to him with such sweet longing, and such unreserved need. His brain tried to focus on a thought—something, *anything*, that might slow his heart rate to normal and restore some measure of his equilibrium. With Sidney draped across his chest, her fingers idly caressing his shoulder, the only concrete image his mind could raise was the view of her incredible face when she'd traveled with him to paradise. He let out a harsh sigh. "Damn," he said aloud.

Sidney smiled against his chest. "My thoughts exactly."

He tipped her chin up with his index finger. "You might have warned me that you were going to try and kill me."

The glow in her eyes delighted him. "I had no idea."

He studied her in the fading afternoon light. "You didn't, did you?" he said soberly.

Her expression turned serious. "Max—"

With a shake of his head, he rolled to his side so he could prop himself up on one elbow. "Honey," he trailed a finger down the curve of her arm, "I want to know why."

She didn't pretend not to know what he was talking about. "Wasn't it all right like that?"

His lips twitched. "Do you have to ask me that?"

She hesitated, then shook her head. "No. You liked it."

"You could say that."

"Then can't we just leave it at that?"

"I don't think so." He smoothed her hair off her face. "I want more from you, Sidney. I want to know everything." A shiver raced through her. Max felt it and frowned. "Are you nervous?"

"No. Yes. Oh, I don't know." Her eyes drifted shut. He could practically hear the gears turning in her mind.

He sensed, somehow, in a remarkable burst of insight that might have shocked him had he taken time to analyze it, that she would find the story easier if she didn't have to meet his gaze. For a man who was widely accused of being the most single-minded individual on the face of the planet, the ease of caring for her was a novel experience. He let it roll around in his head for a few blissful seconds, then eased her onto her back so he could pillow his head on her breast, careful not to smother her in any way.

Sidney's fingers glided through his hair. "It was Carter," she said quietly.

Max concentrated on breathing normally. He supposed he would have to get used to the quick flash of anger that pumped through him whenever she said that slimeball's name in that half-quaking voice. He wished he'd destroyed the smarmy little toad when he'd had the chance. After several seconds, she continued. "Our sex life wasn't exactly ideal."

"The bastard," he muttered against the smooth skin of her shoulder.

Sidney tweaked his earlobe. "It wasn't all his fault, you know?"

He raised his head long enough to give her a censorious look. "Honey, from what I just experienced, you'll understand that I'm having a little trouble believing that."

Sidney's face colored a delightful rosy-pink. "Thanks."

He dropped his head again. "Tell me the rest."

She traced the curve of his ear with her index finger. "Carter had certain, ah, preferences. I didn't care for them."

Max waited. The silence dragged on. He realized that he'd tightened his fingers on her shoulder and willed himself to relax. Sidney drew a shuddering breath that threatened to rip his insides out. "Carter," she said quietly, "found it difficult to enjoy sex unless he felt—" her voice faded away.

Max pressed a kiss to the curve of her neck. "You don't have to tell me."

She shivered. "He liked to feel appreciated."

He met her gaze again, searched it. "Sidney—"

"Weak women made Carter feel appreciated."

His mood was rapidly souring from bad to downright foul. "Did he ever force you?"

She shook her head. "Not exactly. I just…I learned to—endure."

Incredulous, he studied her stoic expression. "You're serious?"

She glanced away, visibly embarrassed. "Yes."

Max gently nudged her chin until she faced him. "The man was an ass," he said softly.

A smile played at the edge of her mouth. "Thanks for taking my side."

"I meant it."

"I know you did."

With the pad of his thumb, he traced the still-swollen curve of her upper lip. "In case you ever had even a second's doubt about this, let me spell it out for you. You could take any man with a pulse straight to paradise."

"I liked it, too," she said quietly.

Max never remembered laughing with any of his lovers. It felt good and natural and incredibly liberating. And, he realized with a deep feeling of contentment, he wanted to keep on doing it—for a very long time. "You don't say?" he whispered.

"Uh-huh."

"Want to, uh, try it again?"

Her laugh spiraled all the way through his insides and wrapped around his heart. "Are you going to keep me locked in here all weekend?"

"It's a thought."

"Do we get to eat?"

"They have great room service."

Sidney linked her hands behind his neck and tugged him toward her. "I especially like strawberries."

With a low growl, he rolled to his back, taking her with him. "I'll have them flown in from Guatemala."

Sidney giggled. "Frozen is fine."

"No way." He nipped her earlobe. "That jerk you married might be the frozen-strawberry type, but I've got a thing for high-class dames who demand the best."

Chapter Eleven

The rest of the weekend passed in a state of near euphoria. Sidney forcibly put aside her lingering misgivings about the wisdom of falling for Max, and concentrated, for the first time in her life, on the present. Philip was always telling her to enjoy the moment. For years, she'd been so worried about the future, about what would become of her, she'd never given herself permission to simply live. For the two days they spent at the Keswick, she refused to let anything mar her bliss.

But by the time they were headed back into the city, she was having more and more trouble quieting the warning voices in her head. She was fairly certain that Max wasn't prepared for the realities of their re-entry into the world. When they were alone in the Keswick's private paradise, it was easy to pretend they were simply a man and woman enjoying their time together. But soon, they'd have to face the fact that Max's world demanded a companion who could fit into his sophisticated lifestyle. With her hand nestled in his, resting on the corded warmth of his thigh, it was so tempting to slide into the sensual web he'd created. Sidney briefly closed her eyes and drew several calming breaths.

"Tired?" His voice rolled over her nerves.

Sidney shook her head. "Not really."

"Should I be offended?" The humor in his tone was unmistakable.

Sidney tilted her head to look at him. "I assure you it's not for lack of effort on your part."

Max grinned at her. "I thought maybe I was losing my touch."

"Hardly."

He shifted her hand in his. "So, you want to tell me what's wrong then?"

One thing she'd learned that weekend—he had uncanny insight. No doubt, the same instincts that made him successful in business gave him a keen intuition. She thought about denying that anything was bothering her, then thought better of it. He wouldn't believe her anyway. "Have you thought about what's going to happen when we get back?" she asked carefully.

"Sure. I'm going to drop you at your place, then head home. I've got some business appointments, and I need to check in with Philip. I'll call you tonight, and we'll make plans. If you want, I can send Charlie out to get you."

She raised her eyebrows. "Just like that?"

"Like what?" His voice turned wary.

"Max, we have a certain, uh, history. People don't think of us as a couple."

"So?"

"So? So, it's going to be a little shocking for them, don't you think?"

"So?"

Sidney rolled her eyes. "So, I don't think I've quite cultivated your disdain for the opinions of the world at large."

"Are you ashamed to be seen with me?"

She choked. "Are you kidding?"

He pinned her with an intense look. "No. Are you?"

"Of course not."

"Are you ashamed for people to know that we're lovers?"

"No, that's not what I—"

"Then what's the problem here?"

She drew a calming breath. "The problem, Mad Max, is

that I don't think your circle of friends—or your family—is going to respond very well when you tell them you're sleeping with your butler's niece."

A hint of irritation pulled at the corners of his mouth. He pulled the car off the highway and glided to a stop on the shoulder. Giving the keys a swift turn, he shifted to look at her. "In the first place, I'm not *sleeping* with you. To say that's what's going on between us makes it sound tawdry. And I don't like it."

Sidney's eyes widened. "I didn't mean it like that."

Max ignored her. "Secondly, in case you've failed to notice, this isn't the fifteenth century. I'm not the lord of the manor, and you sure as hell aren't the scullery maid. Yes, your uncle is my employee, but Philip Grant isn't just a member of my staff, he's my friend. I don't consider you my butler's niece, I consider you the woman I want."

She stared at him. She was beginning to understand why the world found him so formidable. In his present state of determination, he was almost overwhelming. "Oh."

"And third, if *anyone* has a problem with that, then they'd damn well better be smart enough not to mention it." His gaze narrowed. "And if they do, I want you to promise you'll tell me about it."

"Max—"

He cupped the back of her head in his large hand. "Promise me, Sidney."

"Okay."

His fingers relaxed. "Are we clear on this now?"

Hardly, she thought. He might not foresee the inevitable problems that would arise, but she did. "I just don't think its going to be as easy as you think."

"I don't give a damn whether it's easy or not. Do you think I made Loden Enterprises into the multinational corporate giant it is by backing away from obstacles?"

"No, of course not."

"What I'm concerned about is how you feel. Are you all right with this, or not? I think I have a right to know."

She hesitated, then found the answer she needed in his fierce expression. With the sun shining through the windows, and the heat of his gaze searching her face, she decided she could wait a few precious hours before she faced the inevitable. "I'm fine."

"Sure?"

She nodded. "Yes."

"Then you'll let me come to your place tonight?"

"Tonight is my card night with my staff. Kelly and Chip and Licia, my office manager, and I get together for poker the first Monday of the month."

"I love poker."

She drew a deep breath. "Are you sure?"

"Are you?" he asked, his gaze intense.

Sidney nodded. At least they'd be among her friends—people she knew and trusted. It seemed less scary that way. "I'm sure. The game's at eight."

"Good. What can I bring?"

She hesitated a second longer, then gathered her courage. Max was right. If he was okay with it, and she was okay with it, who cared what the rest of the world thought. "A clean shirt and your toothbrush?"

The clouds cleared from his gaze. He leaned over to press a kiss to her lips. "You didn't tell me it was a sleepover."

"I just decided. If we're going to do this, then I think it's past time you tried my specialty of the house."

His eyebrows lifted. "You mean there's something you didn't show me this weekend?"

As he reached for the keys, Sidney laughed. "Not that kind of specialty. I meant I'll make you chocolate waffles for breakfast."

He flashed her a beatific smile, then started the car. "I can hardly wait."

SIDNEY PACED the length of her den as she battled a bout of nerves. For the fifth time that hour, her gaze strayed to the clock on her mantel. Four-thirty. Max had dropped her off four hours ago. She'd unpacked her suitcase, started a load of laundry, made her hors d'oeuvres for the evening, then proceeded to anxiously pace the length of her den.

She couldn't remember the last time she'd been this tense. Damn, but she'd like a cigarette. The craving surprised her. Since she'd kicked the habit six years ago, the urge rarely resurfaced. It must be, she decided, an indication that her trepidation was functioning at peak levels. No matter what Max had said, the same niggling worry she'd felt since he'd first told her he wanted her kept plaguing her: she could never be what he needed. Carter had wanted a society wife, and she'd lost a part of herself trying to please him.

Max was a sophisticated man, who enjoyed the companionship of equally sophisticated women. Root beer, pretzels and poker simply weren't his style. He might think he could grow to like it, might even manage to fool himself into believing it, but he couldn't run in her world anymore than she could run in his.

He was a saltwater fish, she'd decided. Exotic and rare and beautiful and valuable, while she was more the freshwater pond variety. With a weary sigh, Sidney dropped into a wing chair. How had she gotten herself into this? How had she let herself believe that she could swim in the same stream as a man like Max Loden?

Absently, her gaze strayed to the striped wallpaper while her mind drifted to the look of displeasure on Carter Silas's face when he'd come home from a business trip and found the walls painted yellow. Sidney had worked on the project for the three days he'd been gone. She'd loved the color—a cheery pale yellow with a cream wash. She even remembered the name of the shade: Swiss Vanilla. The antique white trim had made the room seem welcoming and bright. It had reminded her of lemon pie. Carter hated it.

Within a week, he'd chosen the striped wallpaper he wanted her to use to cover her paint job. Sidney had hung the wallpaper without comment. She reached out to trace a seam with her index finger. She'd done a great job. Every line was perfectly matched. Carter had thanked her for getting rid of the yellow.

Idly, she plucked at a place where the glue had separated from the wall. The tiny flaw irrationally irritated her. It seemed, somehow, symbolic of the many things that had gone wrong in her marriage. No matter how hard she'd tried, there had always been imperfections.

Imperfections her husband couldn't tolerate. Her finger picked at the loose edge.

Imperfections that had caused a bitter and angry divorce. Suddenly, she was holding a two-foot section of the striped paper in her hand. She looked first at it, incredulous, then at the now bare wall. The yellow-and-cream paint, clearly visible beneath the haze of wallpaper paste, taunted her.

Sidney surged to her feet and reached for a newly loosened edge of the paper. She gave it a hard tug and it ripped a four-foot swath from the wall. Abruptly, she was no longer merely irritated—she was furious.

Attacking the wallpaper with renewed vigor, she began ripping at it. As each piece fell away, she felt a surge of liberating disgust. "Damn him," she muttered as she thought of Carter's smug face and critical gaze. She shredded the piece of paper in her hands and reached for another. "Damn him to hell."

Sidney was wiping the sweat from her brow with the back of her sleeve when she heard the knock on her door. Kelly. Kelly always arrived early on poker night, so she and Sidney could review the calendar for the month. Sidney looked blankly at the piles of torn paper in the center of her den, then walked to the door.

Kelly greeted her with a bright smile and unabashed curiosity. "Hi, Sid. Have a nice weekend?"

Sidney merely stepped away from the door. Kelly gave her a curious look, advanced three steps into the apartment, then stopped. "Uh, when did you decide to do this?"

"Two hours ago," Sidney said quietly.

Kelly glanced from the mess to her. "Really?"

"Yes."

"I like the yellow," Kelly ventured.

"So do I."

"I never thought the stripes were your style."

"They weren't. Carter picked them out."

"Oh." Kelly tilted her head to one side. "I guess that explains it, then."

"Explains what?" Sidney shut the door, then slid her hands into her hip pockets.

"Why I thought your den looked more like a law office than a home."

A giggle welled in Sidney's chest. "I kind of thought that, too."

"So why did you live with it for so long?"

"I don't know. I had other things to worry about, I guess."

"Oh." Kelly picked her way through the debris so she could put her purse down on the coffee table. "Why now?"

"A lot of things changed this weekend," Sidney admitted. "I decided I wanted the yellow back."

Kelly looked around once more, then nodded. "Good choice. Tell you what, I'll help you wash the glue off the walls while we go over the calendar. That way, it'll be clean when Chip and Licia get here."

"Max is coming," Sidney said quietly.

Kelly's face briefly registered surprise, but she masked it quickly. "Good. Maybe he's a high roller."

"You have no idea."

"Then we'd better get started. I want time to relax before I win all his money."

For the first time in hours, Sidney's tension began to ebb. She managed a slight laugh. Kelly had a way of doing that for her—helping her stay connected. "Want some lemonade while you work?"

"You bet."

"Okay. I'll get two glasses, a bucket and some sponges if you'll root out a trash bag and start getting rid of this stuff." She kicked a piece with her toe. "I don't think I want to look at it anymore."

They spent the next hour and a half scrubbing the walls, talking business, and carefully avoiding the subject of Carter Silas. When the bulk of the glue was gone, Sidney was pleased to note that very little of the paint would need touching up. She could probably complete the job in a morning. Tired, but heady with a strange feeling of relief, she dropped into a chair. "It looks great. Thanks, Kel."

Kelly gave the walls an appreciative look. "It really does. Did you do this yourself?"

"Yes."

Kelly sank down on the couch and reached for her glass. "And I thought your artistic talents lay in chocolate. Who knew?"

"I outdid myself." She glanced around. "I think I was trying to compensate for the gloomy state of my life."

"And then Carter made you put up bars—like prison. Geez, the more I hear about the guy, the more I hate him."

"Thanks for your loyalty."

Kelly shrugged. "He was a creep, Sidney. And I'm glad you're finally shedding some of the baggage he left you with."

"You could say that."

Several seconds of silence ticked by. Kelly set her glass down on the coffee table and fixed Sidney with a shrewd look. "Do you, ah, want to tell me about this weekend?"

She drew a calming breath. "What's to tell?"

Kelly's eyebrows lifted. "Is that a serious question?"

"No, I guess not." Sidney ran her hands back and forth

on her jean-covered thighs. "Max and I are—lovers." The word still felt strange.

"It's about time," her friend said emphatically.

"It's a little strange. I've known him for so long—or at least, know of him through Philip."

"Sometimes the best relationships start out slow."

"I know."

"But you're nervous?"

Sidney hesitated, then nodded. "The last time I allowed myself to be really serious about a man, I ended up in a messy divorce with the self-esteem of a slug. I feel like I just finished putting myself back together, and now, here's this."

"Max Loden is a hell of a lot better man than Carter Silas."

"I know he is."

"So why the anxiety?"

"Kelly, how is this possibly going to work? I mean, Max is—spectacular. 'Max the Magnificent,' I used to call him."

"Evidently, he's more than a little keen on you, too."

"So he says."

"You don't believe him?" Kelly sounded incredulous.

"I believe him. It's just that I think he has no idea how hard this will be. How can I possibly fit into his life?"

"The same way he'll fit into yours, Sidney. One day at a time." Kelly leaned forward to brace her hands on her knees. "Look, Sidney. Max Loden isn't the kind of man who settles for less than what he wants. He's shrewd. To hear you tell it, he's brilliant."

"He is."

"So give him a little credit, will ya? If he says he wants you, trust him to know what he's talking about."

The firm knock on the door could only belong to one person. Sidney shot Kelly a nervous look, then took her emotions firmly in hand and went to answer it. Max, clad in a purple shirt and pristine blue jeans stepped over the threshold and pulled Sidney into his arms. "I missed you," he whispered in the instant before his mouth settled on hers. Sidney had no time to react, so she surrendered instead.

By the time he lifted his head, her knees felt like butter. Max's eyes glittered. "I hope you missed me, too," he teased.

Sidney blinked, trying to bring him back into focus. Belatedly, she remembered Kelly's presence. She backed up a step, but Max kept his hands linked at the small of her back. "Max," she indicated Kelly with a wave of her hand, "you remember Kelly."

He grinned at her. "Of course. Thanks for letting Sidney have the weekend off."

Kelly laughed. "Sid's the boss. I just do the dirty work."

Max shook his head. "That's not the way I heard it. Sidney tells me you're her right hand. She's lucky to have you."

"I'm lucky to have her." Kelly's gaze narrowed as she studied Max's face. "Anyone would be."

He didn't hesitate. "Yes, they would."

Another knock on her door saved Sidney from replying. Chip greeted her with a broad smile and a tray of food. "Hey, Sid. I was experimenting this afternoon, and thought maybe we'd try…" He stopped abruptly when he saw Max. "Uh, do I have the wrong night?"

"Max is joining us for poker," Sidney said as she took the tray from Chip.

"Oh." The young man looked at Kelly. "This is an interesting, uh, twist."

Kelly laughed. "Think of the potential, Chip. How much cash do you have on you, Max?"

"Enough to bankroll your pension."

She rubbed her hands together. "I can hardly wait for Licia to get here. I'm looking forward to divesting you of your life savings."

Max shot Sidney a wry look. "You didn't warn me she was a shark."

"You didn't ask."

TWO HOURS LATER, they were comfortably settled around Sidney's table, with piles of shelled peanuts serving as chips. The conversation had turned in and out of their business and personal lives. After the first five minutes, Sidney had completely relaxed, convinced that Max was a virtual social chameleon. He'd slid effortlessly into the light banter and casual business conversations, adding his opinion on occasion, but, more often, asking polite questions of her staff. When Licia had expressed her frustration with the billing problems at one of Sidney's major suppliers, Max, who was accustomed to negotiating billion-dollar deals, had offered advice and empathy.

"So, Max," Chip said as he tossed two peanuts into the kitty, "I was reading in the paper about the Fitzwater deal. The speculators can't seem to understand what Edward Fitzwater has that you want."

Max laughed. "I want his daughter for my sister-in-law."

Kelly nodded. "I can understand that. Miss Fitzwater seemed very gracious."

"Lauren is a gem," Max agreed as he called Chip's bet and raised the stakes to three peanuts. "Greg has outstanding taste."

"But what about Fitzwater Electronics?" Chip insisted. "According to the papers, you pushed hard for the merger."

Max's eyes twinkled. "Looking for inside stock tips, Chip?"

"Sure," the young chef said. "I'm not going to retire on peanuts, you know."

Sidney called the bet as she ate another of Chip's appetizers. "If you keep coming up with recipes like this, you can retire and host a cooking show."

Chip put his hand over his heart. "Thank you for appreciating my talent."

Kelly grinned. "Hey, maybe you could get Martha Stewart and Julia Child to battle it out on your show. Can you imagine the headlines? Duel Of The Whisks. Child vs. Stewart. Death By Meringue.''

Licia shook her head. "I'd like to see the day Chip oversees a duel to the death by anything. Good grief, he's afraid of spiders.''

"Yeah, well," Sidney said, "I'm afraid of Martha Stewart.''

Everyone laughed. Kelly pushed the requisite number of peanuts into the pile. "At the moment, the only thing I'm afraid of is losing the rest of my peanuts.''

Max tapped his fingers on his fanned cards. "I can understand that." He tossed six peanuts into the kitty. "The stakes are starting to get high.''

"But not as high," Chip persisted, "as the stakes in the Fitzwater merger.''

"Chip," Kelly admonished. "Give it a rest.''

"I don't mind," Max explained. "There's really not that much to it. Fitzwater Electronics is the patent holder on a couple of new devices that I want. Edward has a couple of young whiz-kid engineers who have been working on some miniaturization technology for power sources.''

Kelly gave him a curious look. "If it's so valuable, why did Fitzwater let his company get into trouble?''

"Edward is not enough of a visionary to know what he has. Besides, the patents aren't worth much without the innovations our development team has made.''

"What is it?" Licia asked. "The patent, I mean.''

"It's for a self-regenerating miniature power source. We believe we can use it in combination with our interactive microchips. We've been working on artificially intelligent animatronics.''

Kelly blinked. "In English?''

"We plan to introduce a new doll in the Real Men collection that never needs its batteries recharged, and learns to recognize the voice and preferences of the girl that owns it.''

Licia chuckled. "I'd watch out if I were you. Not only will

that make 'Who Gets To Marry Max?' the best advertising slogan of the decade, but you'll have a revolt on your hands.''

''A revolt?'' Max prodded.

''Sure, if those dolls had been around when Keith and I were dating, I might have reconsidered getting married. Once this generation of little girls finds out they can have a Real Men doll who walks, talks and answers to their every whim, they'll swear off genuine men altogether.''

Chip looked affronted. ''Hey. There's more to life than a man who caters to you, you know.''

Kelly laughed. ''Well, I'll admit I'd like to know what it feels like, anyway.''

Sidney shook her head. ''I don't care how good it is, if it can't take out the trash, who needs it?''

Max's eyes twinkled. ''Maybe, but we're banking on the doll being popular enough, and successful enough, that we'll be able to apply the technology to other areas. If we can produce, say, a notebook computer battery that allows the unit to operate for three days without recharging *and* responds to the idiosyncrasies of the user, well, let's just say Chip could considerably pad his stock portfolio.''

''I'll call my broker tomorrow.''

Sidney gave him a wry look. ''Would that be 1-800-Dial-a-shark?''

''Very funny.''

''All I know is,'' Kelly added, ''my sister's kids are going to kill for one of those dolls. Licia is right. 'Who Gets To Marry Max?' is about to become the hottest campaign on Madison Avenue.''

''From your lips to God's ears,'' Max said. ''In the meantime, it's your bet, Chip.''

''I know. I'm thinking.'' He studied his hand a few seconds longer, then dropped it to the table with a disgusted sigh. ''I'll fold.''

The play went to Sidney. She searched Max's expression

for a glimmer of what he was thinking. "I'm going to call," she said quietly, "and raise you nine."

Max looked over the top of his cards and gave Sidney a shrewd look. "I think you're bluffing."

"I never bluff."

"Then you must be a lousy poker player."

Chip laughed. "Don't you believe it. She cleans our clocks just about every month."

Kelly glanced first at Max, then at Sidney. "Well, regardless of whether she's bluffing or not, with the hand I've got, it wouldn't matter. I'll fold. What about you, Licia?"

"No way." She dropped her hand. "All I've got is a pair of twos."

With only Sidney and Max left, the tension took on a strange new edge. Max contemplated his hand a few more seconds, then tossed seventeen peanuts into the center pile. "All right. I'll see your seventeen," he added thirteen more, "and make it an even thirty."

Licia shook her head as she stood. "Too rich for me. Besides, I've got to get home. Keith is going to wonder what's been keeping me."

"No guts, no glory, Licia," Kelly told her.

"Yeah, well, let's just say that I'd rather have what Keith is offering than a pocketful of peanuts." She glanced at Sidney. "I'll let you know what I work out on those bids for the shelving units."

"Thanks." Sidney gave her a warm smile. "I'd like to get that done as soon as possible. The stockroom is starting to look like a war zone."

Licia scooped up her purse, then grabbed one more of Chip's appetizers. "I know. I'll get it straightened out by Monday. I promise."

They told her goodbye and as the door clicked shut behind her, Kelly made a clucking sound with her tongue. "The coward. Can't take the stress."

Sidney studied her hand while Max studied her. "You don't have anything, and you know it," she said.

"But are you willing to risk it?"

She cocked an eyebrow at him. "Are you kidding? I'm not the one at risk here."

"I'm telling you, Max," Chip said. "She has the flush."

"No way." He watched Sidney through narrowed eyes. "There have been ten spades played. There are only two left in the deck."

"It only takes one," she teased. "So I'm going to see your thirty, and raise you thirty." She moved the peanuts.

"It's the flush," Chip persisted. "You'd better cut your losses."

Max's eyes glittered as he watched Sidney. "I'm telling you, she's bluffing.

"Then take the bet."

His gaze dropped to his pile of peanuts. "I would, but I'm a little short. Would you take an IOU?"

"How do I know you're good for it?" she prompted.

"I'd personally guarantee your satisfaction." The subtle shift in his tone was unmistakable.

Sidney found herself captivated by his gaze. "You would?"

"Absolutely."

"How do I know I can trust you for it?"

"Because I'll commit my undivided attention to ensuring that you are?"

Kelly coughed. The room temperature kicked up a couple of degrees, and Sidney felt the answering heat in her blood. She was vaguely aware that Kelly and Chip were watching the interplay with keen interest, but couldn't seem to take her gaze from Max. "Okay," she said softly, "I'll take it."

He leaned closer. "Then show me what's in your hand."

She tipped it toward him. "Full house, aces high. And you can't beat it."

A smile tugged at the corner of his mouth. "Evidently not," he said smoothly as he laid his cards face down.

Kelly abruptly rose to her feet. "Time to go, Chip. It's late."

He gave her a bemused look. "I want to play another hand. We don't have an early event tomorrow."

Kelly gave him a meaningful stare. "Well, it's late and I'm leaving, and you have to walk me to my car. I'm scared to go out alone in the dark."

"Since when?"

Sidney continue to watch Max. His eyes glittered. Kelly walked around the table and grabbed Chip's ear. "Since now. Let's go."

"Oh." He jumped to his feet. "Right. I'll, uh, pick up the tray from you tomorrow Sid."

"Sure." She wondered if they could see the heat shimmering between her and Max.

"Thanks for the stock tip, Max," Chip said.

"Don't mention it." His gaze stayed firmly on Sidney.

In the seconds after they left, a tense silence filled the room. Max tilted his head in the direction of her den. "I like the new paint job."

He knew. She didn't know how, but he knew. "Me, too. I never liked that wallpaper."

"I don't blame you."

"Carter picked it out."

"I'm not surprised." He rose to his feet and offered her his hand. "I'm glad you got rid of it."

And him, she thought. Somehow, Max knew, unequivocally, what it meant to her. She slid her hand into his. "I am, too."

"You ready to make good on that IOU now?"

She rose to her feet and stepped into his arms. "I think I might die if you don't pay up immediately."

His laugh made her shiver with pure, anticipatory delight. "I'll get right on it, babe."

Chapter Twelve

Max spent the next two weeks drowning in his feelings for Sidney, and in the general state of his universe. His brother, for once, seemed content to follow a reasonable course. Lauren was happily planning their wedding. Edward had stopped acting belligerent. The stocks were rising. The shareholders were ecstatic. Colleen and Warren were still vacationing in the Caribbean. And he had Sidney Grant warming his bed almost every night, and brightening his life each day.

Max could never remember a time when he'd felt more content. Or less alone. Somehow, Sidney had knocked the edge off the ache that he'd once thought permanent. She delighted him in a thousand ways. Never, in his entire life, could he remember being with a woman—or another person, for that matter—who seemed to merely enjoy his company. Sidney paid close attention to his preferences and his moods, seeking out the things he enjoyed and listening patiently and sympathetically to his frustrations.

On the afternoon of a particularly tense board meeting, she'd arrived at his office with fresh coffee and a tray of handmade chocolates bearing the Loden Enterprises logo. He'd left his board members happily enjoying the break while he'd trailed Sidney into his office to let her know, in a very graphic and pleasurable way, just how much he appreciated her.

For his part, he was finding that one of the greatest joys of his life came in pleasing her. Her warmth, her energy, her wit, her openness, wrapped him in a cocoon of undiluted happiness like he'd never known.

Increasingly, he found himself counting the minutes until he saw her again. Even his staff had commented on his unusual good humor. "Who Gets To Marry Max?" was becoming the most frequently asked question among his staff and peers. Max took it all in stride, while silently praying that whatever it was Sidney had done for him would continue for a very long time.

He was pleasurably contemplating his evening with her one afternoon when Philip interrupted him in his third-story office. "Max?"

He smiled broadly. "Hello, Philip."

Philip regarded his good humor with little more than a raised eyebrow. "Have you forgotten that you're to meet Mr. Lort in town this afternoon at four?"

"I have not." His hand rested on the wrapped package on his desk. "There was something out here I needed. I'm on my way back into town now."

Philip nodded. "Very good. Will you want Charlie to drive you?"

"No, I'll take the car." Max grinned at his butler. "You and Charlie can get down to a serious game of gin."

"We play rummy, sir."

Max tilted his head to one side. "So you do." The older man didn't budge from the doorway. "Is something wrong, Philip?"

Philip's eyes dropped to the package. "No. Nothing's wrong."

"You're sure?"

Philip hesitated, then met Max's gaze once more. "Please don't hurt her. She's been hurt enough. I'm not sure she can bounce one more time."

Max frowned. "Why the hell would you think I'd hurt her?"

"You can be, er, aloof at times."

"Aloof?"

"Yes. You aren't always open with your thoughts. Some people find you confusing."

"Is that how I got the name, 'Mad Max?'" he quipped.

Philip's expression didn't flicker. "Sidney is a very complicated young woman."

"I'm aware of that."

"I care for her a great deal."

"So do I, Philip."

"I was very in favor of your relationship with her."

"Was?"

"Yes. I wasn't really sick the weekend of your house party, you know?"

He had, of course. He'd seen the cards Philip was clutching under the blanket the morning he'd stopped by to check on him. "You don't say?"

"You knew."

"All along."

"I thought the time was finally right for you and for Sidney."

"It was," he said firmly. He wouldn't even entertain the notion that something might be wrong. "It is."

"She's falling very hard for you."

"The feeling is mutual."

Philip studied him a second longer, then nodded. "I'm sure it is. I'll go let Charlie know you don't need him to take you back into the city."

Max halted his progress. "Philip?"

"Yes?"

"I'm falling in love with her."

Philip looked at him carefully. "That's an exceptional responsibility. You'll want to handle it carefully."

Max felt his frustration mount. "This isn't a corporate take-over, damn it. This is my life we're talking about."

"Yes. It is. And I trust that when you see Sidney tonight, you'll bear in mind that it's her life as well. She's not fragile, by any stretch of the imagination, but she's not as strong as she appears, either. Carter Silas hurt her deeply."

"I know that. I'd like to cream the bastard for it."

"Perhaps you'll have the chance."

"Do you know something you aren't telling me?"

That brought a slight smile to the older man's face. "I know lots of things I don't tell you. That's why you keep me on your payroll."

His fingers tightened on the package. "You're up to something, aren't you?"

Philip hesitated, then nodded his head. "I am. And if all goes according to plan, you'll thank me for it later."

"What if it doesn't—go according to plan, I mean?"

"Then I expect I'll be looking for a new post." Philip pulled his pocket watch from his vest pocket and checked the time. "You're expected in town in under two hours. Should I call Mr. Lort and tell him you'll be late?"

Max scooped up the package. "Hell, no. Ray Lort can sit in my office and stew for all I care."

Swinging open the door, Philip waited until Max preceded him out of the room. "I'll call Lois and let her know you're on your way. I'm sure she'll find something to occupy Mr. Lort's attention."

"Thanks, Philip." He headed down the stairs. "You're way too good to me."

Philip waited until Max disappeared before he said quietly, "You have no idea."

"SIDNEY, stop squirming," Philip instructed her as he adjusted the necklace at her throat. "You'll make me drop it."

Sidney gave him an apologetic look. "Sorry. I'm sort of nervous." That, she thought, had to be the understatement of the decade. When Max had asked her to go with him to the engagement party Edward Fitzwater was hosting for Greg and Lauren, she'd almost panicked. Until now, they'd spent their time alone, or fitting into her world. She'd never tried to make the transition into his.

As it was, she was wearing a dress she'd borrowed from Natalie, and, if Philip could get the clasp to work, a necklace Max had borrowed from Tiffany's. She had on Kelly's shoes and Licia's perfume. Only her underwear was her own—Sidney drew the line at borrowing another woman's undergarments.

At Max's insistence, she'd finally agreed to dress at his apartment. There was no more space than she had at her office, and he'd be able to join her there after his meeting. He planned to take her to dinner before the party.

"I think I have it," Philip said. He straightened the necklace. "It looks wonderful."

"Max has great taste."

"Yes. Why are you nervous about tonight?"

"Why?" She turned to face him. "Are you kidding? You know why."

"Not really. It's just a party, dear. You attend them all the time."

"I *work* at them, I don't go to them. I serve people like Max champagne and hors d'oeuvres. I wear a uniform and blend into the atmosphere."

"Max wanted you with him tonight."

"Lord knows why. With everyone buzzing about the merger, he'd be better off with someone who could carry on a decent conversation about it."

Philip frowned. "You're underestimating yourself."

"Sorry. Old habit. All I'm saying is, I think Max could use someone who fully understands what's at stake."

"I'm relatively certain he never considered Edward Fitzwater as a suitable date."

"Very funny." She gave his shoulder an affectionate poke.

I just don't think Max has a firm grip on the reality of this situation. We haven't been out in public—not *his* public— together. As a couple."

"Perhaps he thought it was past time."

"He didn't think about it all. That's the trouble." She eased away from her uncle to pace the length of the living room. Clad in Natalie's sapphire blue full-length gown, which fitted her like a dream, she felt a sense of unreality. Vaguely, she'd recognized the designer tag on the dress, and knew that three months of her salary probably wouldn't begin to pay for it. Deceptively simple in front, it scooped low in the back, revealing a generous portion of her spine. The sleeves tapered to elegant points at her center fingers. When she'd tried it on earlier in the small apartment at her office, Kelly's praise had been fulsome. "That," she'd assured Sidney, "is a catch-a-man dress."

Looking at herself in the mirror now, Sidney searched her reflection. She barely recognized the person staring back at her. Finally, she met Philip's gaze in the mirror. "I'm not just nervous," she admitted. "I'm completely stressed out. I mean, what if I say the wrong thing to the wrong person and send Loden Enterprises into bankruptcy."

"You're being melodramatic."

"Or what if they get sued because I offend one of their competitors?"

Philip grinned at her. "Or what if you fall down the steps and embarrass Max?"

"Exactly."

"It's impossible to embarrass Max."

Sidney frowned. "This isn't funny."

"I know." The kindness in his voice made her turn to face him.

"Uncle Philip—is this…are you—"

"I'm not as nervous as you are, obviously."

She pursed her lips. "Are you okay with this?"

"With you and Max?"

"Yes."

He studied her for long seconds. "Sidney, would it surprise you to find out that you and Max were, er, my idea?"

"Excuse me?"

"It's true. I've been watching the two of you for years. Max needs you."

That made her frown. "Max isn't exactly what I'd define as the needy type."

"Isn't he? Do you know what it's like to be surrounded by people whose only interest in you is what you can do for them?"

She shook her head. "No, of course not. But that's not true about him. Natalie and Paul, even Colleen and Warren and Greg. They're his family."

"Honey, sit down." He indicated the sofa with a wave of his hand. "Let me tell you something about Max."

"I'm not sure I can sit down in this dress," she quipped.

He smiled indulgently. "It looks fabulous, I assure you."

"I feel like a fish out of water." She eased onto the couch.

"Because of the cost of the dress?"

"No. Because in—" she glanced at the wall clock "—less than two hours, I'll be standing next to Max surrounded by his business and social acquaintances trying to pretend like I belong there."

"You do," Philip insisted as he sat beside her. "Max's world isn't as far removed from yours as it seems."

"Are you kidding?"

"No. The two of you have more in common than you think. Like you, Max grew up detached from his parents. In your case, my sister failed you in a thousand ways, starting with the fact that she didn't know who your father was. You know how I feel about that."

She did. They'd discussed it often. Philip's disappointment with his sister's choices was acute. Sidney took his hand. "You saved my life. You know that."

He raised her hand to his lips to kiss her knuckles. "I think maybe you saved mine, too. Without you, I might have been as lonely as Max.''

Her heart swelled as she thought of the extraordinary changes her uncle had made for her. Despite her difficult relationship with her mother, Philip, who had been feeling his way as much as she, had ensured that she never felt unloved. Max, she was beginning to realize, hadn't been so lucky. ''You were very good to me,'' she said softly. ''I don't know what I would have done without you.''

''In case you ever doubted it, I'm not exactly sure what I would have done without you either.'' He paused. ''I suppose that's why I believe Max needs you. You saved me from an interminable loneliness. You can do the same thing for Max.''

Her eyes widened. ''All this time, I thought you were the one doing the saving.''

His warm laugh delighted her. ''Had you fooled, did I?''

''Completely.''

''Well, I just want to make sure that Max doesn't have you fooled, too. I've known Max all his life. He's an amazing man. He's an intense man. He's a remarkable man.''

''Yes.''

''But he's also a lonely man. He's never had the privilege of having someone love him for who he is rather than what he is or what he has. But you, even from the beginning, you connected with him like no one else.''

''He was very kind to me. I had a terrible crush on him.''

''I like to believe that you saw something in Max that reminded you of yourself. He spent his life knowing he couldn't meet the expectations his parents had placed on him. After they were killed, he bore all the responsibility for Greg, Colleen and Natalie.'' Philip studied her for long seconds. ''In some ways, Max is as dear to me as you are.''

''I know how much you care for him.''

''So I meddled,'' Philip admitted. ''The two of you were taking too long to suit me. I want grandchildren. And I don't want to wait much longer.''

Sidney's eyebrows lifted. "Don't you think you're getting a little ahead of yourself?"

He shrugged. "And," he continued, "I believe the two of you were positively made for each other. So whatever happens tonight, try to remember all the things you know about Max. Don't worry so much about what you think your differences are."

Sidney searched his expression. In the years she'd lived with him, she'd seen that expression register concern, irritation, love, joy, and, on occasion, even anger—but now, she couldn't decipher the odd intensity in his gaze. "Uncle Philip—do you *know* something about tonight that you aren't telling me?"

He smiled at her as he leaned forward to lightly kiss her cheek. "I know that you have nothing to be worried about, and that you and Max are going to have a wonderful time."

"Trying to make time with my date, Philip?" Max asked from the doorway. He winked at Sidney and continued, "Not that I blame you. She's the best looking dame I've seen in years."

Philip rose from the couch. "I see you made it on time. A minor miracle, to be sure."

Max strode into the room. He held a silver-wrapped package in one hand. His lips twitched as he considered Philip's irreverent comment. "Don't chastise. I was tied up with Ray Lort."

"I would never be so bold," Philip said. Sidney marveled that he kept his face straight. Any one who knew Philip and Max, or even the most basic elements of their long association, knew that razor-sharp repartee was the hallmark of their relationship. It masked a deep affection and respect.

Max chuckled. "I don't know who you think you're kidding, old man. You live to berate me."

Philip headed for the door. "It wouldn't be necessary if you didn't give me cause." He glanced back at Sidney. "I hope you'll remember what I said."

"I will," she assured him.

He nodded briefly, then looked at Max. "I'll go lay out your tux. Do you want the black vest or one of the prints?"

"Prints." He flashed Sidney his carefree smile. "I don't want to be outshone by my date."

As Philip left the room without further comment, Max crossed to Sidney. Offering her his free hand, he pulled her to her feet. He bent his head and kissed her warmly. "You're gorgeous," he said against her mouth. "I'll have to fight off men all evening."

She leaned into him. "Thank Natalie. It's her dress."

Max tipped her chin so he could see her eyes. "I'm not talking about the dress. It's you. You're devastating in just about anything. Or nothing."

She felt the tips of her ears reddening. "You'll go to my head if you're not careful."

"I'm very much counting on it." He eased her away slightly so he could hand her the package. "I brought you something."

Surprised, Sidney took the gift. "What is it?"

"Something I thought you should have."

"It's not a laptop computer, is it?"

With a slight laugh, he shook his head. "No way. I learned that lesson."

Carefully peeling away the shiny paper, she shook her head. "You didn't have to do this."

"Consider it a thank-you gift for that tray of chocolates you brought the board the other day. It made them far more amenable, and you wouldn't let me pay you for them."

The paper removed, she tossed it to the coffee table. Beneath the wrapping, she found a white gift box with no identifying markings. "How mysterious."

He tucked a stray tendril of her hair behind her ear. "I hope you like it."

The strange tenderness in his voice surprised her. She gave him a curious look, then opened the box. Nestled in a bed of padded velvet lay the expensive figurine he'd bought that night so long ago to replace the one she'd broken. Sidney felt the tears prick at her eyes. "Oh, Max. You remembered."

He reached inside the box to remove the figure. "I remember everything about you, Sidney."

She took the figure from him as she set the box aside. "Where did you find it?"

His lips twitched. "In my library at the estate."

"This is yours."

"It's ours," he said quietly. "I wanted to get you something that would tell you how much you mean to me. I thought about buying you something."

It was her turn to smile. "Some little trifle like a sky-scraper."

"You want one?"

"No."

"Then don't tempt me."

Laying her hand alongside his face, she caressed his cheek with her fingertips. "You're adorable."

He turned his head to kiss her palm. "I'm glad you think so. I'm rather fond of you, too." Nudging her closer by placing his hands at the small of her back, he bent his head to kiss the corner of her mouth. "I wanted you to have that because I don't think I ever told you what that night meant to me."

"To you?" She tilted her head to one side. "You were the one doing the bailing out."

"Do you remember what you said to me?" he asked quietly.

"I professed my undying appreciation?"

"Not that part." His eyes twinkled. "The other part."

Her expression turned serious. "You mean when you promised to take care of it, and I asked you who took care of you?"

"Yes." He nodded. "Sidney, no one ever asked me that before."

She heard the underlying tenderness in his voice. He looked suddenly vulnerable. Sidney found her fingers tightening on the porcelain figure. "Oh, Max."

"I don't think anyone was interested."

"I'm sure that's not true."

He shook his head. "It is. I was always taking care of everyone around me. I can't remember a time when someone worried about me. Not until you."

"Philip loves you, Max. So do Natalie and Greg and Colleen. I know they rely on you, but it doesn't mean they don't care about you."

"I'm not talking about that—not really." He frowned as he searched for words. "Sidney, other than the people who fear me, I can't say that I've ever had a priority for anyone. I just wanted you to know how much that means to me."

Her throat started to ache. "Max—"

He gave her a slight squeeze. "You don't have to say anything. I needed to do it."

Several seconds passed as she studied his fierce expression. Lord, how she loved this man. Her heart was ready to burst with it. "Thank you," she said quietly. She cradled the figure to her chest. "I will treasure it forever."

The twinkle was back in his eyes. "Sure you don't want that skyscraper?"

"Positive. It doesn't go with a thing I own."

"I could fix that, too."

She laughed. "What would I do with it?"

"Open your own chocolate factory. I could guarantee you a booming business. My board was quite impressed."

Sidney laughed. "No thanks. You've told me how cranky they are. There are two kinds of clients I avoid—irritable and irritating."

"That rules out just about everyone I know."

"Yes." She nodded. "So keep your skyscraper. I'm very happy with my treasure." She traced a finger along the curve of the figure. "Nothing could have pleased me more."

"I'm glad." After one more quick kiss, he released her. "I better get dressed."

"Wouldn't want to keep Philip waiting."

"Lord, no." He grinned at her. "No telling what he might do to me."

"He's so fearsome."

"He terrifies me, I'll tell you."

Sidney prodded him with a poke on the shoulder. "So go. I'm getting hungry. You promised me dinner tonight."

"Have you always been this demanding?"

"Since birth."

Max grinned at her. "I'll try to remember that."

Chapter Thirteen

Two hours later, he surveyed the large crowd in the ballroom and stifled a sigh. His heart wasn't in this tonight. His gaze flicked to Sidney. She stood near the buffet table talking to Natalie and Paul. What he wanted, he admitted, was the same thing he'd wanted since he'd seen her talking with Philip earlier that evening. He wanted to spirit her off someplace, somewhere he could give her his undivided attention for at least a week. Then, maybe, he'd be willing to share her. He was so deep in thought, he didn't even see his brother approaching him.

"Max," Greg said, "I see you're in your usual fine temper." Lauren was with him.

Max blinked. "What?"

With a slight laugh, Lauren laid her hand on his sleeve. "He's just teasing you."

"I am not," Greg argued. "Look at him. He's scowling like a bear."

Max dragged his gaze from Sidney. "I'm—preoccupied."

"Business isn't all there is to life, big brother. Why don't you give it a rest?"

"I wasn't thinking about business, actually." He took a long drink of his club soda.

Greg's eyebrows rose as he followed the direction of Max's gaze. "I see."

"I doubt it."

Lauren poked Greg in the ribs. "Stop goading him. I'm not in the mood to break up a fight."

Greg looked at her wide-eyed. "We aren't fighting."

Max's nod was short. "He's right. Until someone throws the first punch, it's not a fight."

"Good God." Greg stared at him, his mouth agape. "Was that a joke?"

"Only partially," he said wryly.

Lauren laughed. "I swear, you'd think the two of you were still arguing over bicycles and baseball mitts. I suppose I'll get used to it."

Max shrugged. "I suppose."

"In any case," she continued. "I wanted to thank you for recommending Sidney to me, Max. She's been a godsend. I don't think I could have planned this party without her."

Max's gaze slid to his brother. "She's very talented."

Greg met and held his gaze. "I'm sure she is."

Lauren seemed unaware of the tension. "You wouldn't believe the amount of detail involved. If it hadn't been for Sidney, I think I would have gone crazy."

"I know the feeling," Max drawled. He looked at Lauren again. "I'm glad to hear things are going so well. I'm looking forward to the wedding."

"I am, too." She gave Greg a wry look. "I think Greg is a little sick over it."

Greg's face paled. "Don't be silly."

"It's all right, darling." She kissed his cheek. "You'll get over it."

"I'm sure he will," Max said calmly. From the corner of his eye, he saw that a fair-haired man had approached Sidney. A strange feeling nagged him as he watched the exchange. "If you'll excuse me," he said, setting his glass down on the bar. "I'm going to dance with my date."

He picked his way through the crowd, irritated when acquaintances stopped him every few feet. He dispatched with the courtesies as quickly as possible, steadily progressing toward Sidney. A second man had joined her, this one older and, he noted, less pugnacious looking.

"I'm so glad to see you, Henri," Sidney was telling the older man when Max finally reached her. "It's been too long."

"Indeed it has," he nodded to her. "I've missed you."

Max slipped an arm around Sidney's waist, then glanced from one man to the other. The blonde had a malignant expression. Max scowled at him. "Hello, sweetheart," he said softly in her ear. "I was hoping I could get you to dance with me."

Sidney stiffened slightly. "Max. There you are. There's someone I'd like you to meet." She gave him a look over her shoulder that spoke volumes. She was tense, nervous and agitated. Max felt his back teeth clench. She indicated the older man with a wave of her hand. "Henri Dupeaux, this is Max Loden. Max, this is my friend, Henri."

The blonde snorted. Max hated men who snorted. The younger man said, a sneer in his voice, "Henri is responsible for the hors d'oeuvres."

Sidney's jaw visibly tightened. "Henri is the banquet manager here at the Waldorf."

Max extended his hand. "It's nice to meet you, Mr. Dupeaux. My future sister-in-law has been extremely pleased with all you've done for her."

Henri acknowledged the compliment with a regal nod of his head. "We pride ourselves on the quality of our service."

"Then why don't you shuffle off," the blonde said, "and refill my drink."

Sidney took a step forward. "Stop it, Carter."

Max scowled. Carter Silas—Sidney's ex-husband. He remembered seeing the bastard's picture when Sidney had been in the midst of her divorce battle. He'd looked thinner then, and less flushed. With his hairline receding and his waistline expanding, it was no wonder Max hadn't immediately recognized him. Max's hand fisted at his side, but he forced himself to smile at Sidney while he simultaneously tightened his arm around her waist. "Lauren was just telling me, Henri, how much she's appreciated your staff and your assistance." He glanced around the room. "I'm sure this was quite a challenge."

Henri beamed with pleasure. "Sidney did the hard part. I just followed her orders."

Sidney gave him a knowing look. "Sure, I did. I told Miss Fitzwater you'd take great care of her, and I helped negotiate the contract. Really worked up a sweat on that one."

Carter's laugh was distinctly unpleasant. "I would have liked to see that."

No one responded. Henri gave him an irritated look, then glanced at Max. "Actually, you wouldn't believe what she squeezed out of us."

"Six extra appetizers?" Carter said.

Max gritted his teeth. "I think it's time for you to leave, Silas."

Carter glared at him. "You can't give me orders."

"What the hell are you doing here, anyway?" Max asked.

Edward Fitzwater had joined the small group. He frowned at Max. "Is there a problem?"

"Edward," Max said quietly, "one of your guests is making a nuisance of himself."

Carter's too loud laugh drew stares. "Do you think we're all bugs, Loden? That you can just crush us at will?"

Max suppressed a grim smile. The image of grinding Carter Silas into the carpet held increasing appeal.

"That's enough, Silas," Edward barked. "You're out of control."

"What's he doing here?" Max asked.

"He works for me," Edward admitted.

Sidney glanced at Carter, wide-eyed. "You do?"

"Yes." His speech was beginning to sound slurred. "Been

working for Fitzwater since I left you. He pays me better than that bastard Williams ever did.''

Edward took Carter's arm. ''Silas, I think Max is right. It's time for you to leave.''

''You think he's right?'' Carter asked, his voice rising. ''You think he's right? Well, isn't that cozy. You have no idea what that SOB is about to do to you, do you Fitzwater?''

Edward's face turned red. ''What the hell are you talking about?''

''Since we heard about the merger, the boys in acquisitions and I have been doing some digging. You wanna know why Loden here was able to scoop up a tenth of your stock at rock-bottom prices? Do you still want to know?''

Max glared at him. ''I'm warning you, Silas.''

''You're *warning* me? Are you kidding? I'm not the one that spread those rumors to deliberately devalue Fitzwater stock.''

Edward stared at Max. ''What?''

''He's lying,'' Max said.

''Am I?'' Carter demanded. ''Why don't you tell Edward here about your inside knowledge of our research and development team?''

''Patents are public record,'' Max snapped.

Edward looked from Max to Carter, then back again. ''What's he talking about?''

''Insider trading, that's what I'm talking about.'' Carter sneered at Max. ''You think you're above the rest of us, don't you Loden? I know your type. You think you can make your own rules? I know exactly what you did during my divorce.''

Visibly startled, Sidney glanced at Max. ''Max?''

Carter snorted again. Max felt his blood pressure rising. ''I know exactly how you kept me from finding a job. And now you're trying to work me out of this one.'' He swayed slightly as his gaze shifted to Sidney. ''You know, Sidney,'' he sneered, ''I had no idea you were running in such lofty circles now. Loden Enterprises—that's quite a step up from Patsy's Pet Parlor.''

Sidney looked at Max a few seconds longer. "Would you please believe that he wasn't this much of an ass when I married him?"

Max looked at her with a raised eyebrow. "If you say so."

She nodded. "His ass-like qualities took a while to fully develop."

Carter's laugh was unpleasant. "You might think I'm an ass Sid—but I guarantee you I've got nothing on Loden here."

Sidney gave Carter a chilling look. "This isn't going to work, Carter. If you're hoping to make a scene, it's not going to happen."

"A scene." He tossed the remains of his drink down his throat. "I don't know what you're talking about."

Henri reached for Carter's glass. "I'll just take care of this," he said quietly. With a tilt of his head, he brought a waiter to his side.

"Yes, Mr. Dupeaux?" the young man asked.

Henri set Carter's glass on the waiter's tray. "Mr. Silas would like a cup of coffee." He glanced at Carter. "Strong and black." The young man hurried away.

Carter frowned. "You think I'm drunk. I'm not drunk." The denial was weakened by the way Carter swayed on his feet. "Tell him, Sidney. I don't get drunk."

Beside him, Edward was still watching Max through slitted eyes. "I want to know what the hell he's talking about, Loden."

"Oh for God's sake, Edward," Max snapped. "This is neither the time nor the place. He doesn't know what the hell he's saying."

Edward took a menacing step forward. Max refused to retreat. "If I find out," Edward sputtered, "that you deliberately tried to wrest Fitzwater Electronics from me—"

Lauren, Max noted, had joined them. She held out an imploring hand to her father. "Daddy, please."

"Stay out of this Lauren," Edward said.

Carter gave Max a smug look. "You want to tell me how it feels to know you've been caught in the act, Loden?"

Without taking his eyes off Carter, Max carefully guided Sidney to his side. "I think it's time for you to go home, Silas. Why don't you let Henri call you a cab?"

Carter shook his head. "I'm not ready to go home. I want to dance with my wife." He grabbed Sidney's arm. "Come on, Baby. Once more for old time's sake."

Max clamped his fingers on Carter's wrist. "Let her go."

"Carter, please don't," Sidney said softly.

"Let her go," Max said again as he struggled to control his temper.

"Why?" Carter asked belligerently.

"Because you won't like what's going to happen if you don't."

Carter glared at Sidney. "What are you trying to prove here, Sid? You think you fit in with these people? You think they don't know who you are? They know, Sidney. Hell, you've worked for half of them. The only hope you ever had of belonging here was staying married to me."

Sidney wrenched her arm away from him. "I hope you haven't fooled yourself into believing that."

His expression turned ugly as he indicated Max with a nod of his head. "You don't actually think that Loden here wants you for anything other than free party planning and a roll in the hay do you?"

"That's it." Max's temper went straight to the moon. He reached into his pocket and produced his wallet, then handed Henri a platinum credit card. "That should cover the damages, Dupeaux," he said.

Sidney gave him a look of alarm. "What damages?"

Henri cleared his throat and gave Sidney's shoulder a

nudge. "You'd better step back, my dear. This could turn ugly."

"Max—" Sidney laid her hand on his sleeve. "Don't do this."

Seemingly oblivious to the murderous look in Max's eyes, Carter was still swaying on his feet. "Where the hell's my drink?" he demanded.

"You won't be needing it," Max told him the instant before his fist slammed into Carter's jaw. Carter went sprawling into the buffet table.

"Oh, Lord." Sidney buried her face in her hands.

"What's going on?" Greg Loden demanded as he skidded to a stop next to Sidney. A tray sailed to the floor, sending petits fours and tiny pastries scattering across the pristine carpet.

Max ignored the mess as he took an angry step forward and reached for Carter. "I'm going to beat the hell out of him." He jerked him up by the lapels of his tuxedo.

"Max—" Sidney held out an imploring hand.

Max wasn't in a reasonable kind of mood. He buried his fist in Carter's face.

"Damn," Greg said, reaching for Sidney. "Get behind me."

"No! Good Lord, Greg, do something."

"Who the hell is that?"

"My ex-husband."

Max gave Greg a meaningful look. "The bastard."

Greg nodded, then wrapped his arm around Sidney's shoulders. "Why don't you come with me, Sidney? Lauren's been looking for you."

"I'm not leaving. Cripes, Max is going to kill him."

And that, Max decided was a real possibility. He sent Carter flying again. This time, he knocked the ice sculpture to the ground. By now, they'd drawn a crowd. Most of the guests in the ballroom were watching. Sidney looked horrified. Greg looked mildly amused, and Paul Wells, who'd managed to shoulder his way to the front of the crowd looked like he was ready to die laughing. Irritated, Max hauled Carter to his feet and thrust him in front of Sidney. "Apologize to the lady."

Carter swung his head to look at him. His nose dripped blood, his bleary eyes seemed to have trouble focusing. "Lady?" he asked. "Who are you talking about?"

Max hit him again. Carter stumbled, then dropped to the floor at Sidney's feet. Greg dutifully eased her back a few steps. Lauren, who'd come up beside Sidney, slid her arm around Sidney's waist. "It'll be all right, Sidney," she said.

"All right?" Sidney looked at her, incredulous. "Are you crazy?" Carter staggered to his feet. For his part, Max was feeling almost murderous. Sidney gave him a pleading look. "Please stop. Max, please stop. I want to go home."

It irritated him, somehow, that she seemed to be pleading for Carter Silas. And that flash of irritation dimmed his concentration enough to allow Silas to land one well-aimed punch on Max's chin. Max growled and hit him in the stomach, sending him to his knees. He wiped a hand across his mouth where a trickle of blood stained the corner. He searched Sidney's gaze. "I want him to apologize."

On the floor, Carter groaned. Henri cleared his throat. "Why don't I call security?"

Sidney put out a restraining hand. "No, please. We'll leave."

"We will not," Max said firmly. Carter groaned again. Max reached for him.

Edward took a step forward and blocked his path. "Stop it, Loden. You're acting like a barbarian."

"Or a five-year-old," Sidney snapped. "This has gone far enough."

Max put his foot in the center of Carter's chest. "Apologize," he bit out, "to the lady."

Carter coughed. He glared at Max a second longer, then looked at Sidney. "Sorry," he muttered.

Max tightened the pressure of his foot. "Louder."

"I'm sorry," Carter shouted.

"Fine." With a slight nudge, Max sent Carter sprawling to his stomach. "Now, we'll leave."

"Ow." MAX FROWNED at her as she used a cotton ball to furiously pound antiseptic on the back of his skinned knuckles. They were back at his penthouse—and Sidney hadn't spoken to him since they'd left the ballroom.

"Stop acting like a baby," she snapped.

"You're not exactly the Angel of Mercy, you know?"

"Well, I'm a little irritated. Excuse me." She glared at him. The man made her absolutely nuts. She couldn't believe he'd created that scene at the hotel, and, to make things worse, he'd actually had the audacity to tell her on the way back to his penthouse that he'd enjoyed himself. She slapped a bandage on his knuckles. "At least the bleeding has stopped."

Max flexed his fingers. "I'd like to hit him again."

"I think you did enough damage for one night."

"I'm sure Henri will enjoy charging my credit card."

She smacked his shoulder for that. "Not that kind of damage. Cripes, Max. Do you have any idea how that looked? You ruined Lauren's party."

"It'll give her and Greg something to remember for the rest of their lives."

"Oh, sure. They can remember how you picked a playground fight with a stupid drunk."

"He is stupid." Max scowled. "He's even more stupid than I gave him credit for. I can't believe Edward hired him."

"Neither can I."

Sidney finished taping his knuckles. "It's strange, you know. Carter was a pretty good broker—or at least I thought he was. He made a decent salary."

"He stole most of it from his firm."

"No, that money went somewhere else. I saw his actual

paychecks. He did pretty well on commissions, but after those embezzlement accusations, I can't believe he was able to get a job in this city.''

''It makes me wonder what he offered Edward in exchange.''

''What do you mean?''

Max shrugged. ''Just a hunch. I'll check it out later.'' He shook his head. ''Lord, Sidney,'' he placed his hands on her waist as she turned her attention to his split lip, ''What made you marry such a creep?''

Sidney absorbed the comment with a slight intake of breath. With the accuracy and power of a smart bomb, the words sliced all the way to the bone. How could she tell him she had no answer to that? How could she tell him that she'd lain awake for long, chilling nights after her divorce and berated herself with the same question? How could she admit that at least half the damage she'd suffered in the wake of her divorce had been the self-inflicted doubts in her own abilities and intelligence? How could she possibly say that beneath her irritation lay a deep, gnawing fear that at least part of what Carter Silas said was right?

She'd spent four years fighting those internal battles. And tonight, with a few well-aimed comments, Carter had brought them all back to haunt her. Carter's faultfinding she could take, but not Max's.

Deliberately, she concentrated on applying salve to the slight cut on his lip, forcing herself to breathe normally. A knot had formed in her throat, and she was having trouble choking it down. Max must have felt her tense. His eyebrows drew together in a slight frown. ''Sidney? Honey, what's going on here?''

She shook her head, unable to answer him, and dabbed more furiously at the cut. Max captured her hands in his and lowered them. ''Talk to me. This is about more than the fight, isn't it?''

She swallowed. The knot grew bigger. "Don't be ridiculous."

Max shook his head. "It is. Something's wrong."

"I can't believe you did that, that's all. It was stupid and immature."

"The fact that I beat him up just made you mad. But I want to know what put that wounded look in your eyes all of a sudden. What did I say?"

She hesitated for long seconds. When she finally found her voice, it sounded rusty. "I didn't know he was like that when I married him."

"Oh, honey." Max fell back on the bed, taking her with him. His feet still touched the floor. He spread his knees so her legs drifted between his, bringing her pelvis into tantalizing contact with his body. His lips nuzzled her hair. "Sweetheart, I wasn't criticizing you. I'd never criticize you. It wasn't your fault."

"I know."

"I'm not sure you do." He waited. "Please look at me."

Sidney raised her head. "I know it wasn't my fault, but sometimes it's hard not to feel like a fool."

He shook his head slightly. "I'm sorry. I'm so sorry."

To her horror, she felt the sting of tears. She'd promised herself, years ago, that she'd never cry over Carter Silas again. Before she could stop it, one salty drop slid free and plopped on Max's shirtfront. Then another, and another. She squeezed her eyes tight. "I just wanted someone to love me."

"Shh." He cradled her to him. "Honey, don't. Please don't. He's not worth it."

"I know." Furiously, she swiped at her eyes.

Max cradled her to him. "I wish I'd killed the bastard."

Sidney sniffed. "At the time—" she sucked in a calming breath "—at the time I married him, it seemed like a way to quit being uncle Philip's obligation."

"He never thought of you like that. He loves you."

"I know he does, but I couldn't make myself believe that

uncle Philip didn't get stuck with me when my mother—''
Her voice trailed off. The words were too painful.

Max hugged her closer. ''I never meant to hurt you. Please
believe me.''

''I do.'' She wiped her eyes with the back of her hand.
''He's such a jerk. I never wanted to cry over him again.''

Max swept her hair from her face, then gently rolled her
to her back. Bracing himself on his forearms so his weight
didn't bear down on her, he trailed his fingertips along her
cheek. ''Hush. We don't have to talk about it anymore. I'm
sorry I made that stupid remark and you have my permission
to slap me if I ever say anything like that again.''

She laid her hand against his jaw. ''I'm sorry I overre-
acted.''

''To the fight, maybe,'' he quipped, ''but not to that comment. I didn't mean it, and I shouldn't have said it.''

''You shouldn't have hit him, either.''

''It felt good.''

He looked so absurdly pleased with himself that she felt a
slight smile tug at the corner of her mouth. ''You don't have
to look so smug, you know?''

''Can't help it.'' He pressed a kiss on the corner of her
mouth. ''I had the best looking woman there, and she even
agreed to come home with me.''

''Barely.''

His chuckle fanned across her cheek. ''Oh, come on. You
liked it.''

She gasped when his tongue darted into her ear. ''I did not
like it.''

''You did, too.'' He gently bit her earlobe.

''You made a fool out of yourself.''

''Yeah, but I made a fool out of myself for you.''

Sidney's eyes drifted shut from the pleasure of having his
mouth nuzzle her collarbone. ''Oh, Mad Max. Did anyone
ever tell you that you're crazy?''

''All the time.''

She tugged at his head until he lifted it to meet her gaze. "I love that about you," she said quietly.

The teasing glint left his eyes. "Sidney—"

She smiled at him. "I just wanted you to know that."

His expression turned profoundly gentle. "How did I wait so long for you?"

"I honestly don't know," she quipped.

He kissed her, thoroughly, then looked at her once more. "I want to make love to you."

Her fingers traced the curve of his upper lip. "I want you to."

When he shook his head slightly, a lock of his dark hair fell across his forehead, making him look irresistibly boyish. "I want to make love to you—like this," he said softly, as he slowly lowered himself over her.

As his weight came down on her, Sidney sucked in a surprised breath. "Max—"

He waited. When she said nothing, he ran his finger along the curve of her ear. "Honey, please. Please trust me."

She searched his expression. There was nothing but tenderness, and, dare she hope, love in the depths of his gaze. "I do."

He shifted, so slowly, so gently, she could have stopped him at any time. "Are you sure?"

She waited several seconds while she absorbed the feeling of his warm, strong body on hers. To her very great pleasure and surprise, she felt neither stifled nor trapped. He felt solid and safe. The passion thrumming through her blood heightened as she surrendered to the intoxicating sensation. She nodded. "I'm sure."

Something flared in his gaze. "Sidney," he said, his voice sounding harsh. He covered her mouth with his own. When he finally raised his head, they were both panting. "I need you so much."

"I love you, Max."

A LONG TIME later, the words still drummed through his head and down his spine. He'd lingered over her, showing her in every way he knew how that he cherished her. Her trust had nearly ripped his heart out. He had felt himself drowning in her softness. Like those chocolates she made, she was simultaneously sweet and rich and, oh, so very, very tempting. She went straight to his head and his heart and wove a spell around him that left him dazed.

And her love sent him to his knees.

Not in a thousand years would he have imagined himself worthy of that kind of gift. His fingers traced an absent pattern on her bare shoulder as he struggled with a strange sense of panic.

What the hell would he do if he ever lost her? She had, he realized, become essential. Like oxygen. Long ago, he'd sworn not to let anyone get that close. He needed his wits about him—sometimes, taking care of people meant making unpopular decisions. He hadn't even had time to resent the mantle life had thrust upon him. There had been too much to do, too much riding on each and every choice.

In the days after his parents had died, the lives of his siblings had rested squarely on his shoulders. He'd been unable to save his father from self-destruction, but through sheer force of will, he had, so far, managed to keep his brother and sisters from walking down the same path. They hadn't always liked him for it. He knew that, but he had never allowed it to matter.

Until now.

Beside him, Sidney slept quietly, her breath fanning across his chest. His fingers threaded through her hair as he sent up a silent prayer for guidance. He couldn't lose her. He'd die if he did.

"Max?" Sidney's sleepy voice pierced his lassitude.

"I thought you were sleeping."

"Almost." She brushed her hand over his chest. "What about Edward Fitzwater?"

Max frowned. "What about him?"

"What Carter said—"

"It's not true."

"I know that." She tweaked his skin. "But Edward seemed angry. What's going to happen?"

"Nothing's going to happen. Edward's a hothead. It's no wonder he got his company in trouble."

"I hope this doesn't cause problems for Lauren and Greg."

He yawned. "It won't."

"Are you sure?"

"Yes." He gathered her closer. "Now, go to sleep."

Sidney exhaled a long breath. "I hope you're right."

"I am. Once Edward has a chance to calm down, it'll blow over. I promise."

She snuggled her head against his chest. "If you say so."

"I do."

Long seconds passed. "Max?"

He managed to open one eye. "Sweetheart, I'm exhausted. You wore me out."

"I just wanted you to know that I, uh, liked it."

He was suddenly wide awake. And smiling. "You liked it? I thought you were mad that I started the fight with Silas."

"Not the fight," she said, exasperation clear in her voice, "the other thing."

"What other thing?" he teased.

She thumped him with her index finger. "I liked having you on top," she said.

Max nudged her chin up so he could grin at her. "I liked it, too."

She gave him a beatific smile that made his heartbeat double. He had no idea what he'd done to deserve her, but he'd go to his grave believing that the happiness she brought him was the rarest of gifts. He was considering how to tell her that when Sidney began toying with the hair at his nape, distracting him from loftier thoughts. "Do you, um, think maybe you might like to try it again?"

His eyebrows lifted. He'd tumbled into Nirvana, he decided. "Right now?"

"If you're not too tired."

With a joyful laugh, Max pulled her on top of him so he could kiss her. When he lifted his head, he said, "I don't know. What's in this for me?"

Her lips twitched. "Paradise and a tray of handmade chocolates?"

In a seamless move, he rolled her beneath him. "Deal."

Chapter Fourteen

The persistent pounding awakened him. Max cracked his eyelids and squinted at the bedside clock. Six-fifteen. This better be good. He carefully disengaged himself from Sidney's sleeping form and eased out of the king-size bed. Who the hell, he wondered, would beat on his door at this ungodly hour of the morning?

He pulled on a gray silk robe and headed down the hall. For that matter, where was Philip? He hadn't been here when they'd returned last night—for which Max had been eminently thankful, but the place still looked deserted. Odd, that. Philip and Gertie were generally moving around by now.

Max wiped a hand through his hair and jerked open the door. Greg, looking belligerent and disheveled, glared at him. He wore jeans and a T-shirt, and the stubble on his face suggested he'd just rolled out of bed. Lauren, who stood just behind him, and looked only slightly more composed, gave Max an apologetic look. Greg shouldered his way past Max and grumbled. "It's about time."

"What the hell are you doing here?" He glanced at Lauren, who still stood in the hall. "You might as well come in too, Lauren."

With a slight nod, she eased past him. "I'm sorry, Max. He was determined."

Max pushed the door shut before he turned to face his brother. "What's the matter with you?"

Greg thrust a newspaper in his direction. "*This.* Have you seen the papers yet?"

"I haven't been up yet." He strolled across the living room to take the newspaper. "What's going on?"

"You went too far this time, that's what's going on."

Lifting his eyebrows, Max flipped open the paper. The front page of the City section featured a picture of him slugging Carter Silas. It felt just as good this morning, he realized. Max didn't recall anyone taking pictures, but there were always society reporters present at events like that. It didn't particularly surprise him that the episode had made the paper. "They didn't catch my best side, did they," he quipped.

"You bastard," Greg said, his face a mask of rage. "You think this is funny, don't you?"

"Greg—" Lauren held out an imploring hand. "Please calm down."

"Calm down?" Greg began to pace. "How can you say that? For God's sake, don't you see what he's done?"

Without comment, Max scanned the article. It gave a fairly accurate description of the fight. He scowled at the mention of Sidney as his butler's niece. It also gave Carter more credit than he deserved for holding his own during the brawl. The twist the reporter had put on the piece suggested that Max's anger was rooted in Carter's accusations about his takeover of Fitzwater Electronics, rather than in the weasel's comments about Sidney. Still, it certainly wasn't the most damaging piece he'd ever seen, and definitely not the worst thing that had ever been said about him in a newspaper. He glanced at Greg. "You want to tell me why this has you so angry?"

"Why?" Greg's eyes blazed. "Because this time you went too damned far." He waved a hand at Lauren. "Just who the hell do you think you are, Max? God? I don't give a damn what you've done for this family, it doesn't give you the right to arbitrarily dictate the course of our lives."

Max glanced at Lauren. "You want to enlighten me here?"

She sat down. "Daddy thinks there's some truth to what Carter Silas said last night."

His eyes narrowed. "Do you?"

Lauren opened her mouth to respond, but another knock sounded at the door. With a low curse, Max strode to open it. Natalie and Paul rushed in. Unlike Greg, they looked like they'd taken the time to shower and dress before disturbing him at this ungodly hour of the morning. "We just saw the paper," Natalie said as she gave Max a quick hug. "It was on the news this morning, too."

"Great." Greg dropped into a chair.

Paul gave Max a shrewd look. "Edward is on the war-path."

For Lauren's sake, Max didn't voice his opinion about Edward Fitzwater. Instead, he motioned for Natalie and Paul to sit down. Natalie sat next to Lauren and took her hand, while Paul dropped into a wing chair. "All right," Max said. "Everyone take a deep breath." He dropped the newspaper onto the coffee table and began pacing. He wished he knew where the hell Philip was. Philip always knew how to defuse these things.

Greg continued to watch him with a surly expression. "I came here for an explanation, Max. I want it now."

"An explanation for what?" Max snapped. "You want to know why I beat the hell out of Carter Silas last night? Do you?"

Natalie glanced at Greg. "It had nothing to do with what he said about the Fitzwater merger, Greg. You know that."

"Do I? From what Edward told me this morning, he's had Silas and a couple of others working nonstop on this for the past few months."

Max gritted his teeth. "For your information, not that I feel like I owe you an explanation, I don't give a rat's ass what Edward thinks. Carter Silas is a sleazy, self-impressed drunk who doesn't deserve to breathe the same air as the rest of us.

He insulted Sidney one too many times last night, and I finally did what I've wanted to do since the day she married the little bastard.'' He gave Greg a hard look. "And if Edward Fitzwater believes that the word of Silas Carter is worth more than a passing thought, then he's seriously deluded.''

"You can't deny—'' Greg's angry retort was interrupted by another demanding knock.

"Oh, hell,'' Max muttered. He crossed the room in three angry strides and jerked open the door. Colleen and Warren stood outside. Absently he noted that they looked tanned, rested and together. Which was more than he could say for the rest of his family. "Glad you could make it,'' he drawled.

Colleen looked at him for several seconds, then entered the room. "We just heard,'' she announced to no one in particular. "We got back late yesterday. Sorry we missed the party, Lauren.''

Lauren nodded. "That's all right.''

"Sit down,'' Max ordered. Colleen hurried to obey. She joined Natalie and Lauren on the couch. Warren sat across from Greg. Max waited until they watched him expectantly. "I was just explaining,'' he said for Colleen and Warren's benefit, "that no matter what Greg may think, last night's spectacle didn't have anything to do with Edward Fitzwater, his company or the merger.''

Greg leapt to his feet. "Cut the crap,'' he charged. "I knew months ago there had to be a reason you were pushing so hard for my engagement to Lauren.''

"I never made any secret about the merger with Fitzwater.''

Greg glared at him. "You led us to believe—you led Edward to believe—that you were merging with his company because he was in financial trouble. It was a way for him to save face.''

"Oh, good God,'' Max said, beginning to pace. "Don't be naive. I don't toss millions of dollars around on a whim.'' He glanced at Lauren. She was stoically staring at the Monet hanging above his mantel. "Not to mention," he continued, "that I pushed for your engagement to Lauren because I think she's good for you."

Lauren flashed him a wan smile. "Thanks, Max."

He nodded. "I wanted Fitzwater Electronics. I'm not going to deny it."

Greg clenched his fists. "And you were willing to do just about anything to get it, weren't you? Sorry. I've known you too long to believe you did this for any reason other than to expand Loden Enterprises. That damned company always mattered more than us."

Natalie gasped. "Greg!"

"It's true, Natalie. Ask him."

Max shook his head. "I'm not going to answer that."

Colleen brushed her hair back from her face. "Sit down, Greg. Listen to what Max has to say."

"Since when are you on his side all of a sudden?"

"Since I was older than you when Mother and Father died, and I know a little more about what Max had to go through."

Greg glared at her. "Oh, I'm sure it was just hell on earth taking over control of everyone's life like he did."

"Sit down," Colleen said firmly. "You don't know what you're talking about."

He visibly wavered for several long seconds, then dropped into a leather armchair. "Where the hell have you been, anyway? Off finding some other poor slob's business for Max to pirate?"

Warren shifted on the sofa and frowned at him. "Don't talk to her like that."

Greg lapsed into a sulking silence. Max drew a calming breath as he searched for his patience. Lord, he hoped Sidney continued to sleep through this. The thought of her seeing one of these squabbles made him feel queasy. "Paul," he said firmly, "since Greg's clearly not in the mood to listen to me, why don't you explain to him what's been happening with Fitzwater."

Paul nodded. "It's like Max said, Greg. We started looking at Fitzwater before you even started seeing Lauren. Edward is sitting on a couple of patents we need to make some of our new technology work. He wouldn't sell them, so we went after the company." He glanced at Lauren. "Your father still thinks he can do business like he did twenty years ago. His company's financial standing was vulnerable."

"And like a vulture," Greg accused, "Max swooped in and took it."

Max struggled to hold his temper. "If it hadn't been Loden, it would have been someone else."

"But you wanted to make sure," Greg went on. "You wanted to make absolutely sure, so you manipulated me and Lauren, and maneuvered Edward under your thumb."

Lauren looked stricken. "Greg, really."

"Don't be an ass," Max snapped. "I'm not going to lie to you and tell you that your relationship with Lauren didn't make things easier. It did. Edward was more—amenable. Because you and Lauren were engaged, he felt like he was making an alliance." He shrugged. "If that saved his pride, then it did. I don't see the harm in that."

Greg was on his feet again. He stalked toward Max. "The harm, you bastard, is that Edward now knows you deliberately spread rumors on Wall Street to devalue his stock. According to Silas, you pulled strings to make sure everyone believed his patents weren't worth a plug nickel. His stock value kept falling, and you kept buying it. You manipulated me and Lauren into getting engaged so that Edward would feel comfortable with you. And now you're about to execute the rest of this little scheme by taking Fitzwater's patents and padding your own pockets. Do I have it about right, or did I miss anything?"

Max faced him squarely. "That doesn't even warrant an answer," he said.

Greg's face contorted with rage. "Well, by God, you're going to give me one."

Paul Wells rose to his feet. "Greg, if you or Edward would take Silas's word over Max's and mine, then you're fools. Carter Silas couldn't even get a job in this town until Edward hired him."

Lauren looked at Paul. "Why not?"

"Because," Paul explained, "during his divorce from Sidney, Max gathered evidence that Silas had embezzled a significant amount of money from his last brokerage firm."

Natalie gasped. "I didn't know that."

Max shook his head. "No one did. I had investigators digging up whatever they could on Silas. That came out in the wash."

"Then why," Lauren said softly, "did my father hire him?"

Max opened his mouth to respond, but the pounding began on his door again. "What now?" he growled.

Paul headed for the door. "I'll get it."

Edward Fitzwater, red-faced and visibly enraged charged into the room. He still wore his tuxedo from the night before. Bloodshot eyes and a day-old beard bore testimony to a sleepless night. "You son of a bitch, Loden." He waved a sheaf of papers at him. "Do you know what this is? Do you?"

"I assume it's Carter Silas's supposedly damaging report."

"You're damned right it is. I'm going to skin you alive for this. I knew you were up to something. There was no way our stock dropped thirty points in two years without your interference."

"Your stock dropped," Max said through clenched teeth, "because of mismanagement and bad investments."

Edward's face turned redder. "Like hell. You knew what those patents were worth. We were weeks from selling them when the rumors began to spread that they weren't worth anything."

"The ones you're talking about aren't worth anything, Edward. I had them independently tested."

Edward visibly sputtered. "You what?"

Paul nodded. "It's true. We were initially interested in your matrix display. Max hired an independent lab to run a few tests. It's worthless."

"That's not true!"

"It is," Max snapped. "And your own people knew it. If you want to know who leaked the information to the public, then look no further than your personnel roster."

"I don't believe it," Edward growled. "You wanted my company, and you were willing to do whatever it took to get it. But don't think you're going to get away with this. My lawyers have already contacted the Federal Trade Commission. You can expect a full inquiry by the beginning of the week."

Colleen groaned and covered her face. Lauren had started to cry softly. "Daddy, please, stop this."

"Shut up, Lauren," he snarled.

Greg took an angry step toward him. "Don't talk to her like that."

Edward turned his angry gaze on Greg. "You're probably in on this, aren't you?"

"Fitzwater," Paul said carefully, "you don't know what you're saying."

Edward faced Max again. "I do. And if I can, I'll see you in jail for this, Loden."

Max gave him a hard look. "You're out of control."

"I'm out of control?" he demanded incredulously. He dropped the sheaf of papers on the table. "Who are you trying to fool? You're the one who's convinced yourself that you're invincible. Well, you crossed the line this time, and I'm going to take you down."

Paul tried again. "Edward, sit down so we can discuss this. Max and I can document everything we've been telling you."

"Oh, I'm sure you can." His laugh was ugly. "I'm not fool enough to believe you wouldn't have properly covered your ass. But there's one thing you didn't count on. I had Silas."

"Silas," Max said bitingly, "is an incompetent fool."

"Silas," Edward shot back, "had the inside knowledge of you and your company that I needed. Let's not forget that he was married to that tramp you're sleeping with."

A collective gasp filled the air. Lauren held out a hand toward her father. "Daddy, please."

Max's temper snapped. The same rage he'd felt last night was now pouring through him. "Get out of my house, Fitzwater. The sight of you is making me sick."

"By the time I'm finished with you, you'll be begging me for mercy."

Through clenched teeth, Max repeated, "Get out."

Edward indicated the file on the table. "Silas gave me everything I needed to prove just what you were up to. It seems your butler's niece was good enough to fill him in on exactly how, where, and with whom, you like to conduct your shady little business deals. Using that knowledge, Silas gathered enough evidence about you to lock you up for twenty years. Face it, Loden. The day you started thinking with your crotch instead of your head was the day you handed that trollop and her ex-husband everything they needed to screw you." He smirked. "I hope the roll in the hay was worth it, because I'm going to make you pay for this for the rest of your life."

"Get out," Max roared, his temper now shredded beyond repair.

Edward scooped up the folder. "I'm leaving all right." He looked at Lauren. "And you're coming with me?"

Lauren looked from Greg to her father, then back again. "No, I'm not. I'm staying with Greg."

"Lauren," Edward took a step forward.

Max stopped him with an iron-hard grip on his collarbone. "The door is that way, Fitzwater. Use it now."

"This isn't over, you know," Edward blustered.

"I'm counting on it." Max ushered him toward the door. Paul pulled it open, and Max thrust the older man through it.

"Take me on if you dare, but you'll regret it. Don't make the mistake of thinking otherwise."

Paul slammed the door in Edward's face. Max stared at it for several seconds, struggling to regain control of his temper.

"I have something to say." The soft sound of Sidney's voice struck him like a blow to the head. Max felt his heart stop beating.

With panic racing through him, he turned to face her. "Sidney—"

She shook her head slightly. Wearing a pair of dark pants and one of his shirts, she looked almost regal as she confronted them. The blue gown she'd worn last night hung over her arm. "I'm sorrier than I can say that this has happened," she said quietly. She looked at Lauren. "I'm especially sorry your party got ruined last night."

Lauren wiped a tear from her eye. "It's all right."

"It's not," Sidney said. "It never should have happened. And if it hadn't been for me, it wouldn't have happened."

Natalie rose to her feet. "Sidney, that's not true."

"Yes, it is." She indicated the blue dress. "I can borrow your clothes, Natalie, but not your life. That's the thing, I guess. I spent most of my marriage trying to be someone I wasn't. Carter wanted me to be a trophy wife. But I can't do that, and I don't want to. I like my life the way it is, and I don't want to trade it for yours. I—I've known most of you for years. My uncle Philip cares about you very much. It's true, I guess, what Mr. Fitzwater said about Carter's knowledge of Max. It was heightened because of his marriage to me."

Max felt like his temperature was dropping to subzero levels. He had to say something, do something, but he could only stare at her. Sidney flashed him a sad smile. "I guess I was always a little more fascinated with you than I should have been." She drew a shaky breath. "Anyway, there is one thing I think you all should know. No matter what Carter may have told Mr. Fitzwater, and no matter what evidence he has to the contrary, I can assure you that Max's interest in Fitzwater Electronics didn't begin until after the stock started to tumble. Uncle Philip and I had a long talk about it one day.''

Sidney briefly closed her eyes. "Funny thing about butlers. People think they're invisible, but the truth is, they generally know just about everything that's going on. Uncle Philip has always made a practice of listening to Max conduct business—particularly investment business. What better way to build a retirement portfolio than to take stock tips from the best?''

"It's true," Natalie said. "Philip and I discussed it once. He's always invested in whatever Max thought was sound.''

Sidney nodded. "Yes. At last count, I think my uncle's portfolio was worth around one and a half million dollars.''

Max stared at her. He could feel her slipping away. She glanced at Max again and he almost fell to his knees. "He gives very good advice," she said. "Anyway, the point of this is that Philip and I often discussed Max's business affairs. And in this case, I know for a fact that the day Fitzwater stock began to fall was the day Paul and Max had their first meeting about the potential takeover.''

"It's true," Paul said. He looked at Greg. "I can show you the meeting notes.''

Greg muttered something under his breath. Sidney looked at Lauren again. "I know Max pushed really hard for you and Greg to get engaged, Lauren, but I also hope you'll believe me when I tell you it's because he wanted you as his sister-in-law. He confided in me the weekend of the house party that the merger was as good as complete whether you and Greg married or not.''

Lauren looked at Max. "You didn't tell us.''

He shrugged. "It didn't seem important.''

Greg glared at him. "Like hell.''

Sidney kept her gaze on Max. "So, that's what I know.

That, and the fact that nothing Carter Silas says is very trust-worthy.''

Greg swore. "You obviously thought he was trustworthy enough to marry."

Max took a step forward. "Damn it, Greg."

Sidney shook her head. "It's all right. Really," she assured him, then looked at Greg. "Yes, I did. It was a colossal mistake that had colossal consequences." This time, the look she gave Max showed a world of hurt. "I had no idea you were so intimately aware of all those consequences."

"Sidney—" His voice sounded hoarse.

"I should have known, I guess," she continued. "It made sense. I just didn't want to admit that not only had I gotten myself into that mess, but that someone else had to bail me out of it." She searched Max's expression. "I was just one more detail for you to take care of, wasn't I? One more mess you had to clean up ."

"No."

She looked at the group again. "In case any of you failed to realize it, your brother is an amazing man. He's devoted his whole life to trying to take care of you. And most of the time, he gets condemned for it. Maybe he didn't always go about it the right way, and maybe it was hard to understand him sometimes, but he never would have done anything to hurt you." Her gaze turned back to Greg. "No matter what you think."

Max felt a shudder rip through his insides. "Sidney, please."

She didn't look at him. "For what it's worth, I'm sorry," she said. "I'm sorry about what happened last night. I'm sorry about the trouble Carter has caused. I never meant to hurt any of you. Especially not Max." She glanced at him. "I'm so sorry."

"Sidney," Natalie started toward her, "none of this is your fault."

"Yes, it is. I should have known that I was just visiting

here. If I'd done what uncle Philip asked me to the weekend of the house party, and simply paid attention to Greg and Lauren, maybe I could have smoothed the way before this happened. I'm sure if uncle Philip had been there, he never would have allowed the confrontation to take place on Saturday night. Greg," she looked at him, "you've been angry with Max ever since. You told me you were. You told me you felt manipulated the night you argued with Lauren—before you knew about Fitzwater."

Lauren gasped. "Greg—"

"It's not what you think, Lauren," Greg said. He gave Max a resentful look. "I just didn't like having my arm twisted."

"I'm sure," Sidney continued, "that uncle Philip could have handled it better than I did. I was too busy being distracted by Max, wishing for things I couldn't have, to take seriously the job I was supposed to do. I was supposed to be there to help, and instead, I made the situation worse." She sighed. "You'll never know how sorry I am for all of this." Her voice had dropped to a thready whisper.

Max couldn't stand it any longer. He crossed the room to her. "Sidney, listen to me—"

"Not now," she whispered. "I need to go home. You need to talk. All of you." She looked around once more. "And please take my advice. Don't leave here until you've worked this out. I learned from my uncle that family is the most important thing in the world. Sometimes, it's all you've got. You'll never forgive yourselves if you let this come between you."

Max put a hand on her shoulder. "Please don't leave."

She turned to Natalie. "I'll have the dress cleaned and get uncle Philip to return it to you. Thanks for lending it to me."

"God, Sidney." Max reached for her, but she eluded him.

"Please take care of Max," she told them quietly, and then walked out of his life.

FOUR HOURS LATER, Max stood at the plateglass windows in his apartment, staring at the sheeting rain. He felt hollow. The terrible, aching loneliness he'd lived with for so long was back with a vengeance. Only now, it felt worse—intolerable, even—because he knew what it felt like to love Sidney Grant.

"Can I get you anything else?" Philip asked from the doorway."

"No."

"You're sure?"

"Yes." He didn't turn around, but he sensed Philip's continued presence in the room. "I want to be alone," he said firmly.

"Really?" Philip sounded almost amused.

Max turned on him with an angry glare. "Really. This isn't a game, old man."

"I know." His eyes registered deep concern. "I'm well aware of that."

Max studied him for long seconds. "Just what in living hell am I supposed to do now? Or was this part of your plan, too?"

Philip lifted one shoulder in a casual shrug. "I never doubted that the two of you would be volatile. In many ways, she's as stubborn as you are."

"She left me," he said. The words almost doubled him over.

"Sure about that?"

"What the hell is that supposed to mean?"

"Are you certain she left you, or are you merely jumping to conclusions based on what you would have done in a similar situation?"

"She walked out of my life." He glared at Philip. "What other conclusion am I supposed to draw?"

"Has the thought occurred to you that perhaps Sidney merely went home to give your family some time to sort things out?"

It hadn't, of course. He didn't even dare hope for that. "Just where the hell were you when this was going on?"

"I took the morning off. I thought you and Sidney might enjoy the time alone."

Max ground his eyes shut in silent agony. "I see."

Philip continued to watch him from the doorway. "I'm sorry I missed the spectacle."

Max's eyes popped open. "Edward is out of control."

"I'm certain your lawyers will handle it. You aren't concerned, are you?"

"No," he admitted. "We didn't do anything unethical or illegal. Edward's pride is smarting. I could kill him for bringing in Silas. He's going to feel like a fool when he realizes that Silas has been lying to him."

"Carter deserves whatever happens to him because of this. I'm sure Mr. Fitzwater will want, er, compensation for his trouble."

"At the least."

Philip nodded. "So the dust should settle, then, by early next week."

"I think so." Edward would be effectively defused within days. Whatever Silas had given him, it wasn't accurate. The entire mess would simply go away. Except, of course, for the mess in his personal life, he mused, which was probably irreparably damaged.

"Excellent. Just in time for your press conference."

Max scowled. He'd forgotten about that. With the Fitzwater deal complete, the AppleTree Toys division of Loden Enterprises had moved forward with its marketing and development campaign. Max was scheduled to introduce the prototype of the animatronic addition to the Real Men collection at a press conference on Wednesday. Now, the thought made him swear. "I forgot about it. I can't do it."

Philip's eyebrows lifted. "You must do it, if you ask me."

"I didn't. Ask you, that is."

"I see you're feeling surly as ever."

"Well, hell yes, I'm surly." His life was falling apart. Why couldn't Philip understand that?

The older man gave him a knowing look. "If I may be so bold—"

"Oh, for God's sake, Philip, spit it out."

His lips twitched, which Max found incredibly aggravating. "I was going to suggest that if Sidney is really worth the effort to you—"

"You know damned good and well she is."

Philip merely nodded. "Then you may wish to employ that skill you have for strategy and determine how to let her know that. At the moment, my guess is that she's feeling rather superfluous."

"Superflu— Are you serious?"

"Completely."

"That's insane."

"Max," Philip said patiently, "how many truly rational women do you know?"

"Good point."

"If Sidney feels that her, er, association with you has hurt you in any way, she'll not come back to you unless you make it clear that having her in your life is more important than the obstacles your relationship presents."

"What obstacles?"

"Don't be obtuse," Philip told him. "Whether you like it or not, there's a grain of truth in Sidney's concerns. She's not going to change for you—and you shouldn't expect her to. But there are lots of Edward Fitzwaters in your circle. It will be difficult for both of you."

"I couldn't care less what people think, Philip. You know that."

"I do. But Sidney cares very much what people think of you. She always has. If she suspects that her relationship with you is hurting your reputation, in *any* way, she won't come back to you."

Max scrubbed a hand over his face in frustration. "There

are plenty of women who would be perfectly happy to sully my reputation if they could get their hands on my money.''

''So there are. I notice you've never sulked over one of them.''

Max shook his head. ''Sidney's different. She makes me feel—''

''Valued?''

''Cherished,'' he said quietly. ''I can't explain it. She doesn't want anything from me.''

''Except your heart.''

''I don't have one. Haven't you heard?''

Philip's eyes twinkled. ''Then what's that pain you've had in your chest since early this morning?''

Max hesitated, then nodded. ''I didn't know it was there until she ripped it out of me.''

''Maybe,'' Philip said quietly, ''if you ask her, she'll give it back.''

Max turned to stare at the rain once more. ''God, I hope so.''

Chapter Fifteen

"Stubborn as mules, both of them," Philip said as he accepted a cup of tea from Gertie. They sat in the kitchen of Max's Manhattan penthouse. "He's sulking. She's crying. And neither of them will make the first move."

Gertie clucked her tongue. "You knew it would be difficult."

"I did." He took a sip of his coffee. "But I didn't plan on them being irrational."

Gertie's warm laugh chased away some of his sour mood. "Good heavens, Philip. You've known Max all his life, and Sidney for most of hers. They're headstrong and independent, and once the two of them have made up their minds, there's no talking them out of it."

"They're both miserable."

"I know. Max does nothing but brood."

Philip sighed. In the three days since Max's confrontation with Edward Fitzwater, the situation had gone from bad to worse. Max's attorneys had rapidly dispatched with Edward's complaints, but both Max and Sidney had refused to make the first conciliatory move toward each other. Sidney had tearfully confided in Philip that she felt her fears had been validated by the fiasco. She could never hope to be anything but a liability to Max.

Philip had been forced to grit his teeth to keep from deliv-

ering a blistering lecture on the folly of believing anything
Carter Silas had ever said to her. His own sister, he knew,
was more than partially to blame for Sidney's fears. Since
her mother had sent her away, Sidney had heard from her
only four times. Despite Philip's pleas, his sister had turned
her back on her daughter. And in the back of Sidney's mind,
the knowledge that her mother had considered her a liability
had taken firm root. After her disastrous marriage to Silas, it
was only natural that Sidney would fear placing herself in
that position again.

Now, Philip met Gertie's gaze across the table. "I don't
know what to do," he admitted. "I've always known what
to do for her, but now, I'm not sure."

"Have you talked to her."

"I've tried. She won't discuss it with me."

Gertie slid her hand across the table to squeeze his fingers.
"You can't take care of her forever, Philip. You know that."

"I do. I don't like it, but I know it."

"You tried. You did everything you could for them."

"They need each other."

Gertie nodded. "I think so, too."

Philip exhaled a slow breath. "I think I'll go see her today.
Maybe I can talk some sense into her."

"What about Max?"

"I don't know about Max. He seems—preoccupied."

"He has that press conference tomorrow."

"It's more than that. He's planning something, and I don't
know what it is. He hasn't discussed it with me."

"That's certainly unusual."

"I suppose." He set down his cup. "I'm sure it's uncomfortable for him to talk about Sidney with me."

"Yes," Gertie mused. "I suppose it is."

"So," he slid his chair back, "I'm going to talk to Sidney
again. Perhaps she's ready to confide in me."

"Good luck, Philip."

He patted her shoulder. "I'll need it."

KELLY TAPPED on the door of Sidney's office. "You have company."

Sidney looked up from her computer, startled. "What?"

"Company. Your uncle's here."

She felt a simultaneous rush of relief and disappointment. It wasn't Max. "Oh. Send him in."

Kelly gave her a narrow-lidded look. "Sid, are you sure you're all right?"

"Yes."

"You look exhausted."

That was no wonder. She hadn't slept more than four hours a night since Saturday. She'd spent as much time as possible here in the office to avoid going home to her too quiet apartment. "I'm a little tired, but I'm okay." At Kelly's probing stare, she nodded. "Really."

"You know, if you want to talk about it—"

"I don't." Sidney gave her a slight smile to take the sting out of the rebuff. "But thanks for offering. Why don't you send uncle Philip back?"

Kelly hesitated a second longer. "Okay. You know where to find me if you change your mind."

"Yes." She waited until Kelly disappeared to wipe a hand over her face. Would this ache never go away?

"Good morning," Philip greeted her as he strolled into the room, "I hope I'm not disturbing you."

"Never." She forced a smile. "Why don't you sit down?"

He eased into one of the chairs across from her desk. "You don't look well, Sidney," he said carefully.

"I'm just tired. I've been working a lot."

"I see."

When he didn't elaborate, Sidney prompted him, "Is this a social call, or was there something you wanted?"

"Both I suppose." He settled his hands on his knees. "We've talked on the phone, but I haven't seen you since Friday. I wanted to know how you're feeling about what happened."